DEATH WATCH

A NOVEL

STONA FITCH

Also by Stona Fitch

Dark Horse (as Rory Flynn)

Third Rail (as Rory Flynn)

Give + Take

Printer's Devil

Senseless

Strategies for Success

Death Watch

A NOVEL BY

Stona Fitch

Published by Arrow Editions
152 Commonwealth Ave.
Concord, Massachusetts 01742

www.arroweditions.com

Designed by Chris DeFrancesco

This is a work of fiction. Names, characters, businesses, places, events, locales, and incidents are either the products of the author's imagination or used in a fictitious manner.

First edition

ISBN: 978-0-9908059-5-3

For Russell Banks

In this short Life that only lasts an hour,
how much – how little – is within our power.

– EMILY DICKINSON

THE COMPLICATIONS

"Like life, a watch provides complications to keep it interesting." Watanabe sat cross-legged on a low stage while we sat packed around him, students at the feet of a high-art Socrates, all leaning forward to hear his surprisingly delicate voice.

His first name was Sam, but the world knew him only as Watanabe. Dressed in black, his long hair dangling in black-gray strands, he looked like an aging heavy metal drummer. Or he could be a *mononoke,* as Watanabe's many detractors described him—a demon spirit.

Back at the agency, we had done some initial research on Watanabe. He was a political artist who worked with extreme materials, like decommissioned jets and tsunami debris. He wasn't as well known or revered as Banksy or Ai Weiwei. Watanabe was a relentless provocateur, a thumb in the eye of the world. Hearing him talking about something as tame as an old-school watch sounded out of character. But confounding expectations seemed to be Watanabe's specialty.

A woman with pink-streaked blonde hair and red-framed glasses slipped into the Okutama Institute's conference room and slid into the empty seat next to me.

"Flight from L.A. was late, as usual," she whispered, shrugging off her coat. "I'm Renata," she said, "senior editor at *Artforum.*"

"Coe," I said, "from Moriawase."

She tilted her head.

"Ad agency."

She leaned closer. "What did I miss?"

"Introductions. Green tea. Non-disclosure agreements. Awkward small talk. Watanabe just started."

"So glad." She pressed her palms together in thanks. "His work is fabulous, don't you think?"

Renata didn't wait for an answer, just leaned forward to get a better view of Watanabe. Her pale face blossomed with star-struck rapture.

"The usual complications of a watch are actually quite uncomplicated," Watanabe said. "Phases of the moon. A chime on the half-hour. In this way, even the most expensive watch is still simple enough to be used by a child. They are all pretty little toys."

He raised his glinting, obsidian eyes to scan his rapt audience.

"Life can be seen as a plaything as well." Watanabe seemed to pause when he found me, an interloper among the invited guests from the art press and the watch industry. "But this perception ignores the—"

He leaned over to Yohji, his handsome young assistant, who whispered in his ear. "Ignores the verities," Watanabe said. "The unrelenting truths. Like the soul, truth, courage, death."

He turned toward me, his eyes seeking mine—no mistaking it. "The advertisements for these expensive toys make it sound as if each owner is simply taking care of his watch for—" Watanabe's brow wrinkled.

"For the next generation," I blurted, because I hated those ads and the long flight had left me jangled.

Yohji turned and glared at the advertising guy who had broken Watanabe's incantatory spell with his American impertinence. Renata shifted away from me.

Watanabe seemed untroubled. "Exactly. *For the next generation.* As if an object could be a legacy. But let me be very clear about this, my friends. No object is a legacy, no matter how beautiful and well-crafted. Not a watch or an expensive sports car." He gave a small smile. "Not even works of art. What is the true legacy that we will leave?"

No one blurted out an answer.

"The only legacy we leave is the memory of our actions," Watanabe said. "What we did each day and why we did it. For those who choose to remember us, we leave behind these small traces as our gift." He paused, shook his head slowly. "Or warning."

He raised his hand and snapped his fingers as if summoning a waiter. The doors at the back of the conference room opened and the engineers wheeled in a metal cart. They raised a white cloth cover to reveal a glass case the size of a small aquarium.

Inside it glimmered the mysterious watch that my agency was hoping to launch. The emails from Watanabe's team had called it the most revolutionary watch ever created. Having written plenty of hype during my career, I considered myself immunized. I came to Tokyo to be convinced.

"Meet Cassius Seven, my friends. Years in research and development. Now revealed to you, the select few."

Eager nodding among the audience. Renata stared with unrestrained enthusiasm. To me, Cassius Seven looked like any other elegant, understated watch. Its round case held a matte-silver face with tapered black hands. The hours were in delicate Roman numerals. The only unusual detail was a small red dot glowing on its band.

"Looks like any other expensive watch, doesn't it?" Watanabe said, reading my mind. "It is intentional. We are *hiding its light under a bushel basket.*" He spoke the words slowly, as if he had just learned the folksy expression and it delighted him.

One of the engineers inched across the low stage, carrying a bowl of apples in front of him. Watanabe gave an appreciative nod, chose an apple, and held it up to us.

"Temptation, yes? But this is not the Garden of Eden. And we are not innocents." Watanabe nodded and the engineers lifted the glass case. He plucked the watch from its stand and held it in the air, pivoting so everyone could see.

Watanabe turned to the engineers. "Thanks to our team for years of exploration and hard work, leading to this first demonstration of the prototype."

The engineers bowed humbly.

Watanabe fastened the watch gently around the apple. "Once the watch is on, it cannot be removed." He pointed to the band, which had tightened around the apple, then to a small red *1* glowing on the band. "Our watch counts the days you have been wearing it, reminding you to be thankful for each."

Watanabe put the watch-bound apple on the stand and the engineers lowered the case around it like a reliquary. He nodded to one of the engineers, bent over a laptop, who began typing furiously.

Nothing happened.

The engineer stopped and looked up.

Watanabe gave a small smile. "Much of life is spent waiting."

The engineer began slap-typing, but again, nothing happened. My eyes strayed to the conference room windows. In the formal gardens, a breeze set red maple leaves quaking.

The laptop pounding continued until it triggered a brief whirring, then silence. I looked back at the stage to find that the case had turned white. Pulverized apple coated the inside of the case. A slow drip of juice trickled down, then another.

I had no idea what had just happened. Unsettled murmuring rippled through the conference room. The engineers lifted the case to show us the gleaming watch, covered with clumps of apple pulp now, but intact.

Yohji stood and shouted in Japanese. Watanabe's cohorts in the audience jumped up and applauded. We stood and joined the applause as the engineers bowed, then took away the case. Giving a watch a standing ovation seemed excessive, but again, I was unmoved by the fine-watch world. And I had no idea what the stunt with the apple was all about.

Watanabe walked to a small table and waved his hand over a low black box, summoning up a hologram of Cassius Seven.

"Let us take a closer look." He waved his fingers near the slowly spinning image and the watch enlarged. "Cassius Seven is an exceptionally accurate watch. Full-jeweled movement, titanium case, sapphire bezel, small ruby inlaid above each numeral. It has all of the elements of a great watch with none of the gaudiness of a Bulgari or Patek. Or the cloying attention demanded by a Rolex. It looks understated." As he spoke, Watanabe spun the image of the watch to reveal its ordinariness from all angles.

"To be truly radical, you have to appear normal," he said with a smile. "So you can cause more trouble."

Renata opened a small red notebook to capture this insight, as much about the artist as his latest creation.

Watanabe spun the image to reveal the bottom of the shimmering titanium case, engraved with a series of numbers in a circle. "Notice that each watch is unique and numbered. A serial number is not unusual. But here beneath the watch, the singular beauty of

Cassius Seven becomes clear." His hand hovered over the hologram to start an animation. The bottom of the case opened and a tiny silver crescent emerged from the underbelly of the watch, then another, then more. They spun slowly, then in a blur, as Watanabe watched, transfixed.

"Here we see the seven blades, each honed until they are sharp as scimitars," he said. "One by one, the blades emerge from the underside of the watch and pierce the wearer's wrist without warning. At random."

He uttered this incomprehensible detail without explanation, then looked up. "You see, the blades slip down between the delicate bones of the wrist, then spin to sever the ulnar artery, causing violent exsanguination. Or more bluntly, death. In seconds."

The crowd turned silent, then burst into uneasy laughter.

Watanabe smiled. "It might seem like a joke to you. But to us, Cassius Seven is a very serious business. As you will see."

The laughter stopped.

I texted Nathan back at the agency.

Watanabe product demo jst got supr weird

"Oh, come on," a woman in the audience shouted from the audience. "Why would you create a watch that does such a terrible thing?"

The speaker stood and I recognized her from the meet-and-greet before the presentation—Milou Déprit, executive VP of a French luxury goods conglomerate.

Watanabe smiled at her. "Because death is the ultimate complication."

"A deadly watch? That's what you brought us here to see?"

She glared at the gently spinning hologram of Cassius Seven, as if outraged by its existence. "Your watch is absurd. Who would want it?"

Watanabe focused his heavy gaze on the questioner. "There's a market and a price for everything. You certainly know that, Madame Déprit." He held up a long, graceful finger and pointed at Cassius Seven. "Here is something else that you need to understand. The soul of the watch, as it were."

"So your monstrous watch has a soul?" The conference room turned hot and airless as the demonstration veered into uncertain territory.

"Yes, this watch has a soul. Why should so-called sentient beings be the only bearers of souls?" A heckler can throw off a pitch, but Watanabe seemed to relish Madame Déprit's badgering. "The sun has a soul. The moon. Temples. Streets. Gardens. They resonate with all that has passed through them, all that they know."

"What can a watch know? It's just a stupid little machine."

"This watch is far from stupid, Madame Déprit. Only it knows the answer."

"To what question?"

"*When will you die?*"

A moment of stunned silence from the room.

Madame Déprit shrugged her narrow shoulders. "How can a watch know such a thing?"

"An algorithm, trained for maximum variability, determines the moment when the knives will emerge."

"You mean the moment of death."

"Or life." Watanabe paused, tilted his head. "You see, the knives may come out in a week. A year. Twenty years. Or they may not appear at all. The supposedly deadly watch may end up just being a beautiful toy, like its high-end cousins. The wearer never knows what's going to happen, or when. Just like we never know our fate."

Watanabe's dark eyes scanned the conference room, drawing us all in. "When you go to sleep at night, will you wake to live another day? When you walk down the street, will you inhale a deadly virus? Or get shot by a fanatic? Do any of you truly know the answer?"

Silence. Hoping was different than knowing.

"In this way, the watch parallels our own precarious existence. Some claim to be able predict death—from genetic researchers to astrologers. But we must live with uncertainty. We query Google. We ask Alexa. *Where should we travel, what restaurant should we go to?* But the ultimate question, the one so rarely asked and never answered, is simple. *When will I die?*"

"So we are supposed to believe that your ridiculous watch will determine the answer?" Madame Déprit was having none of it.

"Instead of—?"

She said nothing, not citing the usual suspects—fate, luck, God.

"We determine our own destinies. And our own deaths." Watanabe wiggled his fingers like a puppeteer pulling hidden strings. "We court or repel death every day by what we do and how we live. Some put themselves at risk by racing motorcycles or base jumping from mountains. Or they smoke and eat too much, as I do. Others try to extend their lives with exercise and strict diets."

"But that's *our* choice," Madame Déprit said.

"It still is," Watanabe said. "We won't put the watch on our customers like a shackle. They will choose to wear the watch. Or not."

"No one but a fool would decide to put on such a deadly thing." Done arguing, Madame Déprit smoothed her elegant black skirt and sat down.

Watanabe smiled. "Fortunately, the world is thick with fools."

The secret preview of Watanabe's creation devolved into a technical session run by the unsmiling engineers. Somber in their black suits and white shirts, they turned even more serious, as if to distract us from the Cassius Seven's troubling complication. One of the engineers walked through the crowd, solemnly gathering our cell phones in a basket, lest we try to photograph proprietary technology. Then they walked us through the design of Cassius Seven, drowning us in details. I set aside the question of the watch's uncertain purpose and took notes on its innovations—the random timing of the emergence of the blades, the anodized beryllium that kept them sharp, for years if necessary.

My work required understanding complicated machines and arcane tech, at least enough to sell them, so I was all too familiar with product demonstrations, trade shows, and R & D labs. But after listening to the monophonic voices of the engineers lecturing us—no questions allowed—even I was starting to fade. Jet lag set my mind adrift. I stared out the window at the gardens, raked with amber beams of afternoon light. Dragonflies hovered over plum blossoms and pale blue wisteria. I imagined how free they felt, flitting around the Institute grounds. Around me, the other guests in the overheated conference room were squirming like kindergarteners.

Sensing our escalating boredom, the engineers announced a brief break. We rose quickly to cluster around the tea table and started talking in urgent whispers.

The more literal-minded in the group, including the outspoken Madame Déprit, considered Cassius Seven a dangerous toy. "If it's real, it's despicable," she said. "If it's simply a joke, it is not funny in the least." The response from most of the other guests—half-smiles and whispers—hinted at skepticism. Niels De Vries, whose nametag identified him as editor of *Het Moderne Horloge* in Amsterdam, proposed that we were just part of an elaborate prank, one that Watanabe would explain at some point.

"I must say, even if it's all just for a laugh, we need someone like Watanabe to shake up the watch world," he said, eyes sparkling.

"Or to destroy us all." Madame Déprit sipped her coffee.

"I feel as if we are witnessing something truly historic," said Martin Sørgen, an art dealer from Copenhagen. "Even if it's just a prank, the mere concept of a weaponized accessory is sublimely subversive."

"Everything Watanabe creates is sublime," added the besotted Renata.

Sørgen nodded. "He's taking us into uncharted territory."

"Dangerous territory," said Madame Déprit, refusing to give in to groupthink. Her dissent did little to quell the excitement we felt as insiders in Watanabe's latest art project. We huddled close, shocked by the audacity of Cassius Seven. A tagline popped into my head: *The only watch that kills time.* I would have to do better than that.

Watanabe walked back on the low stage, holding up his arms like a street preacher, waving us back to our seats.

He waited silently for our whispering to stop. "You have heard about the inner workings." Watanabe shook his head slowly. "These details are important. But they are not what you will remember about this day."

He nodded toward the engineers, who carried another case toward the low stage. They lifted the black cover to reveal a small white rabbit in the center of the case. Its eyes were red, its pink nose twitched, and a cinched silver watch glimmered around its neck.

A rabbit wearing a watch like a necklace. The sight of it was so absurd that we had to smile, to laugh even.

But we fell quiet, one by one, as we remembered the apple.

"Some in this room consider this project a prank intended to outrage, to get attention. Believe me, Cassius Seven is not a joke. Not at all."

Watanabe nodded at one of the engineers and the inside of the case splashed red instantly, blood dripping down the glass in a slow rain. The watch gleamed at the bottom, its work completed, titanium clotted with dark viscera and pale bone.

The rabbit's quick death left us stunned. Renata clutched my arm. Some shouted, others looked away as if they could pretend it didn't happen. We all looked at Watanabe for an explanation. Was he a heartless sadist? Or just the latest creator to fall in love with his creation?

Watanabe's hands were clasped together, head bowed toward the bloodied case in respect for the untethered soul drifting from its eviscerated remains.

Madame Déprit rose from her seat.

"You are unspeakably vile and cruel." Her voice was loud, clear, angry. "I want no part of this *désastre*."

Watanabe opened his eyes and watched Madame Déprit's quick path toward the door, unconcerned by the disruption. He seemed to welcome it. A small smile played on his face, then faded.

"You sell beauty products that kill thousands of rabbits every year, slowly and painfully, during so-called animal testing." Watanabe's voice was loud and firm, eyes narrowed. "But you cannot witness the painless sacrifice of one well-tended rabbit?"

Madame Déprit turned at the exit but said nothing, silenced by

Watanabe's blistering gaze.

"Perhaps it is *you* who is unspeakably cruel." Watanabe raised his hand, tallying her sins on his graceful fingers. "Fifty million euros in profit last quarter, yes? For handbags of leather, stripped from the carcasses of calves and goats. Clothing stitched in Indonesian sweatshops. Diamonds mined by shoeless slaves—"

The door slammed behind Madame Déprit like a rifle shot.

CAPTAIN LARVAL

I SPRAWLED ON THE FLOOR OF MY SUITE and stared at the intricate beamed ceiling, mind reeling after a long day with Watanabe, the engineers, and Cassius Seven. The idea of a deadly watch was terrible, as the fierce Madame Déprit had pointed out. But it appeared to be a high-art prank, as the rest of us agreed. To my mind, there were much worse hoaxes—from organized religion to the American Dream. By comparison, Watanabe's latest provocation seemed harmless. If I could figure out how to sell a potentially deadly watch, it would do more than earn our agency impressive billings. It would attract a ridiculous amount of attention—and new clients. Nathan had already left dozens of texts. The day was just starting in New York. I should call him with an update. I should call Alta in Darmstadt.

Tomorrow I would have to focus and start coming up with a concept, a campaign, an idea that would sell something as outrageous as a watch that could kill its owner. I would have to return all my calls, emails, and texts. But tonight I could savor my jet-lagged isolation, when I could disappear from everyone's radar and answer to no one.

I thought about reading a book, watching a movie, or ordering room service but instead I fell asleep on the floor—clothes wrinkled, mind unsettled, alone.

The tentative knocking that woke me turned insistent. I stood and felt my way to the door and found Watanabe's assistant, Yohji, standing in the hall.

"Hey." I looked down to makes sure I was wearing clothes. I was.

Yohji smiled widely, revealing perfect teeth—and held up a bottle of whiskey.

"Thanks." Had I ordered a bottle of whiskey? What time was it?

"Compliments of Watanabe." He had been wearing a black suit during the meetings today, but now Yohji wore a T-shirt printed with Ronald McDonald's severed head, baggy below-the-knee gray shorts, and a long kimono coat with a pattern of blobs that appeared to be the blank faces of the Easter Island totems.

"Off duty now," he said, noticing my survey of his wild look. He held up two glasses. "Can I join you? Bad luck to drink alone."

"Uh, *sure?*" So much for my quiet night.

As he walked inside, Yohji glanced around the large suite. "Must be fun to be a creative director." Yohji pronounced my job title with reverence.

I nodded at the couch and low coffee table and pushed my laptop to the side. He set the bottle and glasses between us and poured two whiskeys with a deft hand, sliding a glass in front of me.

He smiled and raised his glass. "To life."

I lifted my glass. Yes, *to life.* So much more preferable to the alternative.

We drank and the first sip burned so exquisitely that I let out a satisfied hum.

"Japanese whiskey is underrated," he said.

"Better than overpraised."

Yohji turned silent for a moment as we tasted the whiskey, listened to the quiet voices of housekeepers in the hallway. We had only spoken once for a few minutes at the Cassius Seven launch. Yohji did something in marketing—and liked fashion, apparently. Beyond that, he was a stranger. During the long awkward silence, we drank and smiled at each other.

I realized Yohji probably wasn't going to say anything else.

"So you work with Mr. Watanabe?"

He nodded.

"CMO?" Chief Marketing Officer would be a reach for someone as young as Yohji, but it would flatter him.

Yohji shook his head. "No titles. We're a collective, built on disruptive democracy." He spoke with the self-assurance of a start-up company before the murk of the marketplace crept in. Nathan and

I sounded the same when we founded Moriawase—confident that our agency was different.

I paused, decided to drill Yohji for insights while he was here. "Got a question for you."

"Sure."

"Is the whole Cassius Seven thing real, or just one of Watanabe's stunts?"

Yohji half-closed his eyes for a moment, nodding his head, then broke into a broad grin. "Can't believe you even have to ask."

"But I do."

Yohji leaned back in his chair. "Can't really say."

"Can't, or don't know?"

"Can't—I'm not supposed to tell anyone."

"Look, I need to know." I leaned toward him. "If the watch is deadly, I'm leaving tomorrow morning. If it's a stunt, I'm all in."

"Well..."

"I've signed an NDA. Would never tell anyone."

Yohji took these details in, gave me an appraising look.

"You can trust me." I nodded. Non-disclosure agreements meant nothing.

"We'd have to be completely cray-cray to make a watch that could actually kill people." Yohji's long dark hair fell in front of his eyes. He reached up to tuck the wayward strands behind his ears. "It'd be way illegal. We'd never be able to sell it. We'd probably all get arrested. Watanabe likes to make trouble, but he definitely wants to stay free."

"So the watch isn't real?"

Yohji's face went blank. He'd only known me for a few hours and I was already asking him to reveal a company secret.

"C'mon, you can tell me." I reached over to give Yohji's shoulder a reassuring squeeze.

"No, it's not real. But the project only works if everyone thinks it is." Yohji stared at the wooden floor. "*Shit.* I'm going to get in so much trouble. Don't tell Watanabe that you know."

"I won't. But thanks."

Yohji exhaled, picked up his whiskey, gulped it down, refilled. "Must be wild, working with Watanabe."

Yohji shook his head. "You have no idea."

"Tell me." I was wide awake now, ready to find out anything I could about our potential client.

"Watanabe's kinda unknowable," he said. "*Soul of an artist. Mind of an anarchist.* That's what he always says about himself in interviews."

I took out my notebook but Yohji waved it away. "Just listen, Mr. Vessel."

"Coe, please." I put away my notebook.

"Watanabe thinks the world's gone insane."

"Hard to argue with that."

"The absurdity of endtime capitalism," Yohji said. "That's his message. Says it in a lot of different ways." He wrote in the air in front of him with loosened fingers. The whiskey was working. "*Make trouble, not money. Generate virtue, not value.* And so on and so on. You get the idea."

Yohji dropped his thin arm heavily, as if Watanabe's ideas were leaden.

I nodded. "So he'll tell people that the watch isn't real?"

"Yeah, eventually." Yohji took the last sip of his whiskey and poured more in my glass, then his. "We'll launch Cassius Seven and get tons of attention. Lots of people will buy the watch. And when he's ready, Watanabe will reveal the truth."

"Which is?"

"They're part of an experiment."

"Proving what?"

"That people act against their own best interests."

I squinted.

"They lead lives that make them sick and miserable. They vote for politicians who can't help them. They delude themselves into thinking everything's okay. So why not buy an expensive watch that might kill them?"

"That they *think* might kill them."

"Exactly." Yohji's dark eyes brightened and he sat up in his chair. "They may feel stupid for a few days, but they'll get over it. After all, they got to feel brave without having to do anything dangerous. Anyway, they didn't buy a watch. They bought a limited-edition multiple from a famous artist. Imagine the aftermarket."

Yohji took a glug of whiskey.

"We'll sell more watches after the truth comes out. That's when collectors will swoop in." He wiggled his fingers to simulate birds in flight. "No matter what happens, we'll take it home in bags."

Watanabe's strategy was brilliant but brutal, and from what I knew about him, entirely in character. "So that's the point, to make lots of money?"

Yohji shrugged. "Of course. Also, to get attention. Watanabe loves attention."

"Who doesn't?" To be honest, I didn't. My job kept me behind the scenes, which was fine by me.

Yohji leaned forward and almost slipped off the sofa. "You need to know something, Coe Vessel."

"What's that?"

"Watanabe's only half-Japanese. Raised in Long Beach until he was fourteen. So don't be fooled by his inscrutable Japanese art-man stuff!" Yohji laughed. "It's part of his act."

"Thanks for that." Thinking back, Watanabe did seem like too much.

"Also—and this is important, so you have to listen carefully." Yohji's voice took on a new urgency.

"Okay."

"We have four other teams competing for the Cassius Seven launch—and they're super-great." He rattled off a list of agencies, all much larger than our boutique agency.

I nodded, tried not to look surprised. Nathan told me other agencies were in the running, but I didn't know they were global players.

"But don't worry, I think Watanabe wants you to win."

"Why?"

"Likes your work."

I smiled.

"And your father's."

My smile faded. My father, Vince Vessel, was a 30-year man at BBDO and an advertising legend. I still lived and worked in

Vince's shadow. But shadow wasn't the right word—more like a solar eclipse.

"Loved those Niagara Juice ads. *Sweet!*"

"Me, too," I said, lying. I remembered my father at the kitchen table, surrounded by samples of the Japanese beverage market, sniffing a plastic cup of plum wine. "If they'll drink this stuff, they'll drink Niagara Juice." He pushed his notebook toward me, his teenaged son with blaze orange hair, a skateboard, and an attitude. His concept—*Taste the Sweetness of Youth*—sounded hokey to me. I picked up his Sharpie and shortened it to *Sweet!* Vince just nodded, knowing a good idea when he saw it. Or stole it.

"Sweet!" Yohji said again, fist in the air this time.

"Yeah, I remember." Vince's TV ads featured *Sweet!* shouted by smiling Japanese children, accompanied by the Black Power fist salute, repurposed to sell grape juice, which flooded the Japanese market with a tsunami of calories.

"Watanabe loves those commercials."

I paused for a moment to summon up *Vince Vessel's Greatest Ads of All Time*. The Niagara Juice campaign turned out to be a huge hit with Japanese kids, who started drinking tankerloads of grape juice. What happened next? Escalating obesity and the country's first cases of juvenile diabetes.

"Not exactly Vince's finest hour." A tell-all book about the campaign, *From Good to Grape*, made my father out to be a modern Commodore Perry, single-handedly destroying the Japanese diet.

"Are you kidding? An ad campaign that messes up *an entire culture*?" Yohji said, incredulously. "It's awesome. Watanabe did a video installation a few years ago with all those ads playing at the same time!"

"Cool." Yohji's relentless enthusiasm was wearing thin.

Yohji refilled his glass. "My father was a fisherman. Yours was a legend. Ever work with him?"

"Used to talk about it. But he thought my work was too weird." There was more to say about why Vessel + Vessel never happened, of course, but Yohji just needed the takeaway.

Yohji bristled. "No disrespect, Coe, but you look pretty normal to me."

"Heard of Mister Mucus?"

"Those gross ads?"

"That's right."

Yohji gave me a loose smile. "Whoa, Mister Mucus is disgusting! And super-funny. Like the commercial where he throws that big mucus ball at a royal wedding. I have a vintage T-shirt with Mister Mucus on it!"

I leaned forward and stared into Yohji's deep mahogany eyes as if I were about to impart wisdom. "I created Mister Mucus."

"No. Way."

"It's true."

Yes, my most famous ad campaign starred a monster made of snot.

Nathan and I had skulked through NYU, sullen English majors in a University Place dorm full of hyper-extroverted actors and musicians. Not fitting in is the best way to find out who you really were. That's the kind of advice I'd pass on to my son or daughter, if I had one. But at the time, our outsider status wasn't making us wise, just unpopular. We spent most of our senior year digging through the book carts outside the Strand, smoking weed in Washington Square, and making fun of our straight-arrow dorm-mates.

Preparing for a retro "Heroes" dorm party, an homage to the David Bowie hit, we dressed Nathan up as a character we called Captain Larval. *We* at that point included Alta Van Schuyler, my girlfriend and future wife. Our concept was pretty hazy—something about how undergraduates were still unformed, lacking the elements (solid skulls, a spine, a fully formed cortex, moral compass) that would enable us to walk the earth like true heroes instead of pretenders. Everyone at NYU was larval, awaiting a metamorphosis. Especially us.

Alta bought three geezer suits in the Village, and I found a place on Canal that sold knock-off Vaseline in gallon tubs. Nathan put on the first suit and we slathered him with a thick coating of goo. Then he put on a slightly larger suit and we added more. By the time he put on the largest suit, petroleum jelly was oozing from his cuffs like ectoplasm.

Barely able to walk, Nathan needed us to guide him, but when he got to the party, he started slamming around the dance floor. He took off one of his coats and flung it at a wall, where it stuck, then slid slowly down. He nuzzled people, messing up their costumes. We got thrown out in minutes.

We trudged from bar to bar, leaving a greasy trail through the East Village. Long after midnight, we came to Dark and Stormy, our favorite dive, and took our regular places at the bar. A cluster of men in the corner kept staring at us. Their wrinkled white shirts and loosened ties, their bloodshot eyes—it all said they'd been there since after work. One of them walked over to the bar and leaned toward us.

"How much?"

My face burned with righteous anger. Did these suit guys really think they could just *buy* my girlfriend?

"*No no no no.*" Suit Guy pointed a wavering finger at Nathan, now staggering through the crowded bar like a greasy zombie. "How much for him?"

"I can't sell him, he's my roommate."

"That get-up, what's that all about?"

"He's Captain Larval."

Suit Guy looked confused. "Who the fuck is that?"

I explained, but whatever I said didn't seem to clarify. He reached into his wallet and handed me his card, bright white with his name and title embossed in an elegant typeface. He was a senior creative director at McCann. "Look, we're doing a pitch tomorrow and need something that doesn't suck." He pointed to the other drunk guys at the table. "These Ivy League douches haven't come up with anything worth a shit."

I told him my father worked at BBDO and that I knew a thing or two about advertising.

"Hang on, your dad's *Vince fucking Vessel*?"

I nodded.

"Be at our office tomorrow morning at nine sharp," McCann Guy said. "And bring your gross friend exactly *as is*. But sober."

"Why?"

"We got a pharma client that's selling a new cold medicine. Your pal looks sick. I think we might be able to use him as a brand character or something."

Alta was listening from the sidelines. "No way."

"Why not?" McCann Guy and I said at the same time.

"You can't just take our work," she said, with the clear eyes of a very sober pre-med student. "We're partners."

"In what?"

I picked up on Alta's lie. "A boutique ad agency."

"What's it called?"

"Moriawase." The word I blurted out came from the menu of the cheap Japanese place near our dorm. It meant *combination platter*.

McCann Guy squinted. "Cool."

"If you end up using our friend in the ad, we want full credit," I said.

"And payment, to be negotiated," Alta added.

McCann Guy squinted. "Payment for what? All I want him to do is show up at a meeting and kickstart our creatives." He pointed at his cohorts, doing shots now. "You kids ought to be paying *us* for the experience."

"No, you'll be paying us for—" I pointed at Nathan, sliding around the bar. I had no idea what I was about to say. "For ... for ... for Mister Mucus."

Ping. McCann guy's face went blank for a moment, then he gave a body-wide palsy, looked at the ceiling of the bar, and pressed his eyes closed.

"*Thank you, Jesus.*"

"*Whoa.* That really happened?" Yohji's eyes glistened like egg whites. He was wandering deep in Whiskeyland.

"It did."

"Then what?"

I summarized the ending for Yohji. The pharma client signed

off on the concept and Mister Mucus became a disgusting but wildly popular cultural icon. In the broadcast ads, Nathan was replaced by an animated Mister Mucus who spewed sputum like a lawn sprinkler. Our brand-new agency ended up on the cover of *Adweek*: MEET THE SNOTTY KIDS BEHIND MISTER MUCUS. McCann paid us boatloads of money and gave us tons of work. We rented an office on Broadway and put out our shingle in the nascent Silicon Alley.

Moriawase—a combo platter of creative services.

During our first dizzying year, we made *New York* magazine's *Best Under Thirty*. Our billings topped $10 million. We poached top-tier accounts from bigger agencies. Alta and I bought our first apartment, a two-bedroom in a white-brick building on West 57th Street. Nathan drove his vintage mint-green Porsche around the embryonic Silicon Alley and got ridiculed by *Gawker*. I turned down a $60 million buy-out offer, insisting that our fledgling agency was worth more.

"Fuck yes!" Yohji gave me a sloppy high five.

I smiled and walked him out, told him I'd see him tomorrow. I closed the door and leaned against it, then turned back to my whiskey-scented suite, dim as a cave. I had left Yohji at a high point in our narrative arc. No need to tell him about the post-9/11 crash, the recession, the pandemic and its aftermath, and other economic lulls that almost pulled us under. About furloughing staff and taking any work we could get. About impossible accounts and difficult clients that we had to haul to small claims court to get paid. About what happened to the *Best Under Thirty* when they hit forty.

He'd find out for himself soon enough.

DARMSTADT

After a few hours of sweat-soaked sleep, I woke confused and convinced that Cassius Seven was a jet lag fever dream. I could be in Tokyo or Times Square. Working on a new account or adrift in the Pacific. I focused, looked around the room, and saw my unopened bag on the floor of my suite, the half-empty whiskey bottle on the coffee table. After Yohji finally left, I hadn't even managed to get my shoes off before I fell asleep. Bright sunlight flooded the suite. I checked my phone. It was just after five in the morning in Tokyo. I did the math to make sure it was a reasonable hour to call our office.

"Hey, you're alive," Nathan said.

"Seems that way."

"Welcome to Tokyo. How's Watanabe?"

"Brilliant, potentially crazy."

"And the watch?"

"Possibly deadly. Impossible to sell."

"It's a watch, Coe."

"This one's different." I explained Cassius Seven to Nathan and let the idea of a weaponized watch soak in.

"Wait, wait. Hold on," Nathan said, perplexed. "This thing *kills* the people who wear it?"

"You never know when it might go off, or if it ever will."

"Okay, okay. It *might* kill someone."

"That's their story."

"Who'd buy that?"

"About to dig in and find out."

"You'll figure it out. You always do."

"You know," I said, "this whole thing reminds me of that dream."

"Which one?"

"The one where you wake up holding some crazy instrument you don't know how to play, then a theater curtain rises and there's a huge audience waiting to hear you make beautiful music. But you're holding some kind of bent metal thing with a bunch of buttons and knobs on it."

"Haven't had that one."

"I'm having it right now."

"You're awake."

"Not really."

"Just stick it out. It's only a week."

"Did you know we're up against other agencies?" No need to tell Nathan that I was also up against the ghost of Vince Vessel—that was my own problem.

"Yeah, they mentioned it."

"So I came all the way to Tokyo to pitch a spec campaign?"

"Could be worth it. The guy's famous. Might get us out of our B2B rut."

By financial necessity, our work had drifted away from consumer brands to anonymous business-to-business clients that sold accounting software, cybersecurity solutions, and other unglamorous products. The work paid well, but it was a grind and took us off the creative radar.

"Cassius Seven's definitely a consumer product," I said. "One that might consume its consumers."

Nathan gave a short laugh, then his focus drifted away from my problems back to his. By now, he was probably reading texts and emails. Nonchalant disinterest defined Moriawase. We helped each other, but not that much.

"If anyone can sell something this weird, it's you." Nathan's phone clicked and he was gone.

I ordered room service and showered while I waited for a large pot of coffee to show up. As the cool water ran over me, I washed away any of the doubts I had about what I was doing, about Watanabe and his motives. I had to buy in heavily. Whatever our clients were selling was the best, most necessary, and fascinating thing in the history of things. Once you began to doubt the product, the game slid off the table. It was like losing your faith in gravity; vertigo would be glad to take over.

I put on a fresh pair of black jeans and a white shirt, then drank two cups of coffee—the first black, the second with a pale orange pill chaser. Cocaine might have fueled the ad world work during my father's long-gone era at BBDO. Now Adderall was the workman-like drug of choice for creatives who needed an extra burst of creativity.

Mind sharpened, I started delving into the specifics of Cassius Seven and its creator, Watanabe. My father liked to say that *the dollars are in the details,* meaning that the best concepts were often inspired by what might seem like an insignificant fact.

Sitting at my suite's elegant desk, laptop open, I explored Watanabe's considerable online presence, which chronicled the stunts of the bad boy of the Japanese art world. No ordinary provocateur, he once had fifty tons of debris trucked to Tokyo and dumped on the front lawn of the Imperial Palace to protest governmental inaction on tsunami aid. He did a series of enormous bronze sculptures of comfort women and installed them in public gardens without asking permission. In light of these attention-getting stunts, Cassius Seven seemed like his latest, most perverse play to remain internationally infamous.

Turning to Cassius Seven, I rooted around online and found that its namesake, *Gaius Cassius Longinus,* was one of the seven assassins of Caesar. Cassius was the main instigator in the attack and the first to stab the emperor, though Brutus somehow managed to get the glow for that, possibly because *Brutus* sounded better.

Never doubt the importance of a memorable name—another lesson I learned from my father.

Cassius sounded too close to Casio, way down on the low price-point end of the watch spectrum. I dove into watch-related etymology. After all, one word had a way of leading to another, and eventually—a new name. The art of watchmaking was called *horology,* a word I had learned less than a week ago. It came from the Greek *hora,* or hour, which had an unfortunate sonic resonance with *whore.* I switched to Latin roots, but found nothing that worked. A new name would have to wait.

I focused on prospective customers, starting with the physiology of their wrists. The ulnar artery, mentioned by Watanabe during the product demonstration, seemed extremely vulnerable. Not without reason did most suicide attempts involve slashing the wrists. If it actually worked, Cassius Seven would make short work of the artery, as it did with the sacrificial rabbit. Any creative approach we took would have to emphasize the watch's ruthlessly efficient design. Selling potential death was hard enough. Selling a painful death was impossible.

Death might be abstract and deniable, but everyone knew pain.

My laughter echoed through suite as I realized that Watanabe and his team had come up with the ultimate category killer, pun intended. No matter how beautiful and precise, no other watch on the market would ever be able to match the undeniable power of Cassius Seven. Other watches could scream status, but only Cassius Seven could deliver death.

Or pretend to.

Thanks to his excellent whiskey, Yohji let the truth slip out last night—Cassius Seven was a sociological experiment, not a sociopathic device. Watanabe's watch wasn't intended to kill its customers, just shock the world. His wan smile during his presentation hinted at a clever trickster hovering behind his carefully curated artist-devil persona.

Now that I knew Cassius Seven's secret, I was more than willing to play along. Watanabe's subversive project dovetailed with my skeptical ethos. The world was teetering because people bought too much stuff—an opinion I came to only after years of selling people too much stuff. But for his scheme to work, I had to convince the world to buy Cassius Seven. It could wind up being the opportunity of a lifetime or a career-wrecking embarrassment. Only time would tell.

I turned to the competition, clicking through dozens of high-end watch campaigns. Powerful men. Sporty sons. Prep schools. Private jets. Country estates with rose gardens and romping black labs wearing red bandanas. The ads were as boring and predictable as the old-school rich.

When jet lag started creeping back in, I drank another cup of coffee and took another Adderall, chewing this one for extra focus.

Then I emailed all the images I'd gathered to the agency with a few words of direction. No need to elaborate. Words were just distractions to Harup, our design director. If anyone could come up with the right look for this campaign, it was Harup—a certifiable genius, heavy emphasis on the certifiable.

Despite all our ad tech, creative directors still had to stand in front of clients and present concepts. Like live music and libraries, advertising managed to stick around after its heyday through sheer tenacity. The golden rule of advertising still held true: *you can't bore someone into making a buying decision.* Pitches still had to be compelling, thrilling even, to seduce a client and win the account.

My concepts had to match the audacity of Watanabe's vision. They had to be the opposite of the lame ads for other high-end watches. Cassius Seven wasn't a watch that you passed on to future generations—unless you didn't like your offspring.

I hovered over my laptop, burning through more and more information, taking notes and looking for angles, paths, ideas. Hidden along the dendritic skein of memories or wading in the debris field of my imagination, glimmering jewels waited for my hand to pull them from the muck. I just needed to find one great pitch for Cassius Seven—and two others to make it look even better. One would be the wrong choice, the straw dog that everyone could feel good about hating. The next would be a middle-of-the-road concept, the good-enough option that no one could get very enthusiastic about, like buying a Prius.

The strongest concept needed to be different, but familiar enough that Watanabe would think he came up with it.

My phone bripped.

"So you're selling death now?"

"Potential death." After Yohji finally left last night, I had emailed Alta, telling her all about Cassius Seven, including the secret I wasn't supposed to tell anyone—that it was all a hoax.

"That it might never go off—that's the clever part," she said. "If you knew for certain that the watch was going to kill you, it would just be a suicide device."

"Those already exist," I said. "They're called guns."

"By the way, Cassius Seven is a terrible name."

"Working on it."

"Just call it what it is—Death Watch."

Ping. When Alta was at Moriawase, she always managed to come up with great ideas on the fly. Now she had handed me another one.

"I'll be using that."

"Glad to help."

"Doesn't it bother you?" Alta's research centered on life extension. Cassius Seven, now Death Watch, threatened to end a life, recklessly, in minutes.

"Doesn't *what* bother me?"

"A weaponized watch."

"Not that different," she said.

"From what?"

"From life. So many things can kill a person. A virus, disease, tumor, their own bad habits. If someone puts on Death Watch, they have an answer—their watch is probably going to kill them. They can still hope it won't. Same as everyone thinks death won't happen to them."

"Until it does," I said.

"Right. But the watch is right there, waiting to kill them." Even on different continents, across an echoing cell connection, Alta's skepticism came through. "It's crazy," she said.

"So are a lot of people."

"Those are the customers you want to attract—crazy people?"

"Still trying to get a bead on our demographic."

"Come on. You're trying to convince people to buy a watch that could make them bleed out and die."

"But the whole thing's a stunt," I said. "I just have to pretend it's serious."

"Good luck with that."

I said nothing. Ours was a marriage of opposites. Alta was rational and deliberate; I was emotional and impulsive. Complementary qualities or incompatibilities, depending on the day.

"I think you're wasting your time," she said, finally. "Just leave now, before you're in too deep."

"Promised Nathan I'd stay for a week."

"Since when does Nathan tell you what to do?"

"Watanabe would be a great client. And this campaign is going to get a lot of attention. Could lead to big projects, better clients."

"Like what? Ads for a Tesla that might decide to drive you off a cliff? An iPhone that could explode? A Burberry raincoat that—"

"Okay, I get it."

"People don't like being fooled. Especially when they pay a lot of money for something. Could backfire on you."

I said nothing, thought about how much work I needed to do.

"I know you'll come up with something great. You always do." Alta paused. "Got to get back to work."

"Zeno needs his ego stroked?"

"Don't go there, Coe." Alta's voice shifted to curt. "Really."

Her phone clicked off, then mine. We had made a deal long before we were married that we would never say goodbye at the end of a call. At the time, it seemed romantic. Now it seemed like we couldn't be bothered.

In the words of my father, his life shaded by my mother's early death—*forget the past*. But after talking to Alta, my mind lurched into our shared history, where personal intertwined with professional. One question kept repeating in my mind like a song worm that never stopped burrowing.

What if we had taken that buy-out offer for Moriawase when we had the chance?

I closed my laptop and stood, pacing through my suite and considering the possibilities.

First, the agency would have died an embarrassing death. The $60 million offer that I turned down came from Zazzy, a Los Angeles-based *digital disruptor* that seemed to be the future of advertising—at least for a gleaming moment. Instead of carefully crafted ads, they paired clickbait photos with a teaser:

See Cardi B's latest wardrobe malfunction.
What really ended *Friends*?
Secret pics show a dark side of Chris Evans.
Docs say stop eating this veggie immediately.

Those who clicked found themselves on microsites pitching sketchy mortgages, time shares in Florida, and nutraceuticals. Didn't matter. Zazzy was all about creating a firehose of web traffic. Zazzy wanted to buy Moriawase *for looks,* one of the executives had told me—to bring the glow of quality to its quantity.

Then again, we'd all be rich. But I wasn't ready to break away from the family business, even if it meant passing up a windfall. Working in Vince's shadow was better than being without it. So I claimed that we could get more money for the agency. When we couldn't, it split the three of us in ways I could never have anticipated. Nathan began to second-guess every decision I made. Alta starting to think of me as a delusional daydreamer, someone whose impulses couldn't be trusted. We began crossing the rocky terrain between being married and being friends.

Finally, Alta might be here in Tokyo, not Darmstadt—with me, not Zeno. Soon after the Zazzy debacle, Alta left the agency to join the Infinity Project, the brainchild of Zeno Zenakas, who called himself a *Greek futurist,* a title as vague and ambitious as the man himself. The Infinity Project was part cult, part company. At its research lab in Germany, Xtensia, its flagship drug, was making its way down the slow road to FDA approval, nudged along by funding from Silicon Valley tech bros obsessed with outliving normal people.

Two years ago, we switched phones by accident on a December morning. I held Alta's iPhone in my hand for a moment, wavering. Then I did what no one should do to someone they love. I guessed her code (her birthday, Alta was super-literal) and started digging beneath the cool exterior of Alta Van Schuyler.

We don't keep secrets anymore. Our phones do, but they can be revealed to anyone. That morning, I opened Pandora's photostream to find hundreds of photos of Zeno—in meetings and conferences, restaurants and hotel bedrooms. I swiped and clicked until my index finger—and my mind—went numb.

Alta wasn't just fucking Zeno. It was much worse.

She was worshipping him.

THE HERO'S JOURNEY

I started by reminding Watanabe's team that all advertising campaigns were collaborations, and that this first pitch was just the beginning. After standing in front of hundreds of clients, I could recite the Moriawase introduction verbatim. It was intended to lull clients into believing that our agency cared about solving their problems, and we did—to a degree that was directly correlated to potential billings.

The press and industry people had left the Institute now, leaving Watanabe and his team in the front seats of the conference room. I had adopted my up-late-thinking-about-your-challenges persona—suit coat over a shirt that looked slept in, uncombed hair. To Watanabe's crew, I wanted to present like a distracted professor searching for answers or an engineer spending too much time in the lab. In short, like them.

The first pitch began. From New York, Harup streamed a steady flow of images on the conference room screen. Shackleton on polar ice, Apollo Twelve on the launch pad, Clayton Kershaw on the mound. Then I started talking, spewing a mix of memorized notes and shit I was making up on the fly. I was a fount of words, if not of wisdom.

"Let's talk about heroic acts for a minute," I said. "Has anyone here saved someone's life?"

No hands rose.

"Pulled someone from the subway tracks? Jumped in front of a bullet. Restarted someone's heart?"

Again, no hands. I nodded, relieved. Once, a middle manager at a software company had chimed in with a story about Heimliching a choking co-worker at a company barbeque. Was dislodging a pork rib heroic?

"People may be good citizens," I said. "But there aren't that many chances to be a real hero in our world. A hero like Odysseus.

Or Hercules. Or Momotaro."

Yohji lit up at the mention of a Japanese hero, my late-night addition to a pitch I had delivered dozens of times.

"Now consider heroes in our context of the work at hand—launching Cassius Seven." I nodded over at the prototype in its glass case on one side of the low stage.

Harup switched to undersea video of divers and shimmering schools of fish.

"Most men who wear a diver's watch aren't deep sea divers, right?"

Nods from the team.

The screen behind me filled with video of Ferraris speeding through French villages, jockeys riding thoroughbreds down racetracks.

"Men who wear chronographs aren't actually racing cars or horses, are they?"

More nods from the team.

"An expensive watch, then, doesn't tell time. It tells lies." I paused for a moment, waited for my provocation to soak in. "It says *I'm a sportsman. I'm a CEO. I went to Harvard.* "So what lie does our watch tell?"

Our watch. My inclusive pronoun chipped away at the agency-client barrier and linked us all in our struggle to bring Cassius Seven to the world.

The screen filled with a sequence that Harup dug up from the archive showing a swirling murmuration of words. *Brave* glowed on the screen. "He or she is brave, of course, for facing potential death." I inserted *she* into the pitch for gender equity, though I suspected few women would be foolish enough buy Watanabe's watch. It was strictly a dude play.

Brave gave way to *Risk-taker,* accompanied by terrifying footage of base jumpers passing through narrow mountain passes, cigarette boats skipping across the waves.

"Our target customers are willing to take risks, because they acknowledge the nearness of death."

Individual pulsed on the screen. "Ultimately, our customers aren't like everyone else. They're different and proud of it."

The words stopped swirling and Harup spewed out a manic montage of bros in action.

"Our target demographic is a male, twenty-eight to forty, a high wage-earner, most likely the owner of a vintage sports car or motorcycle, and a frequent traveler. The brand promise to these potential customers then, is this: *You are a modern hero. You face challenges head on. By wearing our watch, you may die, yes. But you'll face death bravely and on your own terms."*

In the freighted pause while the audience mulled that promise, my phone bripped with a text.

U have got to be fking kidding me.

Nathan must have just walked into the office and checked on our pitch, only to discover that Harup and I were delivering a slightly updated version of *Hero*—the hokey straw dog we used to trot out to make other concepts seem stronger.

I flipped my phone over and kept talking.

"So how will we find these high-net-worth heroes?"

I wasn't sure yet. But I knew how to sling enough ad-speak to make it seem like I did. "We envision an integrated campaign with image-driven ads in all high-end publications—*Robb Report, Wine Connoisseur, Financial Times, Town and Country, Wall Street Journal.* Mirrored online with digital targeting and tracking, of course. We anticipate appearances by Watanabe at ultra-exclusive events in Los Angeles, New York, Basel, Tokyo, Hong Kong, and Singapore."

Yohji raised his hand. I braced myself for a critique from an aspiring young creative.

"What's the price point?"

"Good question." I paused, silently thanking Yohji for bringing us to the part of the pitch that clients liked most—the part about money. "When you're in full production mode we'll have a better sense of the per-unit cost." The chart that Harup and I cooked up last night swirled on the screen. "But let's assume that your cost is about 300,000 yen per watch, including amortizing R&D costs over a decade. From the engineering presentation, that seems about right, yes?"

Yohji stood up and stared at the chart, lost in thought for a moment. "Yes?"

I smiled. The price was a lucky guess at best. I moved on. "We're confident that you can, and should, get a generous margin. So we're recommending a 10x multiple. Which would mean a retail price of about 3 million yen or $30,000 USD."

The audience stirred at this definitive value for their pet project, set at a sweet middle-of-the-pack price point.

I thought back to my whiskey-driven talk with Yohji. "Collectors will see the watch as an investment opportunity."

"That's true!" Yohji jumped in. "An early edition of Cassius Seven will appreciate over time. A rising aftermarket will raise the price even higher."

"Here's our projection." I pulled up another chart showing sales escalating over five years. Did these numbers even make any sense? It didn't matter. We could always say that we did our best but the watch was way ahead of its time.

Low murmurs washed across the conference room as the engineers did the math and realized that we were targeting sales of $75 million in the first year alone. The Watanabe team—a dozen engineers plus a handful of support staff—would probably split the profits. The murmurs grew louder as they calculated their share and came up with a number that made them perk up, which is exactly what I wanted. The potential to transform from intense engineers into instant millionaires inspired new enthusiasm.

Watanabe stood slowly, the way he seemed to do everything—standing, speaking, blinking. He raised his hands above his head to quiet his crew, then nodded toward me. "I'd like to thank Mr. Vessel for what he's shown us here today. Selling Cassius Seven is a difficult challenge, and his careful thinking takes us a great leap forward."

I raised my hand to acknowledge the respectful applause.

"Now I'd like to ask the team to give us a moment to discuss his findings in private."

The engineers stood and filed out of the conference room until only Yohji and Watanabe remained. Then Watanabe turned to

Yohji and gave him a flat stare. Yohji shook his head, long black hair flailing, and clomped away.

Watanabe waved me closer and pointed at the chair next to him. We sat side by side, both facing the low stage where I had just been pitching, Harup's images of heroes still circling around on the screen. To the right, the prototype watch glimmered in its showcase.

"I can't thank you enough, Coe Vessel, for coming here on short notice, for joining us for this—" Without Yohji around, Watanabe seemed to be at a loss for words.

"Journey?"

He smiled broadly, revealing yellowed teeth. "Yes." He put his hand on my arm. "But I need to pass along an insight from our lawyers, one that might influence our approach."

I noticed that the index finger on his right hand was missing its last joint.

Watanabe caught me staring. "Studio accident. I suffer for my art." He gave a wry smile.

I said nothing.

"Selling this watch will be very complicated. We will face legal challenges. We won't be able to advertise or sell the watch through normal channels. Our lawyers tell me it may be classified as a weapon in some countries, since it could be attached to an ... unwitting participant."

I nodded and waited for Watanabe to tell me the truth, that his latest creation was just a stunt.

"I have been following your work for some time," he said. "You have a knack for coming up with the unexpected, for going outside the normal."

I smiled.

"Like your father."

My smile faded.

"*The apple doesn't fall far from the tree,* as they say." This expression seemed to delight Watanabe, but maybe it was just part of his Japanese genius art-man act.

"I've got a lot more ideas I want to show you."

"Of course, we have all week. But as you move ahead,

consider this. Cassius Seven is not just a watch. It's like a deadly virus contained in a titanium monstrance, one that can destroy consumerism."

"Or at least some consumers."

Watanabe smiled. "It's very good to have a good appreciation of the..." He looked around for Yohji but realized that he had sent him away.

I took a shot. "The absurd?"

"Yes." Watanabe brightened. "We're not launching a watch. We're inflicting reality on the absurd world. Think about it that way."

I stared into Watanabe's limitless dark eyes, not sure what to think.

He leaned closer. "Remember this, Coe Vessel. When everything has its price, nothing has value," he said. "When death is denied, life becomes meaningless."

Watanabe could reel off dozens of these one-liners as fast as I could spew taglines, but he stopped himself.

"My son told me he spent a pleasant evening drinking whiskey with you."

"Your *son*?"

"Yes, Yohji is my eldest son by my third wife, an actress. We don't make a point of mentioning it within the company, so he doesn't have to exist *under my oppressive cloud*. His words."

"He told me his father was a fisherman."

"Yohji is young. He tells lies to make himself sound more like who he wants to be."

I nodded. Not for the first time, I considered myself lucky to be childless.

"I'm older, at the point where nothing much matters to me. I'm not pulled one way or the other by desire. But you, Coe Vessel, are in the middle of *the brief song between two infinite pauses*, as one of our poets calls life. You have to decide which road to take. And that decision is not always easy."

"Yes," I said, not sure what I was saying *yes* to.

"Which makes you ideal for launching Cassius Seven."

"Because?"

Watanabe gazed into a dark corner of the conference room, choosing his words carefully. "Because you have a curious mind and a dissatisfied heart, both looking for what they are missing."

Watanabe stood slowly. Our meeting was over. He turned after a few steps. "Perhaps you, Coe Vessel, are exactly the kind of customer we are looking for."

Back in my suite, I looted the mini-bar and poured myself a deep glass of plum wine. "To you." I sat on the bamboo floor and looked up at the intricate ceiling, as if that was where the spirit of Vince Vessel might dwell. The Monkey Bar on 54th Street was more likely.

The first sip was so cold and sweet that it hurt my teeth.

My phone bripped. Dozens of texts from Nathan had piled up. I took a long drink and a deep breath and called him.

"What the fuck are you doing?"

"Calm down, Nathan."

"That was our lamest concept ever."

"I know it sucked."

"Sucked? It was like *Joseph Campbell's Technicolor Dreamcoat.* Where'd you even find it?"

"Harup doesn't believe in deleting content."

"Never pitch the weakest concept first."

"You don't need to tell me that."

"Apparently I do." Nathan was our by-the-book guy, a lover of documented processes and metrics.

"Look, the pitch did what it was supposed to."

"Make us look stupid? Well it sure did that. Did you want to get us knocked out of the running so you could just come home? We need this client."

"I know that."

"Then why the hell did you use *Hero*?"

"Needed to get Watanabe talking." I rolled my eyes. The real answer? I hadn't found anything better yet.

"Just figure out what he really wants. Come up with a concept that doesn't suck. We'll get the account. We'll do a fantastic campaign. We'll get paid. Everybody will be happy. End of story."

Nathan's phone clicked off before I could tell him that it wasn't that simple. Nothing was.

KOI POND

I WALKED ALONG A NARROW PATH through ancient pines and new bamboo. The path was well-manicured, with small aluminum tags identifying the species of every tree and flower. It seemed like the kind of walk that a seeker might take during a meditation workshop or a yoga retreat, a chance to be in nature instead of just in the mind.

I had spent the afternoon locked in my suite doing more research. If Watanabe wanted to pretend his watch was real, I could, too. I dug into silos of information, absorbed online think pieces and trend research, the kind of data that Moriawase devoured and spat back out, lightly digested, as insights.

The Institute's well-manicured grounds were usually filled with visiting thinkers, performance artists, and negotiating politicians, but Watanabe had reserved the entire campus for a week. Emptiness made it feel even more meditative.

I walked in a trance, mind locked on the challenge of selling a potentially deadly watch. The more I thought about it, the more impossible the whole project seemed. Even the mighty Vince Vessel would be at a loss for a pitch. Alta's instinctive dismissal seemed wise. Who would buy a new way to die? Weren't there enough already? Cassius Seven wasn't about splattering apples and sacrificial bunnies. If its brutal little knives ever decided to spin, arteries would open, blood would spray, hearts would stop.

At least that's what Watanabe wanted the world to think.

But I knew better. Cassius Seven would never taste blood and this knowledge freed me from moral restraints, like selling cigarettes that could never be lit or guns without triggers.

I came to a clearing and saw the engineers huddling around a koi pond. They were smoking and taking photos of the fish with their cell phones. Like soldiers on leave, the engineers exuded the casual familiarity of men who had struggled together. When I walked by the pond they looked up and gave small nods and half-smiles, then went back to their selfies with fish. From what Yohji told me, the engineers had been living in their lab for the last few weeks as they perfected Cassius Seven. Their time at the Institute was a reward, one that I didn't want to interrupt.

When I reached the edge of the woods, laughter echoed from the pond. I turned and saw the engineers facing me in a half-circle. One pointed as if I were a strange fish, and the others scolded him until his arm drifted down to his side. Their laughter told me that the watch was an inside joke, one that I was in on. I nodded at the engineers. They smiled and bowed gently, then walked away.

I sat on a redwood bench and stared into a careful stand of birches arrayed in a precise grid, like corn growing in an Indiana field, beautiful and dizzying. Pale green leaves quivering in the breeze lulled me into a half-sleep broken by a polite cough from the bench next to me.

Yohji's eyes were bloodshot and his hands gripped the knees of his lime-green jeans, carefully ripped at the knees. "I've been sent here to apologize."

"For?"

"Lying."

"About what?" I knew the answer, but wanted Yohji to tell me.

"My father isn't a fisherman. My father is Watanabe, of course. The famous artist." He put air quotes around that last bit.

"I get why you didn't tell me."

"Really?"

I dredged up Yohji's own words. "You probably wanted to be out from under *his oppressive cloud*."

He smiled. "Yeah, I did. Exactly."

"My father was a lot like yours," I said. "Larger than life. Ever see *Mad Men*?"

"Binge-watched it. Great costumes!"

"When I first heard about Don Draper, I had to wonder whether a writer on the show had stumbled across my dad's name in old copies of *Ad Age*. Vince Vessel. No one could make up a name like that. When he died, I found out that his real name was Demetri Veselka."

"Not as cool."

"He didn't think so either." My father erased his Czech father and Russian mother and reinvented himself.

"What was he like?"

"Great at coming up with catchy ads. Not so great at being a father." After my mother died, Vince disappeared into his work and dragged me with him. He turned our dining room table into a desk, one end for him, the other for me, so he could keep working even when he got home—and I could help. We lived on Chinese takeout and coffee.

"What happened to him?"

"Dropped dead on 6th Avenue the day before he turned sixty."

"So sorry. How did he die?"

"Advertising."

Yohji's beatific face turned quizzical.

"Stress, deadlines—he carried it all around like a big bag of rocks."

Yohji reached down to pluck a piece of grass and roll it in his fingers, then tossed it back to the ground. "Watanabe eats like several men, drinks too much. Takes drugs. Stays up all night in his studio. Sleeps with women half his age. Shouts at his assistants. And me. Some call him uncompromising. I say brutal."

We paused, our emotional reservoirs emptied by a brief flurry of honesty about our fathers.

"Everyone liked your concept."

"It was just a first try. Next one will be better." At this point, there was no next one, better or not.

"Do you need more whiskey?"

I smiled. "No, but thanks."

"Got an idea for you."

"Glad to hear it."

Yohji took a deep breath. "Okay, maybe one idea would be to show a whole bunch of Cassius Sevens like ... floating down from the sky." He raised his delicate hands then wiggled his fingers to simulate sky watches falling like snow. "They're drifting down on Tokyo and attaching themselves to the wrists of all the people walking down the streets. Like in a Murakami novel. No one knows what the watches really are, why they're floating from the sky. But everyone else just suddenly says *hey, what's this?* And a talking cat walks out of an alley and tells them what the watch is all about."

"Which is?"

"The truth, of course. That they're all going to die."

"Why does a cat tell them?"

"Because cats are wise."

I paused for a moment and mulled Yohji's pitch, not that different than the skunkweed-fueled ideas that Creative used to send down to my father at BBDO. "But if we act like the watch is for everyone, no one will want it. Watches are about exclusivity. In our case, extreme exclusivity."

Yohji shook his head to clear his idea about the floating watches. "We're not making one-of-a-kind runway pieces, like Comme des Garçons. In the end, we need to sell a lot of units, like the Gap. Well, maybe not quite the Gap, but you get it."

Yohji had just handed me a clue. "We could sell a few watches for big bucks, or a lot of watches for short money," I said. "It's all about scale."

"Sure, whatever works." Yohji seemed uninterested in the crass details. He looked around, saw that the engineers were clustered too far away to hear. "You talked to my father about the ... regulatory issues?"

"Yes."

"Did you tell him what I told you? That Cassius Seven doesn't work?"

"Didn't mention it." Clients never liked to admit that they were selling vaporware. Watanabe was no exception.

"Good. Please don't tell anyone."

"I won't." I had already told Alta and Harup, who told Nathan, who definitely told the rest of the agency, which spread the news to a wide swath of Manhattan's creative class.

Yohji stood up and walked silently down the path toward the Institute.

I might know Cassius Seven's secret. But I still needed a pitch that did more than please Watanabe. I needed a pitch that would make Vince Vessel proud.

THE POWER OF SEVEN

As I BEGAN MY SECOND PITCH, Watanabe stared at me from the audience, dark eyes wide with anticipation, waiting for me to break out a blistering Coltrane solo of adspeak.

I started with a question designed to engage my all-male audience. "What do men want?" The screen filled with images of actors, musicians, and even a fleeting image of Watanabe in his studio.

I didn't wait for an answer. "Do they want to be famous? Probably," I waved fame away with a swipe of my hand.

"Do they want to be known as the smartest guys in the room?" Images of Jobs and Gates pixelated into Zuckerberg and Musk. "Of course. Or at least to think that they are."

The screen went blank to make our audience focus.

"What men really want is to be part of the chosen few. Members of a highly selective club. Our second concept leverages this desire. We call it *The Power of Seven.*

A glimmering circle of stars emerged from the darkness. As they brightened, the image came into focus, revealing a ring of diamonds that encircled the familiar silver face of Cassius Seven, thanks to Harup's meticulous retouching.

"This is the Cassius Seven, of course, now with a diamond-studded bezel."

Slow nods from the audience. I suspected that they didn't like seeing their elegant watch turned into bling, but they would get over it when the money started rolling in.

"Let's explore the possibilities."

On the wall behind me, the watch split into a seven small watches, which spun slowly, then faster, diamonds blurring, like the spinning blades of the Cassius Seven. The watches faded as Harup's montage began with sepia photos of hundreds of workers digging in mud.

"We're looking at the *Groot Gat* mine in South Africa in about

1895. It was one of the world's first diamond mines, and people said it was the deepest hole in the earth ever excavated by hand. By low-paid diggers, of course. Unsafe conditions, heartless owners, brutal deaths. The usual."

A photograph of a bug-eyed man with a prominent forehead and a droopy moustache filled the screen. "Meet Cecil Rhodes. Prime Minister of the Cape Colony, later Rhodesia. White supremacist. Architect of apartheid. A terrible man. But most relevant to us, Rhodes founded the world's most successful diamond cartel."

No reaction from the audience. They had dropped into obedient student mode.

"Our history lesson ends here. Now we move to economics."

I paced the stage slowly, images of diamonds filling the screen behind me. "What can we learn from Cecil Rhodes?"

No answers from the audience.

CONTROL IS FREEDOM. The phrase appeared behind me, giant words filling the screen. "There are a lot of diamonds in the ground. Careful control over supply gave Rhodes and his successors the freedom to charge whatever they wanted."

Three new words splashed on the screen behind me. SCARCITY DRIVES DEMAND. "Today's high-end consumers want extreme luxury items—the kind that only an elite few can have, or afford."

The parade of embarrassing luxury goods appeared on the screen behind me. "A diamond-encrusted gold iPhone—$16 million. A diamond dog collar—$4 million. Your own private island in the South Pacific—$50 million. A luxury apartment in New York—$240 million. It goes on and on. And up and up."

The screen faded to black.

"Luxury goods aren't worth those ridiculous prices, of course. The price is set by what people are willing to pay for them, right? That's what our market-driven minds tell us."

Mild agreement from the Watanabe team.

"Free-market capitalism has been hammered into our heads from the day we're born." Watanabe's dark eyes opened wider at this bit. I was singing his song.

"Yes, *the market speaks.* But it can only tell us what commodities are worth based on supply and demand. I'd like to propose the opposite for the Cassius Seven. Like diamonds, our watch is worth whatever we're brave enough to charge for it. After all, we control the supply. Since there's no competitor, we can set the price very, very high."

A rolling set of numbers spun on the screen now, going higher and higher. I waved my hand and they held at $500,000.

"Not enough." I waved my hand to send the numbers spinning again.

They stopped at $750,000. "Still not enough for a device as beautifully engineered as Cassius Seven." The engineers smiled at this game-show stunt.

The numbers stopped at $1,000,000. "A million used to be a lot of money when I was growing up. Not anymore." I waved and the numbers started spinning again.

"Should I stop now?"

A couple of tentative hands rose.

The numbers spun. "Now?"

More hands rose now, accompanied by murmurs of protest. But I let the numbers keep spinning until all arms were jutting in the air, hands waving, people shouting at me to stop.

The tally came to rest at $10,000,000, exactly where we planned it to land, of course. "Ten million dollars," I said. "Or more than one billion yen. Does that seem fair to you?"

No one said anything, stunned by the sum.

"Of course it doesn't. Because you know the cost of the watch, the materials and labor that go into it. But try to forget all that now, and imagine this."

The image of the seven spinning watches reappeared. When they stilled, I got ready to deliver the ultimate line of the pitch, rehearsed for hours in my suite late last night.

"Imagine the Cassius Seven, taken literally," I said. "Only seven watches in the world. Each costing ten million dollars. Purchased by seven elite customers. Generating seventy million dollars in revenue."

The engineers seemed intrigued by the idea of making fewer watches and still earning more millions.

A hand shot up. "But what happens after those seven watches

sell out?"

"Either you're done, or you introduce another line, slightly different. But only seven. We keep the brand exclusive. A club for billionaires who need to prove that they can buy anything. Even if it might kill them."

Yohji stood up quickly. "But billionaires are difficult people to reach. How will we sell to them?"

"We'll target a deep influencer among a rarified cohort, like investment bankers, tech executives, or art collectors. Watanabe will tell our story to this individual and offer him the chance to be the first man to wear a Cassius Seven. And to get all the attention that will go with it."

Yohji nodded approvingly and sat down.

I kept going. "Others will come to us organically. The hyper-wealthy are pack animals. The only problem we'll have is fending off hundreds—or thousands—of buyers."

The engineers huddled with Yohji while Watanabe walked in a slow circle around them, eyes down, like Thelonious Monk in a funk. After a few circles around his team, Watanabe stopped in front of me, reached over and touched me gently between my eyes with two fingers. Whatever that was about, it seemed to please him.

"You see clearly, Coe Vessel. The potential and the problems. You have made very much progress in your time here."

"We are getting closer, much closer. But—"

Here we go, I thought. His early praise was about to veer into thorny weeds.

"The world already knows that the super-rich will buy anything, even our subversive watch dressed up in diamonds. The seven greedy men who buy a Cassius Seven would quickly move on to buying other things. Our watch would be lost in their endless stream of trophy purchases."

What could I say to that? Watanabe was right. I'd managed to come up with a second concept almost as dead in the water as my first.

NEW NIHILISTS

"Now we've finally got something good." Wren, our Chief Awareness Officer, served as our harshest in-house critic. We'd been on a brainstorming conference call for three hours and she had shot down every idea we tossed up in the air. Until now.

"I'm sending you some data now," Wren said. "There's a generational split you need to know about." Smarter than the rest of us, she tracked the zeitgeist for Moriawase like a relentless huntress.

"Which means?" I had about an hour before my next pitch started.

"Your target audience may be younger than you think," she said. "I mean, you guys grew up pre-9/11, right? The carefree years of Nirvana, skateboards, Bill Clinton, and the DotCom bubble. Am I right?" She knew the answer was *yes,* just moved on. "My generation got darkness and wars—on terror and democracy, not to mention sexual freedom and women's rights. We got the death of ambition, unaffordable housing, and the daily ego erosion that comes from being extremely online."

"Sorry your world sucks," Nathan says. "But this matters because?"

"Because Cassius Seven might not seem as crazy to Generation Z as it does to you," she said. "So even though you're old-adjacent, tilt toward a younger crowd."

I cringed at Wren's brutal honesty. "Will do."

"Sending you more data, now."

I checked my phone. "Not much time."

"Just skim the studies. There's some big-picture stuff from McKinsey. They've got a name for the emerging demographic you're talking about."

"Which is?"

"New Nihilists," she said.

Ping. The concept clicked into sharp focus.

"Buying you a large coffee when I'm back in New York," I said.

"Maybe even a blueberry muffin."

She laughed. "Just don't fuck it up, Coe. Those last two presentations sucked big time."

"Agreed," Nathan said. "Suckfest."

"So glad to have the support of my comrades," I said. "Any parting advice?"

"Stick to the data," Wren said, "instead of just saying a bunch of shit like you usually do."

"Try not to suck?" Nathan added.

Harup didn't say anything. He never said anything.

"Nihilists get misunderstood, like artists and anarchists." I glanced at Watanabe, who considered himself both. "The word comes from the Latin *nihil*, meaning nothing. So we think that nihilists believe in nothing, that they care about nothing, that they reject everything—religion, love, life. But that's not true."

The engineers glanced at their phones, wondering when this last presentation would be over so they could get back to work. *New Nihilists* wasn't a Hail Mary pass, but close. I was pitching a message I hadn't refined, based on data I had scanned minutes ago. The Moriawase team was listening in via my iPhone and I could almost hear Nathan's teeth grinding.

I paced the low stage of the Institute's conference room, which seemed so airless, suddenly.

"The original nihilists were about acceptance, not rejection." I paused in front of Cassius Seven's reliquary. Inside the glass case, the prototype glimmered beneath the low lights of the conference room. "They accepted that the world was a mess. And remember, this was 1900. Imagine what they'd think of the world now."

Knowing glances all around, then their eyes strayed. I needed to amp it up.

"Maybe nihilists sound like an idea out of the past." I paced the stage faster now. "They're not. I live in New York, a three-hundred-square-mile petri dish of human behavior. When I walk around, when I take the subway, when I go to parties, I don't see power and money, or anger and desperation. You know what I see?"

I kept circling the stage, talking, exactly what Wren had told me to avoid.

"What I see is hopelessness and acceptance. People have gotten used to the fact that the world is spiraling. Burning. Self-destructing. Being taken over by forces they can't control. Diseases they've never heard of. Storms and fires. Greed and corruption."

On cue, Harup unleashed the greatest hits of climate change on the screen behind me. Fire swept over Northern California, a dust storm darkened Morocco, floodwaters poured through Piazza San Marco in Venice, down the streets of Miami Beach, and glaciers calved in Greenland.

"The rich are starting to realize that no amount of money can protect them. Everyone else knows that the dream is over. Kids will never have the opportunities their parents had. The environment isn't going to fix itself. When there are too many disasters to count, people quit caring. See too much violence and the world turns into a global first-person shooter game. You give in to terminal ennui. Call it *new nihilism*. I feel it. Maybe you do too."

"I do!" Yohji stood and held his hand high, his orange, bamboo-patterned shirt glowing in the dim conference room.

Watanabe closed his eyes and gave an almost imperceptible shake of his head, the universal gesture of a father with an incomprehensible son.

"I'm one of those people," Yohji said. "I don't care about anything. But I wouldn't call myself a New Nihilist."

"Of course not." I leaned down toward Yohji from the low stage. "We're exploring a frontier demographic. One that barely knows it even exists."

Beaming, Yohji sat down.

Watanabe squinted at me. "How will we find these so-called New Nihilists if even *they* don't know who they are?"

"We won't." I shook my head and went silent, letting the mystery deepen as I dredged my short-term memory for answers.

"So you're saying that we won't have any customers?" Watanabe leaned forward, dark eyes glinting. "To get our message out, we have to sell many watches."

"We'll sell plenty of watches," I said. "And we'll find lots of customers. Or more accurately, they'll find us."

"Explain, Coe Vessel." Watanabe settled back in his chair.

"The forest near Mount Fuji, the one where people go to kill themselves. What's it called?"

"Aokigahara," said most of the room in unison.

"*Exactly*. You all know about Aokigahara, also called Suicide Forest. Where it is and what it is. Did someone have to brand it, name it, sell it? Did a Travelocity ad for it ever pop up in your Twitter feed? *Feeling sad? Visit the Suicide Forest.* No. But more than two thousand desperate people, most of them under thirty, sought it out last year because they *needed* it."

Thank you, Wikipedia.

"What are you getting at, Coe Vessel?" The once-taciturn Watanabe was turning prickly and impatient. Time was running out.

"Plenty of people are depressed, right? But if they put on our watch, maybe they wouldn't need to commit suicide. Maybe the *possibility of death* would be enough for them."

The engineers looked grim. They wouldn't get rich from Cassius Seven if we just targeted potential suicides.

I moved on. "As part of this campaign, we need to rename Cassius Seven so people remember it. Like Suicide Forest."

"What are you suggesting?" Watanabe shouted. "We've called the watch Cassius Seven for years. There's no need to change it." After a long week at the Institute, he was getting frustrated. I couldn't blame him. He had flown in the son of Vince Vessel and he didn't have a winning concept yet. Now I was messing around with the name of his latest creation.

"From now on, we're calling it something more powerful and memorable." I circled the display case and pointed at the prototype as the words CASSIUS SEVEN appeared on the screen, faded, and were replaced by DEATH WATCH.

"Death Watch," I said.

A squint from Watanabe, a quizzical stare from Yohji, some chatter from the engineers.

I barged ahead. "Death Watch delivers the possibility of escape to anyone frustrated with our broken world. Anyone who sees the future getting hotter, sicker, and more desperate. Anyone who feels excluded, rejected, or left behind. Who are they? The silently suicidal. The hopeless. People who used to care but don't anymore. People waiting for the end of the world." I paused, squatted down to stare into Watanabe's eyes. "These are the New Nihilists. These are our customers. There are thousands of them, maybe millions. And they'll find Death Watch. Because they need it, badly."

I expected *New Nihilists* to trigger an emotional response, or at least some response. Instead, crickets. As Watanabe's team started to squirm, I was filled with the queasy realization that my final pitch had failed to hit its mark. I kicked myself for setting the price too high during my second pitch. Watanabe's crew was probably worried that there weren't enough New Nihilists to make them instant millionaires.

Watanabe held up his hand to pause the meeting. The engineers huddled and murmured.

Sleep-deprived and frustrated, I stole a page from the Vince Vessel playbook. *When all else fails, make noise.*

I walked over to the prototype, lifted the cover that protected it, and tossed it across the stage.

It shattered with a crash and glass skittered across the stage.

The engineers looked up, shocked. Watanabe tilted his head.

I reached out to lift the prototype from its stand, felt its weight in my hand, and held it up like a glimmering trophy.

"Audacious and over-the-top. That's what your campaign needs to be. Not careful and conservative. Choose our agency and we'll sell thousands of watches together—I know it. Death Watch is the accessory of the end-time. It's the taste of poison that might save the world from itself."

I slipped the prototype on and felt cool titanium on my left wrist. When I closed the band around my wrist it tightened like a noose. A small red number *1* glowed on the clasp.

The engineers stood up in unison and applauded loud and long, as if I had just finished playing a finger-breaking piano concerto. I stood on the low stage, nodding, accepting their enthusiastic applause and cheering. But for what? *New Nihilists* was an interesting concept, but not fantastic. A standing ovation, really?

Watanabe bounded toward me, his half-smile blossoming into a broad grin. He smiled and gripped my shoulder with his heavy hand.

"Congratulations! I knew you'd come through for us. We have officially selected you and Moriawase to launch Cassius ... Death Watch!"

"Really glad we'll be working with you," I said.

Watanabe leaned closer. "Whatever you do, don't take off the watch, for now. Please follow the instructions like any other buyer."

"Because?"

"You can experience the watch—and tell the world about it."

I said nothing.

"It's going to be fantastic, Coe Vessel. We'll teach the world a lesson it will never forget." Watanabe slapped my back and I stumbled forward.

Leaving me in his wake, Watanabe walked on to the low stage and stood under the spotlight. He thrust his heavy arms straight in the air, sending his wild hair flying. He let out a feral scream, echoed by his team.

The light in the conference room dimmed and loud music kicked in. Waiters appeared with Champagne flutes on trays. The engineers rushed toward the waiters and the final pitch morphed seamlessly into a party. One of the engineers near me smiled and bowed deeply, as if I were some kind of hero. I looked for Watanabe, but now he was the center of his own instant party, surrounded by his crew, swigging from a magnum of Champagne and shouting over the music.

Yohji threw his arms around me. "We did it, Coe. We did it!"

"Right." What had Yohji contributed—the idea about the floating watches and the talking cat?

Yohji carried a whiskey bottle and two glasses.

"Aren't you excited?"

"Yes?" I was glad that my patched-together pitch seemed to have worked but I still wasn't sure what was going on. Normally, I would take a new client to an expensive dinner to celebrate signing their account. Now Watanabe was throwing a Tokyo-style rager.

Yohji pointed at the gleaming watch on my wrist. "The prototype! Serial number *zero-zero-one.*" He leaned closer. "Doesn't work, of course. But it'll be super-valuable someday."

I pulled at the band, tightened around my wrist. "How does it come off?"

"It doesn't, or the experiment will be a failure," Yohji said, as if explaining the incredibly obvious to the remarkably dense. "People would just buy it and take it off whenever they wanted. This way they have to wait until the end—*captive audience.*" He put air quotes around the last bit. "Get it? You're supposed to be part of the audience."

He put his hand on my shoulder.

"But don't worry, Coe Vessel, I'll get the engineers to send you a special code that unlocks the clasp. Just don't tell anyone."

Together, we watched Watanabe—enigmatic Gargantua of the art world, drinking and spinning from one engineer to another, slamming into them like they were in an old-style mosh pit, shouting over the music. My work was done and I could go home. That alone was worth celebrating.

"We're all going to be stinky rich," Yohji shouted. "Time to celebrate!"

I held out my glass, Yohji filled it, and we started drinking whiskey like water.

I pulled the lavender-scented sleep mask from my eyes and tossed aside the airline blanket. All through the cabin, passengers sprawled and slumped like a business-class crime scene. I had only slept for a few hours, according to Death Watch, gleaming in the dim light. The red number *1* on the metal band (the *bracelet*, as watch pros called it) throbbed slowly, like the lights atop distant radio towers. I wasn't used to wearing a watch, so it felt more like a handcuff to me.

Out my window hovered a layer of clouds, silvered by moonlight, the dark ocean below. We still had some of the Pacific and all of America to fly over and I knew I should sleep while it was dark, just like the seasoned travelers were doing. But I was too excited—about going home, coming up with a pitch that didn't suck, and getting the Watanabe account.

I took my notebook out of my backpack and started writing down ideas for the Death Watch campaign. But then I paused and pressed the button to summon a stewardess, to order a gin and tonic for me and a second one for Vince.

THE HOLY ROTOR

Like every hustler, my father needed an accomplice. In the beginning, it was my fast-witted mother. But after she died, he turned to me.

Vince worked in BBDO's Midtown offices most of the time. But when he had to travel to important client meetings, he would pull me from school and take me along. He would introduce me as an intern and I'd take my place near him to watch and learn—and occasionally blurt out an idea or a tagline that he had fed me. *Can you believe it? The kid nailed it!*

We had our moves down like a comedy duo or Times Square scammers. At fifteen, I could tell a shitty concept from a winner. I could spot a derivative campaign or off-brand message. I knew that whatever we were creating was as much about theater as results. It was the mid-90's and data hadn't taken the fun out of everything yet. Metrics were just a glimmer in some nerdling's eye.

Midair somewhere between New York and Minneapolis, my father had briefed me, his adolescent acolyte, on our upcoming meeting—Vince's idea of a vacation. He explained that Driscoll Dryers was paying BBDO millions to raise its visibility in the marketplace and make every restaurant in the world ask for cloth napkins that had been washed, dried, and sanitized with Driscoll's WhisperJet™ process. My father would be pitching the final creative work to the marketing team tomorrow morning.

As he swizzled his third gin and tonic with a red plastic drink-sword, Vince taught me the vernacular of Driscoll Dryers. Every client had one. Learning it was the price of admission to their world.

He described how a newly laundered restaurant napkin gave off a finely calibrated scent—fresh without smelling of detergent or masking the cooking aromas drifting from the kitchen. This quality was known as *scent neutrality*. It needed to feel crisp but not scratchy, soft but not slick. This quality was called *finger feel.*

And behind these qualities waited the quality that towered over all the others—*optical opacity*. The napkin had to look brand new, even if it was on its hundredth trip through the dryer. Dining out was all about the future, not the past. No lipstick traces. No grease spots. No stray crease from previous foldings. A napkin had to be immaculate.

Before he popped a Valium, pulled down his eyeshade, and checked out for the duration of the flight west toward Minneapolis, my father handed me a thick background binder crammed with data sheets, press clippings, and annual reports. All of the 747's reading lights went off but mine as I studied the industrial apocrypha. The binder my father handed me was from the real world, not Trevor Day School. Studying the minutiae of industrial laundry machinery seemed more important than learning French verbs or studying European history. Advertising was hard and about mastering the details—and life seemed pretty much the same. I would learn that lesson for myself eventually, but my father wanted to give me an early warning.

The next morning, we sat in Driscoll Dryers' corporate boardroom high above Minneapolis, the city below bleak in midwinter. The meeting started with some back-and-forth between the BBDO guys and the clients. But their chatter was freighted with anxiety. The future of the account hinged on getting these commercials approved.

Despite the tension, Vince introduced his team's work with studied nonchalance and humor, like he was about to screen a home movie instead of four broadcast-grade commercial spots that had burned through a massive budget.

The lights dimmed and the final cut played on a giant monitor for the executive team.

East Wind showed a beautiful woman looking down from a fire escape, her silk blouse rustling gently in the breeze. Her boyfriend joined her to watch the crowds of people teeming through the city on a Friday night.

To me, it looked like fifteen seconds of evocative beauty, the kind that moved the romantic in me.

North Wind showed Minneapolis in winter, a couple walking along the snowy shore of Lake Superior. They turned to face north, closing their eyes as the wind ruffled the fur fringing their parkas.

South Wind was set in New Orleans, in the thrumming French Quarter, where an older couple (hitting all the demographics) looked down from a balcony and smiled as a Mardi Gras parade passed.

West Wind featured a dewy couple standing at an overlook on the winding coastal highway, staring out at the Pacific at sunset. Cars drifted by the background, evocative headlights raking across the couple. Then the west wind ran through their hair and rippled their clothes.

The woman delivered a sultry voiceover. *WhisperJet. Like the wind. Strong. Natural. Clean.* Then the call to action faded in.

WHISPERJET. ASK FOR IT.

The executives at the table seemed to like what they saw. And so did I. The commercials were beautiful. The call to action was taut and cleverly constructed, with parallel structure and a half-rhyme at the end. At the time, the glowing mid-1990s, I didn't realize that I was watching the last gasp of old-school advertising—or as Wren liked to call it, *manvertising.*

"I only wish there were more kinds of wind," one of the execs said, finally. "Beautiful work, Vince."

More compliments, graciously deflected to the entire BBDO team by my father. He didn't explain how hard it had been for the dozens of people involved in creating ads *for a dryer.* Didn't describe the weeks of site scouting and permitting, the test shots with dozens of models in four cities. Didn't complain about the arguments with the petulant copywriter or the long nights with the director in the editing room.

Vince was the consummate pro. He made his work (and his life) look easy even though it wasn't.

"But when will we show the WhisperJet 5000?" This question

came from an older man in a dark blue suit at the other end of the conference table.

My father gave the creative team a look that said *what the fuck*—and this was before WTF. A loose cannon had come unchained.

"You mean at trade shows?" my father said. "That's up to the marketing team."

"No, I mean *in the commercials.*" Dark Blue Suit's face twisted and he rose up suddenly as if my father's words had probed his sensitive prostate. "WE HAVE TO SHOW THE WHISPERJET 5000. IT'S A DAMN FINE-LOOKING MACHINE."

"Thanks for coming today, Mr. Driscoll," said the nervous woman who headed the marketing team, as if talking to a kindergartener instead of a blue-suited mummy, son of the company's founder and chairman of the Board of Directors. "We didn't know you would be here."

The marketing chief stood and looked Mr. Driscoll in his gin-clear blue eyes. "Let me explain. During our initial visioning, the marketing team decided to go for a higher-end look. Showing machinery is for trade shows. These 15-second spots are—"

"Don't call them spots, dearie." Mr. Driscoll flapped his pale hand at her. "We hate spots."

Hahaha. Nervous laughter from the team.

As the Driscoll team's intra-company spat escalated, my father looked over at me and wiggled his fingers, summoning me. The meeting was veering into the weeds. I leaned toward him.

"I need you to go over and spin that metal thing on the wall," he whispered in my ear, then glanced at a plaque on the far wall. "But not until I tell you to."

I nodded and drifted away from the conference table.

"What you need to do is figure out where to put the Whisper-Jet 5000," Driscoll shouted. "Because I'm paying for this expensive marketing hoo-ha and we're gonna show the unit."

Show the unit. Was there ever a more dickish instruction?

My father decided to dive in. "Mr. Driscoll. You know the saying *sell the sizzle, not the steak*, right?"

"We don't like steaks either, friend. They're greasy." Old Man Driscoll laughed and pointed at my father. "Who the hell is this guy?"

My father smiled, killing with kindness. "I'm Vince Vessel, senior creative director at BBDO. The ad agency your impressive company hired to stop hemorrhaging sales to the competition in Japan."

"Listen. You may think you know our business, but you don't." Driscoll reddened and sputtered. "I spent three decades at the helm. I know what our customers want. They want to see a big, shiny unit that like a million bucks but costs a lot less. They want to know the discount. And they want to know the local distributor. Maybe we could just have them all listed at the end, alphabetically, like we do in the brochures."

Vince surveyed the conference table, taking stock. Stunned and queasy, the BBDO account team had taken an intense interest in the backs of their hands. My father gazed one by one at the other Driscoll executives, who had enthusiastically supported the *Only the Wind* campaign moments ago. Suddenly, their spines had turned limber.

He nodded at me, his accomplice, standing across the room near the far wall, thick with awards.

I'd been activated like a sleeper cell.

One of the plaques held a small five-bladed thing that looked like a boat propeller. I reached out and touched its cool metal, then gave it a hard spin. But it didn't spin. It just flew off of its plaque, ricocheted off a table, then hit the floor, where it broke into dozens of pieces.

The meeting stopped cold.

"Oh *blessed Jesus,*" Driscoll shouted. "The rotor!"

Mr. Driscoll stood and tottered toward the debris. He dropped down on his hands and knees and began collecting the pieces, as if the True Cross had splintered in the conference room. Then he grabbed his chest, lurched forward, and face-planted into the carpeting, blue and red—the corporate colors of the Driscoll Dryers brand.

The same colors Mr. Driscoll turned as he went into cardiac arrest.

I had destroyed the very first rotor used in an industrial dryer, a breakthrough innovation hand-hammered in 1922 by Daniel Driscoll, company founder and father of the current Driscoll. It was made of battered, age-brittled brass and wasn't worth anything, but it was the core of the company—used as its logo, on the cover of its annual report, and even on the company T-shirt. The softball team was the Rotors. The annual sales award went to the Top Rotor. It went on and on.

Mr. Driscoll disappeared into the hospital for a quadruple bypass. His heart condition had been sent into hyperdrive by me, the young intern who had destroyed the holy rotor beyond repair. He recovered, but never set foot in headquarters again. In his absence, the marketing team regrew its spine and approved the *Only the Wind* campaign, which went on to win a Cannes Lion and three CLIO Awards. Driscoll Dryers remained a lucrative BBDO client for years.

My father bought me my first drink on that long-ago plane ride back home from Minneapolis, when we raised a toast to ourselves—mentor and student, father and son, survivors. Now, flying back from Tokyo, I raised my plastic glass to Vince, to honor my father and keep his uneasy spirit at bay.

MORIAWASE

"Welcome home, conquering hero." Nathan met me at the reception area and gave me an awkward hug. I had come directly to the agency from the airport, so I had the wrinkled, stunned look of an international arrival. I shoved my suitcase in the front closet and we walked through the agency. Our designers and copywriters, the digital marketing team—earbuds in, eyes on their laptops—looked up for milliseconds and blinked in my general direction. It was the Moriawase equivalent of a standing ovation. Despite their studied nonchalance, my cohorts seemed more engaged and awake, leavened by a new account, one that promised to be more interesting than designing a trade show booth for a waste management company.

Harup wandered around in the back of the workroom, a murky exception among the young designers, black metal to their chrome. Pale and unshaven, tall and thin, Harup's look could be described as *disgruntled art punk.*

Lothar, the agency's long-suffering cat, a cranky black-and-white mongrel named Lothar, came over and rubbed against my leg. When I bent down to scratch him behind the ears he started purring like a misfiring engine.

Wren circled closer and hugged me. She wore her *invisible-in-the-city* outfit, spring version—black shorts, white T-shirt, denim jacket, black Converse high tops.

"Missed you," she said.

"Really?"

"Well, a little. Kinda quiet around here without you."

"Thanks?"

Nathan steered us toward the conference room. "I know you're exhausted, but let's do a quick debrief." We walked across the agency through beams of late-afternoon sunlight. I remembered the long weekend when we pulled down the suspended ceiling to reveal the skylights, polished the cement floor, and painted the brick walls high-gloss white. That was twenty years ago.

Nathan nodded at Harup and Wren and they followed us toward the conference room.

"Let's see it!" Wren rushed close and I held up my left arm to show her Death Watch, its band blinking a tiny *2*—tallying the days I had been wearing it.

She pulled out her iPhone and took a few pictures. "You look really tired. Got double bags under your eyes."

"Here." I handed Wren a bottle of duty-free Icelandic gin from my backpack. "Maybe if you drink this you'll get nicer."

"Probably not, but thanks." She put the bottle in the low cabinet cluttered with our awards—a couple of golden Clios, some silver Webby Awards, and a bunch of ANDYs from the Advertising Club of New York. We kept them in uncurated disarray to show that we cared, just not that much.

"What'd you get me?" Nathan asked.

"A cool account that'll make us a boatload of money?"

"Thanks for that."

"Your last presentation killed," Wren said, raising her fist in the air. "New Nihilists forever!"

"Your research inspired me."

Wren shook her head. "And you did a great job." She looked at me and steadied her deep brown eyes. "Every once in a while I'm sincere."

"Something to look forward to."

We slid our vintage white leather Eames chairs up to the green glass conference table, Nathan and Wren to either side of me, Harup across from us in his favorite seat. Nathan polished his wire-rimmed glasses on his shirtsleeve and put them on. "A quick update—Watanabe already signed the contract and the purchase order. Wiring an initial payment in the morning."

"Cool for us." The impending arrival of serious money meant we had to get moving.

"What's Watanabe like?" Wren asked.

"Hard to figure," I said. "Even his own son says he doesn't really know him."

"That Yohji guy?"

"Right. Also a bit of a cipher."

"Need to figure him out," Nathan said. "He's our client contact for the Death Watch campaign. Good name, by the way. Cassius Seven sucked."

"Alta came up with it."

Nathan nodded. "Not surprised."

"Yohji's young and slippery, but seems smart. He's got some wild clothes." I scrolled through my photos, shared one of him wearing his lime-green Doc Martens. "Can't say I miss him."

"Well, get ready," Wren said. "He's flying in for the campaign kick-off meeting next week."

I paused. "Really?"

Wren checked her Apple Watch. "Gets here on Thursday at two."

"We need to get our act together. Can't let him go rogue on us." I told them about Yohji's idea about the floating watches and talking cats.

"No no no no no." Nathan shook his hand in front of him and Harup gave his *I hate people* look.

"They liked *New Nihilists*, right?" Wren said. "We can build on that."

"Yes." I opened my notebook, read the notes I had scribbled on the plane. "We could do a new take on *a day in the life*. Make Death Watch seem like a lifestyle choice."

"For who, exactly?" Nathan asked.

"People who don't particularly like living?"

They laughed, even Harup.

"Funny," Nathan said. "But if the watch really worked it would be tragic."

"It doesn't," I said, remembering Yohji's promise.

"Then what we're running is a bait-and-switch campaign," Nathan said. "Like Orson Welles, back in the day."

"*War of the Worlds?*" I said.

"Yeah."

"Is that a gamer thing?" Wren looked confused. "Like *Mortal Kombat?*"

Nathan tilted his head at Wren. "Look it up, buttercup."

Wren did, clattering away on her laptop at Olympic speed. "*Wow*. Oh, yeah. This was before that actor guy got all fat. Fooled people that Martians were attacking. Cool. *Mars Attacks*. That movie sucked. So what were they doing? Trying to fool people and scare the pants off of 'em?"

"Wanted to cause a panic," Nathan said, "and get attention."

"And prove how gullible people were," I added, "believing everything they heard on *the big wind*."

"Cue Fox News." Wren clattered away at her keyboard, absorbing details.

"Here's the thing," Nathan said. "We need to sell a lot of watches. Then at the end of the project, when Watanabe tells people the truth, we'll make a clean exit. We don't want to look like assholes who fooled a bunch of sad people into putting on a watch that they thought might kill them but actually can't."

"Which is pretty much what we're going to do," I said.

Harup tilted his head and looked at us as he started texting from under the table, so adept that he didn't even seem to be moving, like a ventriloquist. His text flashed on my phone.

Theres fooling ppl. Then theres fukking ppl.

Harup wasn't mute. But he thought his heavy accent sounded silly, and Harup was definitely not silly. So Harup communicated via text only, sending messages pinging off distant cell towers to show up on our phones across the conference table. Nathan had tried to get him to cut it out, since it made clients nervous. But Harup continued to be a quiet island in an ocean of noise. When he texted, it mattered.

"Good point," Nathan said. "We want to fool them in a way that seems—"

lik we're not ttl assholes

I pointed at Harup. "Right."

"And if any negative buzz comes out of the whole thing," Nathan said, "we need to make sure Watanabe owns it."

"Oh, he will. Loves attention, good or bad. He's definitely going to want to be front and center."

"About that." Nathan opened a folder and turned some pages. "It's in the contract that he announces the watch and stays visible in the campaign."

"Uh, yeah, but—" Wren wrinkled her face.

"But what?" Nathan closed his folder.

"He's a bore," she said. "Like Karl Marx without the sense of humor."

"Pretty sure Marx didn't have one," I said.

"Exactly," Wren said. "If we give Watanabe the pulpit, he'll bore the shit out of the congregation. I've watched his online stuff. Art-speak with a side of cigarette smoke."

"He's a celebrity, kind of." I said. "People definitely know him."

"But they don't particularly like him." Wren clacked away at her laptop. "He's got about a twenty percent positive ranking across social media. Banksy has about seventy. Ai Weiwei is at eighty. The best thing we can do for Watanabe is limit his exposure."

"It's his watch," I said. "And his narrative."

"But you're the one wearing it," Wren said. "Maybe it's your story."

My cohorts turned to stare at my left wrist.

"Quit being weird," I said. "Tell me what you're up to."

A long pause. Then Wren chimed in. "Death Watch—early adopter tells his tale."

"You're a natural," Nathan said. "Perfect fit."

"No way." I shook my head. "I went to Tokyo on spec, sat through the weirdest product demo in the world, scraped my brain for concepts, and got the account. I've done my part."

"Well, you're the first customer." Wren reached out and flicked Death Watch with her fingers. "You're super credible. We're thinking the campaign could take a creator-customer approach, like Apple used to. First Watanabe announces his brilliant creation, then you, the first customer, tell the world why you bought it."

"There are other ways to go, of course," Nathan said. "But we don't have a lot of time."

"What do you mean?"

Nathan opened his folder, scanned the pages. "There's this accelerated sales clause."

"Which means?"

"Sales have to start coming in within ten days of launch."

"Or what?"

"They can move the campaign to another agency."

"You mean fire us?" I said. "We just got the account."

Nathan nodded, closed his folder.

"That's fucking impossible," I said. "Why didn't you tell me?"

"Had to hurry. Sooner we signed, sooner we got paid."

"We could have negotiated."

"The first draft said sales had to start in a week."

"Thanks for fighting for three extra days."

"No need to be snarky," Nathan said. "We'll come up with something great. We always do. Ten days is forever in Internet time."

"It's not," Wren said. "And no one says *Internet time* anymore. Or *snarky*."

"Thanks for that." Nathan stood up and pushed his chair in carefully. "Look, I know it isn't ideal."

"It's impossible," I said.

"We've done really hard campaigns in a few days." Nathan shrugged. "Why not this one?"

I said nothing. Nathan still didn't seem to get that Death Watch was a very different sell.

He looked around the conference room. "Got a great team."

Harup lowered his head on the conference table, done with us all.

Wren broke into a big fake smile, as if Nathan had just given her a raise instead of a ridiculous deadline.

"Gooooooo team!" Wren stood up and raised her arms as if shaking pom-poms, then jumped in the air. "Go Death Watch!"

CIVIL TWILIGHT

I SET DOWN MY BAG, clicked on the lights, and wandered through the apartment, opening shades and windows to let in the warm spring breeze. The sun had already set behind New Jersey, but it was still light—the palpable thrum of Midtown winding down after work, a slow, beautiful evening ahead.

No apples rested in a bowl on the breakfast table, no vegetables waited in the refrigerator—just takeout packets of soy sauce, sriracha, and hot mustard. As I stared into the bright void, I had to wonder if our life together was as empty as our refrigerator.

In the bedroom, I opened the closet, slowly emptying of Alta's clothes as she migrated more of her life to Darmstadt. Staring at the depleted closet offered another opportunity for my thoughts to slip into a maudlin key. Instead, I unpacked my bag, sorted the dirty laundry, and filled the dry-cleaning bag. I undressed, took a shower, put on new clothes, and set up my laptop on the dining room table.

We would talk later. I would find out how the Xtensia trials were going and Alta would hear more about the Death Watch campaign. Our life together would continue ahead, even if we were far apart, even if our apartment wasn't really a home, more like a hotel room that Alta and I shared between work trips.

We would sell the apartment someday, but not soon. We hadn't been in a hurry to move in together and now we weren't in a hurry to officially move on. We weren't dissatisfied or satisfied. We just were—and sometimes that was enough.

Alta and I had fallen in love at NYU, started Moriawase with Nathan, and got married at thirty. Our love was born too early and failed to thrive—that was the story we told ourselves until it stuck. Since we didn't have children, we could feel lucky that no one else had to suffer when we drifted apart and ended up back where we started—as friends.

I sat at the dining room table, sorting our mail and the Amazon boxes. In hindsight, our slow dissolution began at this table, a vintage Swedish piece made of light wood—functional and elegant. I could sell it to rid the apartment of a resonant object, but that wouldn't erase the memory of Zeno, sitting at the head of the table, being smart and charming. Being annoyingly confident and more than a little full of himself.

Being Zeno.

Alta met Zeno when she was working for Merck and he was looking for funding to start the Infinity Project. Merck wasn't interested, but Alta was. She was a fan of his bestselling book, *Live, Forever!*, which straddled wellness, self-help, and life extension. Like any budding guru, he had a wandering eye. So he invited Alta to his annual retreat in Sedona. She came back glowing, fit, and thoroughly charmed. He was assured and optimistic, and to my mind, tinted by more than a hint of grift. He was a radiant sun, attracting matter, attention, funding, acolytes. I was more like a wayward asteroid spinning through the universe, trying to avoid smashing into anything solid.

Soon Zeno was sitting at the head of our Swedish dining room table on a Sunday night, sharing an enormous tureen of a green soup that Alta had painstakingly prepared. No salt. No meat. Just the subtle flavor of lawn.

Zeno was a decade older than us, but with his full head of wild black hair and blazing dark eyes he seemed more vital and alive. He was thin and strong, nimble and wired, spewing life energy. *Chi,* as the Chinese put it. So much chi that our apartment seemed unable to contain it all.

Like Neil deGrasse Tyson explaining the universe, Zeno could summon deep silos of scientific data about maximizing life and make it interesting to mere mortals. He was also a shameless name-dropper of his famous friends, longevity-obsessed Silicon Valley tech bros who ate nothing but nutritional goo that Zeno concocted. Zeno made it seem like living longer was not only possible, but mandatory. It just required a punishingly Spartan diet and elimination of all *anti-life* behaviors, from negative thinking to smoking. A WASP by birth, Alta was hard-wired for self-denial. During that first dinner she had looked on in awe as Zeno spoke, and spoke, and spoke.

"I love your apartment," Zeno blurted after finishing every drop of his verdant soup. He waved his arms as he took in our not particularly lovable one-bedroom, bought with the easy cash of the early Moriawase days.

Alta leaned forward and whispered, as if the condo board was listening. "We want to buy another apartment someday and put them together."

"Of course you do." Zeno leaned back in his chair like an eighth-grader, balancing on two legs of a dicey chair I had dragged in from trash night. Behind him, the wall was adorned with an oatmeal-colored wall hanging, also from the curb. In the presence of our vivid guest, it looked like the unraveling flag of the Nation of Etsy.

"Of course you do," Zeno said, repeating himself louder now, beaming. "Why wait? Seize pleasure. You live on 57th Street, the boulevard of billionaires."

Zeno was right, but our 1950's white-brick building was on the far western frontier of 57th Street, a rotten molar among shiny glass incisors. Glenn, our sullen doorman, smelled like weed and salami and our trash chute kept clogging with deliquescing diapers.

"Buy *all* the apartments on your floor, friends. Turn it into your kingdom."

Our eyes widened with amazement. There were six other apartments on the seventh floor.

"Reach further." Zeno flailed his arms like a faith healer. "Make the world your own! Make your own world! Own the world you live in!"

I looked over at Alta, her eyes wide, nodding slowly, like a lucky-cat bobblehead in a Chinese restaurant. She was caught up in the moment, the dream, the delusion.

Then the delusion became the plan.

"Here's what you do. Buy an apartment every year." If stone tablets had been available, we would have carved them with Zeno's commandments.

"Wait until you have them all, then—"

Then what? We needed guidance. We were innocents. We knew nothing of Zillow or StreetEasy.

"KNOCK DOWN ALL THE WALLS." Zeno dervished through our apartment, swinging a metaphorical sledge, one that could cut through illusion as well as drywall and studs.

He stopped and stared at me, then Alta. "I know what you're thinking, friends."

I was thinking if I didn't get hopping on a spec campaign for a last-minute hotel site, RoomsWithaYou.com, we'd never get the account. What was Alta thinking? I couldn't tell. They were born opaque on the Upper East Side.

"You're thinking it's impossible."

Of course we were, because it was.

"Well it's not. Go beyond the limits. Of life. Of health. Of yourself. Even of your imagination. Why should you do something this crazy?" Zeno was asking the question we were both thinking. "Because—"

Because *what,* we wondered.

"Because *if you keep doing what you've always done, you'll get what you've always gotten.*"

Years later, I'd find that Zeno had lifted this fun-sized insight from Tony Robbins. But at the time, it hit us hard. A few years into our marriage, we were definitely doing the same thing over and over. Working late. Eating *mu shu* whatever from a 24-hour Chinese place that delivered. Watching DVDs on Alta's laptop in bed while we drank piney white wine from Slovenia. Starting every bleary morning held together by caffeine and routine. Wondering if this was why people had kids—so life had a purpose in their thirties. Knowing that there were much worse problems to have, that we should be thankful but weren't.

"Stay with the plan, friends. An apartment a year. Two if you can swing it. *Monetize. Optimize. Leverage. Transform.* MOLT!"

Alta smiled broadly at the catchy acronym.

"Soon you'll have your own kingdom in New York City. You'll live as gods among men."

I just wanted to live as an adman among the swaggering money managers who were colonizing the city. Survival seemed like an aspirational target. But Zeno was all about reaching for the stars.

Also, even then, reaching for Alta.

He put his hand on her shoulder. "Alta—I want you to offer what you've learned to the world. Leave Merck and come work on my team."

He pointed his finger toward me. "Coe, I want you to help me brand the life extension drug I'm working on." Nathan would be really glad that I brought in a new client.

"*Pro bono,* of course."

My smile faded.

My phone rang and woke me from an unsettling dream about going swimming in the ocean and finding a sea urchin attached to my throat. I shook off the dream and answered.

"You're back." As always, Alta sounded impossibly awake.

"Sort of." I sat up on and rubbed the left side of my face. I had fallen asleep on the living room floor.

"How're you feeling?"

"Shitty, but okay." I rubbed my cheek. "Got some kind of rash on my face."

"You're allergic to wool. Don't fall asleep on the rug."

"Didn't plan on it." I stood and wandered into the kitchen and gulped a glass of water.

"Drinking Japanese whiskey?"

"No, just water. Had enough whiskey for a while." I took a long drink. "I'm half-awake, so don't ask me anything hard."

"How's the campaign going?"

"Like I said."

"Just tell me a little."

"Nathan likes Death Watch. Told him you came up with it."

"Remind me to bill him."

"He and Wren hatched a scheme while I was gone."

"Sounds mysterious."

"Just annoying. They want me to be the poster boy for Death Watch when the campaign kicks in."

"You?"

"Thanks for that vote of confidence."

"Didn't mean it. You're a natural."

"I'm in advertising. I don't want to actually *be* advertising. Kind of like breaking the fourth wall."

"Kills the illusion."

"Right."

"Might work," Alta said. "Keep the agency way in the background. Put you out front like an Everyman. Then maybe the world won't figure out that Death Watch is a big joke."

"Not a joke," I said. "It's an experiment."

"Drug trials are experiments. This thing's just an art project. But it'll be okay. And you'll be fine. You always are."

Less sure, I said nothing.

"Hey, I got an email from Krishna."

"The blue deity?"

"I think that's racist."

"Just culturally insensitive."

"Krishna's the nice guy renting the place upstairs, remember? He had a family emergency back in Mumbai. May have to break their lease."

"Oh, got it." We hadn't followed Zeno's plan. But during a plush year, we did manage to buy the apartment directly above ours, planning to create a duplex at some vague point in the future. In the meantime, we rented it out to medical residents, who were perfect tenants—tired, quiet, rarely home.

"Krishna said he had emailed you about it, but didn't hear back."

"I was in Japan."

"Where you can't get email?"

"I was busy." As its *de facto* landlord, I was supposed to be keeping an eye on the extra apartment. But like most of my chores, it slid right off my plate.

"Check on them, will you?"

"Will do," I said. "But first, I'm going to fall asleep."

"In bed, okay? Not on the floor. You're not a grad student. You're the face of Death Watch."

I clicked off my phone.

When I woke up again it was past midnight. I tried to force myself back to sleep so I'd be back on a normal schedule but I couldn't.

I got dressed and walked into the kitchen to rummage around in the Drawer of Babel, jammed full of hotel key cards and pens, crumpled euros and yen. Debris from our work trips or artifacts from the last gasp of late capitalism? Only time would tell.

I found the keyring and walked out of our apartment. Most of the other apartments had been snapped up by investors, so our floor was almost always empty. I took the back stairs. Upstairs, the smell of sautéed onions hovered in the entryway—the unvanquished scent of the Langersteins. We had inspired them to move to Long Island City with a generous offer for their untouched-since-the-Kennedy-era apartment, directly above ours.

I slipped quietly into the living room.

The dim apartment was empty and immaculate. In the kitchen a thank-you note and a bottle of red waited on the counter. I read Krishna's note, found that his mother was very ill and he and his wife Lakshmi had to go back to Mumbai. He apologized for leaving on short notice. In my mind, I apologized for being a shitty landlord.

I'd have to call Alta's father, Robert, head of Neurological Surgery at New York Presbyterian. He could send some new medical residents our way, though the cusp of summer seemed like a tough time to rent a gloomy apartment in Midtown.

I wandered through the apartment, turning on lights and looking around, finding almost no evidence of its previous tenants.

Our plan had been to charm the co-op board, get approval to combine our two apartments, then get access to the roof and build a private deck. There would be workspaces for both of us so Alta wouldn't have to hunch over the kitchen table and I wouldn't have to work from the couch. We would create a luxury mini-penthouse and seize pleasure just like all the other hedonists of Manhattan. But time, inertia, and the pandemic derailed our plan, which even downsized, still bore the mark of Zeno. After I killed the Zazzy offer, we didn't have the money we would need to MOLT, though we ended up owning a second apartment in Manhattan.

Even I hated us a little bit for being so lucky. But like all good luck, ours looked a lot better from afar than it did up close.

I checked the bathroom for flooding or bugs (neither), made sure the fridge was empty (it was), and cracked the windows in an attempt to air out the apartment (good luck with that). I shut off lights as I walked back through the apartment to the entryway, where I leaned against the doorway and took one last look, one floor upstairs but decades back in time.

Alta never ventured up here, seeing our extra apartment as a broken dream. But I liked the dim apartment in much the same way that my father, connoisseur of an older, more authentic New York, would have. It was a fading relic from the time before a golden wave of money swept over the city and tainted it forever, a prewar cave dwelling from before billionaires turned their attention to life on Mars.

TEAM DEATH

"So good to see you again!" Yohji grabbed my hand and shook it maniacally, as if we were old friends, reunited after years. He took in the Bauhaus-ness of Moriawase—the skylights, the glossy white workroom. "This is so cool!"

Yohji's cinnamon-colored suit might be exquisite in Tokyo, but it made him look cringingly Wonka-like in our white office, blazing in the noonday sun.

Lothar emerged from the tech closet, annoyed at the arrival of a stranger with a loud voice.

"You have an office cat!" What was it with Yohji and cats?

Lothar sniffed Yohji's lime-green Doc Martens and strutted back into his lair.

I introduced Yohji to Nathan and Wren while Harup lurked in the background. We drifted into the conference room and took our places at the long table, glossy white and immaculate.

Team Death's first official meeting was underway.

"So, Coe tells me you did some ad work."

"Yes!" Yohji broke into a smile. Nathan's bond-building opener worked.

"Did you work on Watanabe's other projects?"

We all looked at Yohji, waiting for the answer we already knew. Harup and Wren were info-sleuths, and Yohji was an open book online.

"Worked on his last project," he said.

"Maybe we could hear a bit more," Nathan said. "You know, find out how it went. Could be helpful as we get a new campaign going."

I beamed silent thanks to Nathan, master of client management.

Yohji opened his laptop and looked around for the cable to connect to the screen on the far wall. Harup pointed at a black box about as big as a pack of cigarettes, which connected every device a client might drag in. He hated awkward moments.

"Cool." Yohji squinted at his laptop screen, searching.

Harup stood up to leave, but I shot him a look. He sat back down, opened his laptop, and stared at the screen.

"Yeah, uh, here it is." Yohji sounded like a grad student who hadn't prepared for his seminar. "Been a few years. Here are some photos from the campaign."

The screen filled with a photo of a beautiful woman standing in the middle of Times Square, wearing a long white dress and a jeweled breathing mask, her piercing green eyes staring at the camera.

He clicked and the next photo came up—another model in a blood-red dress, standing in the middle of a crowded hospital ward.

The next photo showed a trio of pale models standing in a field, arms around each other, wearing nothing but bejeweled masks.

We glanced at each other, wondering why Yohji was showing us what seemed to be pandemic porn.

Nathan leaned forward. "Maybe you could give us an overview of the campaign, Yohji, to make sure we're aligned."

"Oh, yeah." He searched on his laptop and smiled when he found what he was looking for. "Here's the press release," he said. "The project was called *Money Can Save You*. Watanabe wanted to show how money makes people feel invincible, even during, you know—a pandemic." He rolled his eyes.

"But it can't save you," Wren said.

"Right. But he came up with a great readymade." He dug around in his white-leather backpack. "Helps to see it."

He took out a black case and set it in front of him like a ceremonial object. He looked at each of us, then opened the case to reveal the glittering mask. "The jewels around the outside are garnets, but the center stones are rubies, diamonds, and star sapphires. The stuff that looks like wire is actually woven strands of 24 carat gold." He slid the case over to Wren.

She looked at it carefully. "Wow, looks better from a distance. Up close it looks like someone bedazzled a Halloween mask."

Nathan rolled his eyes at Wren's complete lack of filters.

"*Uh,* what do you do here again?"

"Chief Awareness Officer." Wren's voice was even and direct, not pulling rank, just reminding Yohji that her opinion mattered, even though she was wearing a denim jacket.

"Do you know how much that mask cost, Jen?"

"It's Wren. And no, I don't."

"Five hundred thousand dollars." Yohji looked up, expecting some *oohs* and *ahhhs*, getting nothing.

"Kinda over the top," she said. "But I guess that's Watanabe's schtick, right? Takes normal stuff—tsunami debris, a medical mask, a watch—and politicizes it."

Yohji startled at her ruthless insight. "Pretty much."

"So how many did you sell?" Nathan was a bulldog for results.

"Like twenty." Yohji shrugged. "Mostly to art dealers and fashionistas. Did pop-up stores in Dubai, Marfa, Basel. Jewelers swooped in when the price of gold went way up and they realized we had underpriced the mask. They cut them up and melted them down, sold the gemstones. Really sad."

Yohji looked around for sympathy, found none. Harup had drifted into his *imagining-all-the-other-places-I'd-rather-be* fugue state.

"Sounds like the project didn't work." Wren knew how to cut to the chase.

Yohji looked flummoxed for a moment, then rallied. "That's true. We didn't get a lot of press and most of it missed the message—the irony of a half-million-dollar mask. They just said Watanabe had gone all Versace. But to be honest, we stole the design from Alexander McQueen."

Wren leaned toward Yohji. "So the mask is another lie, right?"

Yohji squirmed in his white chair like he was being interrogated. *"What?"*

"The mask promised something it couldn't deliver," she said. "It couldn't save people who put it on. Same as Death Watch can't kill anyone."

Yohji stood and pointed a shaking finger at me. "You told them!"

"Yeah, I did." I shrugged. Secrets were for telling.

"Why?"

"They're on the team, Yohji. In fact, they *are* the team."

"You said you wouldn't tell anyone."

"You said your father was a fisherman."

He opened his mouth but didn't say anything, for once.

"Anyway, they have to know what we're selling or we can't create a great campaign."

Yohji thought about it for a moment, settled, sat back down. "Okay. Just don't tell anyone else. Any of you."

"We won't," Nathan lied. "But we have to move fast, before people start to figure out that it's a prank."

Yohji gave Nathan a hard stare. "Do *not* call it a prank."

"Then what should we call it?"

"An experiment. All of Watanabe's works are social research."

"Okay, so we'll call it an experiment," Nathan said. "What did you learn from the last experiment?"

"Good question." Yohji stood up and stretched, then peered out the conference room window down on Grand Street, slick with spring rain. He was relishing the role of client. Pretty soon he'd be asking for lunch to be brought in.

He stayed silent for so long that Harup started playing with his phone.

"I guess the main thing we learned was not to start an experiment during a global crisis. We ended up getting lost in the shuffle. The mask just kind of disappeared in the midst of all that ... bad news." Yohji waved his hand in front of him to clear away the memory of millions of people dying.

"Let's turn to Death Watch," Nathan said. "That's why you came all the way from Tokyo."

"Okay, Watanabe emailed me this last night." Yohji tapped on his laptop screen. "I'm supposed to show it to you." He clicked and a bulleted list flashed on the screen.

At the top of the list was a header that said GOALS FOR THE CAMPAIGN.

"So here are the goals for this campaign."

Thx mr master of th obvious

I gave Harup the look that said *give it a rest.*

"We want to get lots of attention. That means not just from the art press. Lots of outrage. Tons of controversy."

"Getting attention for Death Watch is going to be a breeze," Wren said. "There's nothing else like it."

Nathan and I looked at each other. We always had to remind Wren to make our work sound harder so we could bill more. Telling clients their project sounded easy opened the door to a discount.

Yohji smiled. "Yeah, we want to make sure that we go wide. Global."

"You're already getting strong early buzz—word's leaking out about the watch." Wren held up her thick blue bible of media contacts. "When you launch, we'll get you tons more."

"Exactly." Yohji moved the cursor and the list disappeared. "*Shit.*"

Harup jumped up like a roadie, did a few virtuoso keyboard moves and the list reappeared.

"Thanks, dude!"

Harup gave Yohji a tight smile and sat back down.

"Okay, next point. We want to get a Death Watch into a major museum collection. You knew who really pisses Watanabe off? Damien Hirst. He gets all kinds of attention for work that doesn't—"

I raised my hand to stop the distracting art-bashing. "What do you want to happen right after we launch Death Watch?"

Yohji shut up and thought for a moment. "We want to see momentum. Lots of people joining the experiment. Buying a boatload of watches, quickly."

"We need to talk about the schedule," Nathan said.

"Already did." Yohji stared into the far corner of the room. "You have ten days."

"There's no way we can hit that deadline," Wren said. Most agencies just told clients what they wanted to hear, but not Moriawase, and definitely not Wren.

"Why not?"

"Not an easy sell," I said. "Wren's going to build awareness and get attention. But New Nihilists are a niche audience."

"Then find them, or we'll find another agency that can."

We said nothing, surprised to find a ball of ice at Yohji's core.

Nathan held up his hand. "We'll do the best we can."

"Let's hope it's good enough." Yohji gave an uncertain smile, then gathered up his laptop and fled the conference room, done with working.

We sat in silence for a moment.

Wren nodded toward the black case. "Dude forgot his fancy mask."

Harup took a seat across from me in our usual table. He didn't say hello, just nodded. He wore black jeans, a black T-shirt, and a heavy black leather jacket on a warm night. We came to Bar Dog right after work, so it was more crowded than Harup preferred. He avoided strangers, crowds, clients, dogs, other designers, germs, anyone in costume, tourists, and sunlight.

Tracy, our long-suffering waitress, froze when she saw us then ran back behind the bar.

She came back with our drinks on a small tray and set Harup's glass carefully in front of him. He inspected the latest iteration of the salty dog, their signature cocktail and his personal favorite. Highball glass. One ice cube, not two frozen together. Evenly applied salt on the rim without any empty patches. As Harup had informed me many times, without salt, a salty dog was just a greyhound.

Harup eyeballed his latest drink to confirm its symmetrical placement on a Bar Dog coaster with a matching bar napkin to the right. Then he raised the glass, lightly sweated in the warm bar, to test its composition—three and one-third ounces of grapefruit juice (fresh, not canned) and one and one-third ounces of gin (Hendricks, not some weird botanical stuff from Germany).

He looked up with a radiant smile, as if Tracy just delivered a highball glass filled with liquid gold over silver ice cubes, salted with diamonds. She sighed with relief and disappeared behind the bar.

I couldn't even begin to tally the ridiculous tips I had left for Tracy and hundreds of waitresses and waiters all over the world for dealing with Harup.

Serving Harup was easy. He always ordered the same thing. Serving Harup was hard. He demanded perfection. Being his friend was much the same.

I set my phone on the table in front of me, screen up.

Let me see yr watch.

I lifted my left arm from the table and pulled my sleeve back to reveal Death Watch, its gleaming metal reflecting the bar's strings of colored lights. The number 7 glowing on the band. We had spent a week together, me and my shiny new friend.

It was the first time Harup had taken a close look at Death Watch but he just nodded. The watch could have been spewing flames and Harup wouldn't have been excited. Years ago, on a Sabena flight to Brussels, thick smoke had flooded the cabin somewhere over the North Atlantic. Oxygen masks dropped and even the libertine Belgians started praying. But Harup just kept eating kale chips and playing *Go* on his iPad.

Unflappable or insentient, the jury was still out on Harup.

He texted.

Oldskool pitchman. Hahahaha.

"Thanks, buddy." I took a long drink of red wine. Wren and Nathan had overruled my many objections and now I was the official voice of Death Watch, Mr. New Nihilist.

I felt queasy, not just from Bar Dog's house wine, but because I would be the voice (and face) of the campaign Wren was already putting together.

"I don't want to do it," I said. "It's bad luck." My father appeared in an ad once, part of a public service campaign for safe driving—hilarious because Vince never drove. He told me it felt like being scalded by spotlights.

I didn't want that.

Harup reached out to put his hand on my shoulder, an uncharacteristic gesture from my phobic friend.

Jst a gig. It'll be ok.

"Alta said the same thing."

Bettr than th last quote nquote xperiment

"What do you mean?"

Harup jabbed at his phone for a bit, then spun it toward me. I read while he savored his drink. The story was from a Slovenian photographer, Anton Krajnc, who shot the *Money Can Save You* campaign for an agency in Ljubljana. From what I could tell from the auto-translated blogpost, the photographer and his crew didn't want to set foot in the hospital but Watanabe insisted. They dodged security and got the shot, the one that Yohji had showed us during his visit to Moriawase—a photo of a beautiful model wearing the bejeweled mask with a chaotic hospital ward behind her.

But not far enough.

The model contracted a virulent strain of the coronavirus and died, her death lost among millions of others. The photographer ended his post by demanding that the art world boycott Watanabe's work.

I pushed Harup's phone back to him. He rubbed the screen on his leg and texted.

Nd to be careful.

"This project isn't as dangerous," I said.

Ppl r gonna get pissed off at the watch and u

"People will do whatever they want," I said. "We'll just have to play it out and stop if it gets weird."

Harup shook his head.

Once ths thing gts strted theres no stopping it

"Maybe it won't even get started," I said. "Who's going to buy Death Watch in just ten days? It's impossible. Besides, it costs $50,000. Not exactly an impulse buy."

Yeh, we're fked

Harup shrugged, savored a sip of his salty dog, then put his drink down carefully on its coaster.

"Really?" I reached over to pick up his drink, licked the salty rim. "Mmmmm."

He backed away so fast that his chair almost tipped over.

WTF!

Harup picked up his sullied drink and put it on the floor.

Tracy rushed over from the bar. "Everything okay?"

Harup nodded, pointed at me.

"I messed up his drink," I said. "But don't bring him another for a few minutes. I'm mad at him."

"Please don't get too freaky tonight, okay?" Tracy rushed back to the bar.

I leaned forward, licked the salt from my lips. It tasted pretty good. "Remember that crazy German guy who invented that zero-alcohol cocktail? The gross red one?"

Beets 'n Tonic?

"We drank Beets 'n Tonic. And we came up with a campaign, because we're good, really good. And because we don't give up, even when whatever we're pitching seems impossible to sell."

He went silent.

"There's always an angle." It was one of my father's favorite lines.

Harup sat staring at his phone. Maybe he realized he had let me down. Or maybe he was just sad about his drink.

I waved Tracy down.

Harup perked up when she delivered yet another perfect salty dog, which he pulled closer to protect. "So are you going to help me, or are you just going to bail?"

Harup took a sip.

Better than fkn Beets n Tonic.

"I'll take that as a *yes*."

Harup nodded.

We sat silently in Bar Dog, the air warm and still, aware of the television over the bar but not watching it, close but not saying anything—our version of friendship. It worked for us.

Harup pulled my notebook across the table, opened it and wrote something, then spun it around to reveal a name and a phone number.

"Who's Vanessa?"

Shes any1 and everything.

Harup gave an inscrutable smile.

"And I should call her because...?"

Needs an apt. Tld her you got one. Jst call hr.

"I will.

Harup gave me his skeptical look, knowing I let things slide, lots of them, most of them.

Shes got $

My interest in Harup's friend ramped up. I could have a new renter upstairs by the time Alta came back to New York. One problem solved.

"I will. I promise." We raised our glasses to Vanessa, Death Watch—and the uncertain future.

PERSONAE

Wren walked to the white board, picked up a marker and stood still for a moment, lost in thought. Through the conference room windows, I could see the workroom emptying out, designers packing up, turning off computers, heading home. Team Death had been sequestered in the conference room for hours, brainstorming about the launch of Death Watch, drinking so much coffee everything we said seemed clever. But now we were getting down to the very unfunny business of figuring out how to sell potential death.

WHO'S GOING TO BUY?

Wren underlined it, then started making her list, her hand a blur, as if she couldn't scrawl her ideas fast enough.

MEN WHO WANT TO LOOK BRAVE BUT AREN'T
MEN TRYING TO OUTDO EACH OTHER
MEN WITH SOMETHING TO PROVE
HEINOUS FINANCE DUDES WHO THINK THEY'RE ROYALTY
PEOPLE WHO ARE SICK OF THE MESSED-UP WORLD
ARTY NARCISSISTS LIKE WATANABE
ANTI-NATALISTS

I squinted at the last line. "What's an anti-natalist?"

"They hate their parents for giving birth to them. Sometimes they sue them."

"Really?"

"It's a thing. They resent being born into such a shitty world, so a potentially deadly watch might look good to them."

I nodded—another reason to be glad Alta and I didn't have kids.

Wren handed the marker to Harup like a baton. He approached

the white board tentatively. The whole thing seemed too analog at first but then Harup got over himself and started writing.

ART COLLECTRS WHO DIDN'T READ TH FINE PRNT
PPL SURE ITS TH ENDTIME
DEBTORS LOOKING 4 WAY OUT OF DEBT
GAMBLERS WHO THNK THEY CAN BT THE ODDS
PPL DONE GIVING FUKS

Harup stared at the whiteboard for a moment, then handed me the marker.

I added to our growing list.

NEW NIHILISTS
PEOPLE WHO DON'T WANT TO LIVE TO SEE THE NEXT DISASTER
WOULD-BE SUICIDES WHO DON'T MIND WAITING
DISENCHANTED LEFTISTS
DISENCHANTED CONSERVATIVES
DISENCHANTED PEOPLE
PEOPLE WITH LOW IMPULSE CONTROL, LIKE ME

I handed the marker to Nathan. He stood in front of the white board and stared at the list for a long time. It was hard to imagine what he could add. We'd covered a lot of ground already. He started writing.

ANYONE WITH $50,000

He underlined it three times, capped the marker carefully, and sat back down at the conference table. We contemplated the prospective customers for Death Watch. Each group needed something that was missing from their lives and we knew what it was.

They needed Death Watch.

All we had to do was convince them.

"Here's your persona." Wren slid a folder across the conference table.

"What?" I'd come up with countless brand personas for our

clients over the years. But never had one of my own.

"Like you but a little different, more in tune with the New Nihilists."

"Thought I was just supposed to be the voice of the customer."

"You are, but adjusted a bit to be more ... on message."

Nathan laughed. "Did you think we were just going to let you start saying shit like you usually do?"

I gave it some thought. "Yes?"

"*No.*" Wren, Harup, and Nathan shook their heads.

I stood up and walked over to the window. A guy in a yellow cellphone costume was walking down the sidewalk, trying to drum up business for the Verizon store. I pictured myself wearing a silver watch outfit, doing a little dance on Grand Street, singing a jingle about Death Watch.

Hankering to die?
Give Death Watch a try!

Somewhere in the spirit world, creative souls division, Vince Vessel shook his head in shame.

Wren walked over and stood next to me at the window. "Look, you just have to play the role of customer for us until Watanabe reveals the truth. Then we can adjust our strategy."

"I'd like that."

"When you guys went to NYU," Wren said, "didn't you do any acting?"

"Kinda?" I remembered Mister Mucus and beamed that thought across the table to Nathan.

Nathan smiled, flailed his arms in a credible Mister Mucus impersonation.

"Enough, weird dudes." Wren led me back to the table.

I opened the folder and read Wren's detailed media plan and talking points about why I decided to buy Death Watch.

"This is fantastic." Wren was the best strategist and copywriter in the agency. Only Alta was better, but she was gone.

I handed the folder to Nathan.

He read for a few minutes, adding notes. "It's okay, but you're selling the problem not the solution."

Wren rolled her eyes. It was one of Nathan's standby criticisms.

"*The world's a mess and it ain't getting better*. That's not news to anyone. We don't need to make our audience feel bad. We need to make them feel like buying Death Watch, fast." Nathan scrawled more notes on the back of the draft and slid it across the conference table to Wren.

"It's an incremental sell," Wren said.

"By that you mean *slow*?"

"I mean complicated. It's like trying to convince someone to join AA, but luring them in with death instead of coffee."

"That's funny," Nathan said, not laughing. "But you heard Yohji, right?"

Wren nodded. "I know, I know. We need to sell a bunch of watches fast or we lose the account."

"Not just lose the account," Nathan said. "We lose the billings. We lose a client who might bring in more projects and money. We lose all the free PR we'll be getting when the quote unquote experiment is revealed. Which would pull in other clients and more projects and even more money. Because if we can sell death, we can sell anything."

"I get it, Nathan, really." Wren's face reddened at being called out. Nathan had two modes—detached and dickish.

"I don't think you do."

I held up my hand. "Drop it, Nathan. Let's move on."

"Move on to what? This is serious, Coe. We need to make some sales fast or we're gone. Anyone got an idea?"

Silence.

Wren?"

She stared at the conference table and shook her head.

"Harup?"

Quit bein a dick?

"Thanks for that. How about you, Coe?"

"I think we just need to stick with our plan. Get Watanabe a lot of attention when he announces Death Watch. Then we'll sell as hard as we can."

"So you're hoping that someone, somewhere, will hear your fascinating pitch and buy Death Watch?"

"That's pretty much the definition of an early adopter ad campaign, Nathan."

He tossed his pen on the conference table and it spun like a compass. "Not enough."

I pressed my eyes closed. Nathan could be annoying, but he was usually right.

I remembered a thick cream-colored envelope waiting in my stack of mail on the dining room table. "Okay, here's an idea. I have to go to this annual fundraiser thing my father-in-law puts on for his hospital. Artists, collectors, lots of big money people." Robert's circle of friends tilted toward wealthy and weird. "Maybe we'll find some early buyers. Or at least we'll learn something."

Wren looked intrigued. "Old-school field research."

"Very," I said.

"Sounds okay." Nathan nodded. "When is it?"

"Tomorrow night."

Wren did her cheerleader pom-pom shake. "Team Death field trip!"

After everyone else had gone, Harup turned toward me, his dark eyes set on *stun*.

Did you call Vanessa?

I said nothing, which meant *no*.

Harup shook his head.

Shes got to gt out of hr apt. Like NOW.

"I'll call her, I promise."

U already promised and didn't do it

Harup stood and his white leather chair knocked into the wall.

He wiggled his fingers impatiently until I handed him my phone. He punched in a number, pressed the green button, and set my phone down on the white conference table.

I listened to my phone ring on speaker, wondering what he was up to. Security guards had hauled Harup out of client meetings when he got too weird. And not just once.

As I stared down at my phone, Harup gripped my shoulder and slowly forced my head down until my cheek was pressed against the cool white conference table.

"*What the fuck—*"

"Who is this?" The woman's voice sounded angry.

Harup poked me in the back with his bony finger.

"Vanessa?"

"Yeah?"

"It's Coe, Harup's ... friend?"

"Been waiting for you to call," she said, voice shifting softly. "Just in time."

SECRET SUBLET

I WAITED FOR VANESSA in the bar of the Madison Hotel, where we had agreed to meet. When Harup had pinned me to the conference table, Vanessa sounded professional but urgent, as if she were on a deadline. She suggested that we meet in person, and soon. I walked over from the agency after work and staked out a booth in the back of the bar.

Now Vanessa was already half an hour late and every minute that passed convinced me that she was just a flaky friend of Harup's who needed a favor.

I decided to give her a few more minutes before I headed home.

I looked around the half-empty bar. When I was in college, Union Square bars had been thick with editors and authors talking about books and politics. Now there was just a handful of underemployed tech bros and tourists, not many women among them. I wasn't sure I'd recognize Vanessa from Harup's hazy description—dark clothes, pale skin, reddish hair, a beautiful voice. Could be anyone from Julianne Moore to Ed Sheeran.

I started to leave.

A stylish woman wearing dark sunglasses slid into the booth across from me. "Coe, right?"

I nodded. "Vanessa?"

She nodded. Her look tilted toward smart and serious—black skirt, black silk blouse, leather laptop bag, silver necklace. She might be *anyone and everything* to Harup, but to me Vanessa looked my cousin Sandra, who taught art history at Yale.

"Was just about to head home," I said.

"Figured."

Had she been watching me the whole time? I didn't ask, just settled back into the booth.

"So you're a—"

"Friend of Harup's, yes." She took off her sunglasses, set them in front of her.

I nodded, waited for her to tell me more. Her pale blue eyes darted around the bar, as if searching for a lurking shooter. Her fingernails clicked on the tabletop.

I gave a disarming smile to put her at ease. "I've known him since before he went text-only."

"Me, too," she said. "I'm his best friend."

I paused, stunned. Wasn't I Harup's best friend? We had traveled the world and collaborated on hundreds of campaigns. And I had put up with his weirdness for years. But he had never mentioned Vanessa until a few days ago. "Really?"

"Yes, really. Let's order drinks." She brightened at her idea, waved down the bartender. A glass of Minervois for me, a mescal neat with an extra lime for her.

I jumped the gun during the awkward lull while we were waiting for our drinks. "Harup didn't tell me a lot about you, Vanessa. Just your name."

She shook her head. "Not my real name."

"Because?"

"Long story." She said nothing else. Apparently, she wasn't going to tell me that story.

When our drinks arrived, Vanessa took a generous gulp of mescal, its smoky scent wafting to my side of the booth. It seemed to calm her.

"Harup said you were in some kind of trouble."

"That's an understatement." Again, no details seemed forthcoming. I decided to wait out her silence.

After another sip of mescal, she clicked on her phone and pushed it across the table to me.

In grainy video, a man in black jeans, combat boots, and a T-shirt stalked down a dark street, picking up trashcans from the curb and throwing them at the entryway of an apartment building. He was shouting but I couldn't make out what he was saying.

"What am I looking at?"

"What does it look like?"

"A *fuck the police* thing? Antifa? Anti-antifa?"

"It's security video from outside my apartment last night."

"Who's the psycho trashman?"

"My boyfriend," she said. "My *ex*-boyfriend."

Questions popped into my mind. Who was this boyfriend? What made him so angry? But now didn't seem like the time to ask Vanessa, eyes still searching the bar.

"Does he know you're here?"

"Hope not," she said. "But he could be tracking me or something. Tim works in tech. Super-smart and—"

"Really pissed off?"

"Always."

"Why?"

"Long story."

"You seem to have a lot of long stories."

She thought about it, nodded. "Guess I do. This one's pretty simple. I met Tim through work and we started going out about a year ago. Everything seemed okay then he turned into a complete control-freak monster. Now he's out in front of my place almost every night, screaming and throwing stuff. I have to get out of my place, fast. Harup says you have an apartment for rent."

"I do."

"Good. I need a bolthole. No lease. Untraceable." She took a sip from her mescal. "A secret sublet."

I thought about the Langersteins' apartment, oniony and dark, and couldn't imagine Vanessa there. "You should know that the apartment is kinda gross."

"Don't care." She shook her head. "Just need a place where I can hide and work until this shitstorm blows over."

Vanessa seemed nervous, and after seeing that video, I could see why.

"I don't think so." I wasn't being heartless, just skeptical of a *damsel-in-distress* scenario. "We like to rent the place for a year at least."

"I can pay for the summer up front if that helps," she said.

"Not about the money."

"I get it. You're worried." She leaned toward me. "I'd be worried, too. You just met me. I showed you a video of my creepy ex. I'm nervous. Guzzled my mescal."

"Completely understandable."

"But I'm not going to be a problem." She pointed at my phone. "Just text Harup about me if you're not sure."

"The apartment is right over ours," I said. "The building sucks, so we can hear a lot of what goes on upstairs." I was starting to miss Krishna and Lakshmi, so drama-free.

"I work at home, but I'm super quiet. I'll take off my shoes."

"What kind of work?"

"Freelance marketing." Vanessa smiled broadly, as if marketing was thrilling.

"For?"

"Any client who needs my help."

She leaned toward me, her eyes tearing up a little, upper lip quivering. If she was putting on a show for me, she was very, very good.

"Look, let me rent your apartment, Coe. If you're not happy about anything, absolutely anything, I'll be out in a couple of days. No questions asked. Promise."

Was I stepping into a crazy renter-landlord nightmare—the kind that showed up regularly in the Metropolitan section of the *Times*—where I'd never be able to get rid of Vanessa even after years of throat-slittingly expensive lawsuits? Then again, if I rented the place now, I wouldn't have to call my father-in-law Robert and beg him to send us new medical residents.

"You'll have the apartment rented before Alta gets home from Germany," she said. "Problem solved."

"*What?*" I froze. "How do you know about that."

"About what?"

"About where my wife happens to be right now."

"Harup tells me everything."

"About me?"

"Sure. Talks about you all the time."

It was unnerving to meet a stranger who seemed to know so much about me, like being blindsided by an unauthorized biographer.

She leaned forward, as if she was telling a secret. "You met Nathan and Alta at NYU. Your father was a famous ad guy, Vince Vessel, so you've got some legacy issues. You turned down a really good buy-out offer for the agency and pissed everyone off." She pointed at my wrist. "You tend to leap before you look, so you put on Death Watch without thinking it through. Now you're stuck with it."

"*Whoa*, anything else?"

"Alta is in Darmstadt with Zeno Zenakas and she's—"

I held up my hand. "Enough, Vanessa, or whatever your name is."

"What I'm saying is, I'm not a stranger," she said, backing away. "I'm a friend who knows you, even if you don't know me, at least not yet."

A friend. I couldn't be sure about that. I had become a professional-grade skeptic. From the start, my father taught me to be wary of any offer that sounded too good to be true. Because behind that offer waited someone who wanted something. Given the mercantile tilt of our world, that usually meant money, or its clever cohort, power.

I stared into the far corner of the bar. I didn't want to even think about the apartment right now. I needed to focus on the Death Watch campaign. If Vanessa turned out to be a problem, Harup could deal with her.

I turned back to Vanessa, waiting anxiously. "Okay. But only if you agree to keep it down, not get weird, and leave if we ask you to."

"*Yes, yes, yes.* Thank you." Vanessa pressed her hands together in faux-prayer. "You won't even know I'm there."

I would definitely know she was there, this stranger who seemed to know everything about me. I waved the waiter toward me to pay our bill but Vanessa shook her head.

"Already put it on my room," she said. "Hiding out in the hotel tonight."

We slipped out of the booth and Vanessa put on her black jacket. She leaned down toward me, her long auburn hair trailing in her face, hazel eyes locked on mine.

"Thank you, Coe," she whispered.

I nodded, still not so sure.

"Just give Harup the keys tomorrow morning at the office. He promised to help me move in."

If Harup had already promised to help her move in, that meant they already knew I'd say *yes*. Which I did. By the time I figured it out, Vanessa had already disappeared into darkness, leaving me stunned in her wake.

MOVING DAY

EARLY SATURDAY MORNING, a white truck pulled up on the sidewalk and a squad of burly men started hauling what looked like Vanessa's worldly possessions up the service elevator—plastic-wrapped couches, tables, dozens of shipping boxes. The scale of it all made me wonder what I'd gotten myself into. The hammering and scraping from upstairs ramped up and by noon I couldn't work, read, or think. Just worry.

I took the elevator downstairs and talked about the Yankees with our doorman. Glenn was convinced they didn't have a shot, which he said every season. Then I walked north into Central Park to clear my mind of spiraling worries.

A sun-drenched early summer weekend. Young couples pushed squirming babies in Swedish strollers. The summer left-behinds sat in the grass, reading books, staring at their phones. Mixed among them, weathered wanderers dozed in the grass. Above us all, jet contrails cross-hatched the hazy blue sky. Fanatics could convince themselves that they were seeded with poison from the Deep State. To me, they looked like a child's chalk marks on a blue playground wall. We see what we want to see.

I had walked through the park with my father as a boy, with roving packs of friends in high school, and with Alta before she migrated east. Even now, I wasn't alone. With every step, Death Watch sparkled in the sun, a gleaming reminder that I had work to do—and also, that I could die at any moment.

When I got back to the apartment later that afternoon, a bottle of Volnay waited at my door with a note taped to its neck, a tasteful Kandinsky notecard. From the MOMA gift shop, if I had to guess.

Thank you, Coe, a thousand times, for letting me rent your apartment. I know it probably seems weird to you, but I promise it will be fine. Sorry about the noise. Harup is such a klutz. The place is great. It may take a few days, but I'm going to find that onion.

P.S. I'm working tonight. Stop by. We'll celebrate.
– V

I sat at the kitchen table and examined the note word for word, like a forensic editor, searching for hidden meaning. The note was nice, but not too gushy. Vanessa was right about Harup, he was impossibly clumsy. I'd watched him lurch down hundreds of airplane aisles, bashing passengers with his backpack. One thing was certain—there was no way she would ever clear the onion smell from the Langersteins' place.

The postscript was the stumbler. She was *working tonight.* I still wasn't sure what she did—some kind of creative freelancer, which covered a lot of ground. But on Saturday night? And what were we celebrating, exactly? Her single-letter signature seemed a little much, like she had developed her very own symbol. That said, it was just a *V.* For victory. For peace. For Vanessa.

At about nine, I decided it would be rude to not at least stop by and welcome Vanessa to the building. After all, we lived in libertine New York. If I didn't show up, she might think that I didn't trust myself to be alone with her.

I took the backstairs, the air warm and stale. Most of the top-floor apartments in our building were owned by foreign investors, so the eighth floor felt abandoned. A second Kandinsky notecard waited on the door of 801, our second apartment, now Vanessa's secret sublet.

Finishing a call, but come on in.

I slipped quietly inside. The hallway floor, scarred by decades of visitors, was covered in a dark rug now. I passed by the kitchen, its vintage appliances gleaming, fresh fruit filling a blue ceramic bowl on the counter. I walked by the bathroom, lit by a flickering candle, its salty ocean scent filling the hallway.

Vanessa had converted the apartment into a very elegant bolthole.

The Langersteins would shit.

So would Alta. Residents from the hospital never decorated, just threw down a futon and stocked the kitchen's knotty-pine cupboards with instant noodles and coffee.

The far end of the living room was brightly lit by torchieres in each corner, floor covered by a dark-gray rug, walls lined with a row of framed Japanese woodcuts, windows darkened by drapes of plum-colored velvet. I sensed that Harup had been art directing all day. But the rest of the room was empty—bare floor, a couple of boxes, no furniture—making it look like a stage set.

Vanessa sat on the edge of a plush, indigo-colored couch. Two studio lights glowed above her, casting even light on her pale face, dark-red lipstick, thick auburn hair restrained by a hammered copper barrette. She held a cigarette in one hand and a cellphone in the other. She wore a black leather skirt with a tight, sheer white blouse. Beneath it I could see vague tattoos and the shadow of a black bra.

She didn't look like she was working. But what was she doing? Vanessa turned toward me, caught my confused stare, waved, and nodded me toward a metal folding chair on the edge of the bright circle of light that held her at its center. I sat on the edge of the chair, tentative, wondering why I had been invited to watch a performance by the woman who had thoroughly colonized our extra apartment.

Harup had some explaining to do.

I watched Vanessa with cautious fascination. She had transformed from the skittish woman I had met at the bar. She looked completely focused and in control, her gaze locked on a cueball-sized webcam perched on a tripod a few feet in front of her, its red light blinking in a slow throb.

A laptop rested on a chair in front of Vanessa, and on it I could make out the head and shoulders of a hunched man, about thirty, with thin sandy hair, and a tidy beard. His wire-rimmed glasses were a little too small, giving him a spidery look. His white shirt flared in the bright light of what seemed to be a home office.

Was she talking to a client, co-worker? It was Sunday night, late for a Zoom call, even for a freelancer.

"Take the new job." Vanessa spoke slowly and clearly, each word a command.

"But I'll have to move to Kitchener." The spidery man's voice sounded thin, nervous.

"The new job pays more, doesn't it?"

"Yes."

"Then move," she said, without hesitating. "How much more does it pay?"

"Thirty thousand dollars more a year. Plus better benefits."

"Your benefits mean nothing to me, Phillip." Her voice held an edge—not a razor, but definitely a knife. "Canadian dollars, *yes*? Not worth as much, are they?"

"About sixty-seven cents, USD."

Vanessa stared at the camera and shook her head, disappointed, as if Phillip was responsible for the shitty exchange rate. She brought her cigarette to her lips and sent a plume of smoke toward the ceiling of our non-smoking apartment.

"So your raise isn't that impressive, is it?"

The man on the laptop screen pressed his eyes closed. "No, it's not. I should have asked for more."

"But you *will* send me more money."

"Yes," he said. "I suppose I can."

"You suppose?"

"I mean, I haven't started yet and—"

"I'm raising you up to $700 a session." Vanessa's voice turned even more commanding. "In real dollars, not yours. You're ready to move up to that, aren't you?"

Phillip said nothing.

"If you have to think, Phillip, I'm gone. Don't be an *er*."

"What's an *er*?"

"A banker without bank. That would make you an *er*."

"*Yes,* I can do it." Phillip's small eyes popped open and he was breathing hard, as if Vanessa had just suggested something much more erotic than a raise.

I looked around the room but my gaze circled back to Vanessa on the blue couch, the rising smoke from her cigarette, the glimmer from her crystal drop earrings beaming across the ceiling. Her gaze never strayed from the webcam and her expression stayed neutral, without even the hint of a smile, sultry or otherwise. She reminded me of my steely high school English teacher, who took absolutely no shit.

Vanessa said nothing, just raised up her phone like an auction paddle.

He fumbled around and the image turned jagged. "Hang on a sec."

Vanessa shot a glance at me, rolled her eyes.

More bashing around, then Phillip was staring down intently at his phone, revealing a circular bald spot. "There, payment sent."

Vanessa's phone pinged. She looked at the screen and nodded.

"It's so little money, really," she said. "Same again."

"*What?*"

"Tip me, Phillip."

"That's not really a tip, it's like paying twice."

Vanessa shrugged. "Then pay me. You have the money, don't you? Or did you waste it on food and beer?"

Phillip's eyes closed again.

Vanessa held her phone high. "Do *not* make me wait."

Phillip gave a resigned shake of his head and Vanessa's phone pinged again. She checked it, then reached toward the laptop. "Time's up, *Phillip*."

She said his name like a medical condition. The laptop screen went blank and Phillip disappeared back into the Canadian night.

Vanessa dropped her cigarette into a kombucha bottle and it sizzled. "Sorry. Special request. Phillip's bitch mother smoked and it signifies power to him. Don't worry, I won't stink up the place. I mean, more than it is already. She waved me toward her, patted the blue couch next to her. "C'mere."

She had transformed again, from a warlike goddess demanding tribute to a friendly upstairs neighbor who wanted to chat.

I stood up from the visitor's chair and sat next to Vanessa on the couch, but not too close.

"Vanessa?"

"Yeah?" She took a long drink from a bottle of sparkling water.

"What's going on?"

"I'm working," she said. "Like I told you."

"You told me you were in marketing."

"I am. I market myself."

"That could mean a lot of things. S'plain."

Vanessa scooted closer and looked into my eyes. "I monetize the male gaze."

I stared at her, said nothing.

She tilted her head. "I explore the desires of my clients and deliver a custom solution." She uttered business-speak with a hint of disdain.

"By desires you mean—"

"Sexual desires." No disdain now, just directness.

"*O-kay.*" I wasn't expecting that answer. What was Harup thinking? "So you're a sex worker?"

"Of a sort, yes," she said with a shrug. "And it really is *work*, believe me."

I ran through the possibilities—high-end escort, cam girl, porn star, or something new on the sexual frontier that I had no clue about.

"But I specialize." She held up her hand. "I control submissive men who need to be dominated by a woman, sexually, intellectually, or my favorite—financially." After each category she extended a finger, then waved it all away. "*Findom.* Heard of it?"

"Kind of." I knew the word and that it involved men giving money to women, but that was about it. Did Harup think I needed a dominatrix? That I had extra money to hand over to anyone?

"Well, that's what I'm doing, for now."

"Why didn't you tell me?"

"Harup said you probably wouldn't rent your place if you knew what I did. I hedged a little."

"A little?" I looked around the living room, lit up like a community cable studio slash bordello. "I think you need to move out, Vanessa."

"I thought if I let you see what I was doing tonight you'd know it was okay," she said. "But Harup warned me that you'd probably freak out a little. Since you're kind of a normie."

"I am not freaking out," I said. "And I'm definitely not normal."

"Well, now's your chance to prove it." She smiled, reached her hand up, tugged on her auburn hair, and tossed it on the floor.

I stared at the red mop of hair lying on the rug like a fox pelt.

"That's my *going online* wig," she explained. "Gets stupid hot under the lights."

The unwigged Vanessa had dirty-blond hair, one side shaved so short her scalp showed through, the other slightly longer. She looked gamine and slightly dangerous, like an edgy Jean Seberg.

"I need your help, Coe. It's serious."

"Really? Maybe you're just making it seem serious."

"I'll explain. Did you bring that wine?"

I nodded, handed the bottle to her. She reached down and opened it deftly with a hotel corkscrew.

She poured wine into two glasses on the low glass table in front of us and handed me one, holding hers out.

"To truth," she said.

I held my glass back. "I don't even know your real name."

"Okay, to *eventual* truth," she said.

We drank.

"That guy, Phillip? He's a client?"

Vanessa nodded. "Low-end, but yes."

"Have you met him, you know, in person?"

"You mean, will there be weird men showing up? No, absolutely not."

I had to admit, potential visitors were on my mind.

"What does someone like Phillip get out of the whole ... arrangement?"

"Look, if you have to ask," she said, "you probably won't understand."

"Try me."

"Short or long explanation?"

"Let's start with short."

Vanessa leaned back. "Phillip works in a bank in Toronto. Back-office job. Sees millions of transactions blur by on his screen every day—money has become meaningless to him."

"So he gives you some of it."

"He gives me what I *tell* him to give me." Vanessa gave me a wary look. "I really don't think you're going to get this."

"I'm a quick study." I rolled my hand in front of me to keep her going.

"Why do you want to know?"

"I'm curious."

"About what?"

"Almost everything."

"Okay. Phillip has all kinds of issues—he's balding, a little heavy, doesn't have a girlfriend, complicated mother issues, socially awkward. It makes him feel good to surrender to me, to let me be in charge so he can just forget about everything for half an hour a week, sometimes more."

"I get it." The idea of putting all those worries on hold was completely understandable. Paying $700 for that brief pause seemed extravagant and possibly self-ruining. Then again, men had paid much more for less, from boating to gambling, sports cars to ... watches.

"It's a mental fetish. No intimacy involved." She pointed to her buttoned-up blouse. "Not even a peek."

"Really?"

"Maybe on special occasions."

"You don't humiliate your clients?"

"What, like telling them how bad they are, calling them *worms* and *cash pigs*?"

"Something like that."

Vanessa shook her head. "That's for amateurs. Findom 101. That's not what I do. More like at the grad school level. Maybe post-doc."

"Can't say that I understand it, but it's fascinating."

"It is," she said. "Ever open an oyster?"

"No."

"Lived in New Orleans for a while after college. Worked in an oyster bar on St. Charles. The oyster shucker used a beat-up table knife. Said it wasn't about a fancy knife or strength—just about finding the vulnerable point, the place that wanted to be opened. Every oyster had one. But they were all different." Vanessa took a sip of wine and put down her glass. "Kind of reductive," she said. "I mean, bivalves aren't exactly bipeds. But they're not that different."

"Right." I took much the same approach to getting new clients to sign a purchase order.

"Best of all, I never have to meet anyone in person or know their real names," she said. "That's the beauty of findom," she said. "It's transactional, not emotional. No spending time with clients, no long dinners listening to their boring tales about their genius life decisions, no having to touch old men with hairy backs." She shivered.

"Is that something you do?"

"Not anymore," she said. "I did some escorting when I first moved to the city. Then some sugaring."

She noticed my confusion.

"Spending time with a sugar daddy. Older. Richer. Getting paid for it."

"For *it*?"

"For lots of things. Some okay, some pretty awful. Never going back. Too gross. Too dangerous. Way too personal for me." She pointed at the dark laptop. "Through the wonder of technology, I can stay safe."

"Except when your boyfriend tracks you down."

Vanessa paused, wineglass suspended. "About that."

"Yes?"

"I should probably clear up some details."

"Please do."

"That wasn't my boyfriend throwing trashcans."

"There's no Tim, then?"

"Right."

"Who was it?"

"It wasn't one guy. It was a bunch of incels. Involuntary celibates. Know about them?"

"Pissed-off young men who don't have sex?"

"Maniacs who blame women for not having sex with them even though they're repulsive," she clarified. "Incel is just a new word for asshole. They blame women for everything and chase us down. I don't get freaked out easily, but they're spooky."

She pushed her phone toward me and showed me another video. "This is from the security camera outside my apartment last night."

More dark figures in terrorist-wear, men shouting, trashcans flying. "Why are they so pissed at you?"

"I ran a stupid hustle and they got burned."

"What kind of hustle?" If Vanessa knew everything about me, I wanted to know something about her.

Vanessa held her phone toward me again. The photo showed what looked like a teenage boy's PhotoShop edit of Vanessa—tight black corset with silver clasps, a sly smile, and thick makeup that made her skin looked like unglazed porcelain. Curls from her auburn wig fell on her bare shoulders. Smiling, her hand hovered near her generous cleavage, ready to release it. The words WHAT'S NEXT? glowed in pink and below waited a bar of click boxes for one dollar to a thousand.

"What happened next?"

"Men fell for the dickbait. They clicked. They shared. It went viral."

"Why?"

"Because men are delusional?"

"No argument here. But why?"

"They thought something good would happen if they tipped me. I'd unleash my tits. They'd get a free video clip of me taking a shower. Or maybe I'd just show up at their door wearing nothing but a pair of cat ears, scratching to get in."

My imagination rushed to envision Vanessa naked and mewling but I reined it in.

"What happened next?"

"Nothing," she said.

"*Nothing*?"

"Absolutely nothing. Except the money started rolling in."

"How much?"

"A little more than a hundred grand." Her eyes glistened. "It was amazing."

"Wow." My smile broadened. What's Next? wasn't even *bait-and-switch*, just *bait*. "That's incredible."

"Not exactly." Vanessa took a long sip of wine. "So many people complained that Twitter shut down my account. Then Instagram, the camming sites, and PayPal. The ban hammer came down hard."

"Sucks." If Moriawase got shut down every time we overpromised, we'd all be in jail.

"Not only that. Angry old dudes lawyered up. Angry young dudes got rage boners and went vigilante. Then they doxxed me, spread my address around, and you saw what's been happening outside my apartment."

"You didn't rob them, you just fooled them." I thought about her hustle for a moment. "They gave you their money freely, like customers or investors. If they didn't get what they thought they would get is their problem. Unrealistic expectations and all that."

"Doesn't matter." Vanessa shook her head. "They're crazy and still pissed. That's why I'm glad to be here."

"I'm glad, too, I guess."

"I don't have to pack up and leave my new Midtown penthouse, do I?" Vanessa gave a royal wave, as if adoring fans packed the half-empty living room.

"You can stay," I said.

"Feels like home already."

"Sorry the gold-plated towel heaters aren't working."

"Meant to tell you, the butler seems a little grouchy."

"I'll talk to him. He's been working here for decades. Kinda considers the penthouse his own."

"Put him in his place, please. Or I will."

"Wouldn't want that."

Vanessa yawned and stretched out her strong, pale arms. "Long day. Time to turn in." She pressed a button on her phone and her set went dark, reverting the living room back to Langersteinian gloom, lit only by a couple of dim sconces.

"We'll talk more tomorrow." She reached down and tucked her red wig under her arm, smoothed her skirt with her palms, and walked away—kicking off her high heels and unbuttoning her blouse as she sleepwalked toward the bedroom.

"Come up for coffee in the morning if you want." Her voice floated from the hallway.

I said nothing. I hated to admit it, but like the men who clicked so eagerly, I wanted to know what was next.

MANIFESTO

Wren hyped Watanabe's mysterious announcement relentlessly in the run-up to the Death Watch launch, sending out hints on Twitter and planting rumors in the dark corners of Reddit. Watanabe had been silent long enough that his followers and fans were starved for any word from their shambolic master. Finally, the morning of the launch came and we gathered in the conference room to hear Watanabe deliver his message to the world.

Watanabe appeared onscreen, dressed in a black shirt and jeans, sitting on a tall wooden stool in his cavernous Tokyo studio. We insisted that the video camera be positioned slightly above him, looking down, which made him look less intimidating, more likable. Or at least as likable as someone as intense as Watanabe could appear to be.

His dark eyes stared into the camera, then disappeared behind smoke from his cigarette, which drifted above him like the haze from a forest fire.

"I told him not to wear that," Yohji whispered to me. "Looks like Tokyo Johnny Cash."

Having Yohji at the launch was raising our anxiety level from yellow to red.

"It's okay," I said. "It's on brand."

"Or close enough." Wren stared at the screen. "Quiet, I think he's about to say something."

Wren had edited Watanabe's rambling diatribe to a succinct one-minute manifesto and coached him through it. But who knew what he would do? He was the all-powerful Watanabe. We sat at the white conference table and watched like nervous parents of an unpredictable child.

"I am Watanabe. Artist and citizen of the universe." And so the launch of Death Watch began with Watanabe's invocation of his muse—himself, fully immersed in his inscrutable Japanese art-man act. "Tonight, I am announcing Cassius Seven, a radical new work." The corners of his eyes crinkled with an almost kindly smile.

Watanabe stood and walked to the wooden table where Death Watch waited in its case.

"I have been working on this project for many years. There have been many rumors about it. Now is the time to introduce it to the world." Two assistants lifted the top of the case and the camera zoomed in to show the gleaming Death Watch. "The ordinary often hides the extraordinary. What appears to be just another beautiful watch is so much more than that."

I looked at Nathan and we gave an almost imperceptible shrug that said *so far, pretty good.*

The screen split to show an animation of the watch activating. "Inside the watch are seven tiny, carefully honed knives. These knives emerge from the watch, pierce the wearer's wrist, and spin—causing rapid exsanguination. In other words, death. Many are already calling it Death Watch, for this reason."

The screen split again to show video taken at the meeting in Tokyo—the innocent rabbit's pink eyes, Death Watch fastened around its body, the sudden evisceration, and the shower of blood.

Harup gave a quick shiver. Nathan and I looked away.

Wren looked worried. "Didn't know he was going to show that. Might be over the top."

"Nothing is over the top anymore," Nathan said. "You know that."

The video ended and Watanabe returned onscreen, lighting a new cigarette from the butt of the old one.

Yohji stood up, raised his arms. "STOP SMOKING!" Yohji seemed to have lost his cool detachment. From across the conference room, we could see the sweated-out patches that darkened the underarms of his yellow suit jacket. Harup shivered at the grossness.

"The watch might activate in days or months, a year or many years. Or perhaps never. Its wearer never knows the chosen moment, randomly selected, when the watch may end their days. They only know that the possibility is always with them as they work, travel, live."

The split screen transitioned to show images of the thrumming streets of New York, London, and Tokyo that Harup had edited into a montage that suggested isolation as much as crowds—shorthand for the modern condition.

"No matter where we are, what we do, how we think, we are all human, not immortal. There is no afterlife. There is hardly any life at all, just our brief time on earth. To be truly free, we must strip away the illusions of an otherworldly future. We must reclaim the one life that we have been given. We must take control of our lives, and bravely acknowledge and anticipate our inevitable deaths."

The crowds disappeared, replaced by images of ocean waves, a birch forest, the moon. "Cassius Seven is a constant reminder of the short time we have to live, love, and create on this remarkable, besieged planet. It puts your destiny under your control, not in the hands of deities, doctors, or your own delusions."

Harup cringed at the tacky alliteration.

"We didn't write that," Wren said. "Watanabe's off script."

Yohji shrugged.

"Unlike a tattoo, Death Watch cannot be removed," Watanabe said. "If it is tampered with in any way, it will activate immediately. Nothing can remove it. In a provisional time, it demands a lifelong commitment."

I pulled Yohji toward me by the radiant yellow sleeve of his Nehru jacket. "My watch will come off, right? You were going to going to send me a special code so I could take it off."

Yohji gave a nonchalant shrug of his narrow shoulders. "Oh, that. There isn't one. But don't worry, your watch is just a prototype."

"Which means?"

"It's missing a lot of component thingies."

"Like what?"

"The engineers would know for sure, but they're busy. To be safe, I'd say just keep it on."

"To be safe?"

Nathan looked down the conference table and shook his head to remind me I was talking to a client.

"You told me the watch wasn't real. Now you're saying it is?"

"Of course it's real," Yohji said. "It's on your wrist, isn't it?"

"Does. It. Work?"

"You saw for yourself in Tokyo."

"I saw what you wanted me to see."

Yohji shrugged. "Everyone sees what they want to see, hears what they want to hear."

"But does my watch have seven knives inside?"

"Maybe?" Yohji wasn't reassuring me. He slid his chair closer. "Yes, your watch is different, Coe Vessel," he whispered. "But you have to make everyone else believe *their* watch is real. That's your role." He leaned closer still. "I thought we explained this all to you when we picked you."

"Picked me for what?"

"To be our first customer, of course." His smile revealed his small teeth, so white they glowed.

I felt the conference room floor shift a little. "You didn't pick—"

"*Shhhh.*" Wren waved at us. Watanabe's manifesto was coming to an end, as he geared up for the call to action. I set aside my worries, attributed them to launch jitters.

"I invite you to reset your life to its original potency. To embrace life by recognizing the potential of death." Watanabe flicked his cigarette on the ground and exhaled a thick stream of smoke.

"ENOUGH WITH THE CIGARETTES," Yohji shouted.

"Perhaps my new work disturbs you, as it should. We are living in very disturbing times. Join us in this revolution, this celebration of mortality. Who is ready to take the cure for uncertainty? Who will be the first to wear Death Watch?"

I knew the answer. I *was* the answer.

Watanabe's gaze turned so intense that his dark eyes seemed to be drilling right through me. Then he gave a beatific smile and his image faded out, leaving the words LOOK FOR IT ON THE DARK WEB to glow and fade.

Nathan stood up, looking concerned. "Harup? Wren?"

Harup held up one hand to keep Nathan at bay as he clattered away on his laptop with the other. Next to him, Wren focused on her screen like an astronaut coordinating a risky landing.

We watched them and waited for early results.

"Trending heavily." Wren smiled. "Pretty much everywhere. People are going apeshit about the bunny."

Harup nodded, his version of enthusiasm.

Nathan started applauding and I joined in.

"Thank you, all of you." Yohji stood, blinking, as if delivering his Oscar night speech for Best Costume. "For all that you've done, for all that you will do, to bring our miraculous experiment to the world. To make them *believe.*" Yohji covered his face with his hands suddenly. He might have shed a tear or two.

Nathan led Yohji out, issuing his ritualistic post-meeting reassurances—*so glad to be working with you, the results look excellent, more ahead,* bullshit, conjecture, wishful thinking.

Walking through the agency, Yohji looked calm, relieved, as if he just passed a test, though he didn't do much to help with the launch except pepper us with texts asking how it was going. Yohji waved to our designers, who smiled and pretended to care because he was a client who helped pay their salaries.

"Watanabe must have put him in charge of the campaign as some kind of test." I watched Yohji go with more than a little relief.

"Pleasing Daddy," Wren said. "So much wrong with that—don't even get me started." She shut her laptop and left.

I locked the doors behind her and stood next to Harup.

"Hey!"

Harup looked up, saw it was just me, slipped back into Dataland.

I sat down at the conference table, kicked his skinny legs. "Why didn't you tell me about Vanessa?"

Told you she needed an apt, fast.

"Not about that," I said. "About what she does."

Wd you have rented yr place to hr if u knew?

I thought about it. "Maybe?"

That's why I didn't tell u.

"Do you think I have extra money I need to get rid of. That I need findom-ing?"

Harup shook his head.

"I watched her working last night," I said. "Talking to some guy named Phillip. "Is that what she does for you—yells at you? Gets you to give her money?"

Harup shoved his laptop away.

1—no. 2—fk no.

His dark eyes glinted. Whatever he was doing with Vanessa wasn't any of my business, of course. But I had read stories about psychics and other opportunists siphoning off hundreds of thousands of dollars of men like Harup, smart but naïve. "So if Vanessa's *anyone and everything*, what's she to you?"

Harup stared into the far corner of the conference room, vacillating between telling me to fuck off or answering my question. He stared down at his phone and started to text, fast and hard.

Vanessa is my professional confidante. You won't understand but it matters to me. And I need you to know that it's okay. That she's amazing. You'll see. I would never have sent her to you if I didn't know that it would be fine. More than fine. So quit worrying. And also, fuck off.

Harup only texted in full sentences when he was serious. He looked at me, dark eyes softening, one corner of his mouth crinkling, straightening.

I stared at Harup, my partner for years, a collaborator whose creative brain was connected to mine with a psychic HDMI cable, possibly my closest friend—and realized that there was a lot I didn't know about him.

DARK ROAST

"THE LEGENDARY WATANABE, shadowy provocateur of the art world, announced his latest work last week—a watch called the Cassius Seven, named after one of the assassins of Caesar, but known by its more memorable name, the one on every pundit's lips—Death Watch. Why? Well, listeners, high-end watches may give you sticker shock. But only one might kill you. That honor goes to Death Watch alone. For a sweet 50k this ticking tautology can wrap around your wrist and remind you to live life fully—or it just might end your life."

The buttery voice of Jeremy Wood slid through my headphones and entered my buzzing brain. The local NPR veteran's morning show served as an intellectual antidote to drive-time DJs. But *ticking tautology*?

Wren mimed gagging at the overwrought introduction. She chose to do our first interview with Jeremy Wood because his demographic was Upper West Side intelligentsia who were awake and on their treadmills, earbuds in, at 7 AM. It was a perfect soft launch of my new role as Death Watch pitchman. Still, my mind pinballed and a river system of sweat trickled down my ribs.

"What is it about this watch, or should I say cultural weapon, that's attracting so much controversy?" Jeremy Wood asked himself, still deep in solipsism. "Is it a dark-souled sign of the end-time? The inevitable next step as we shuffle toward national nihilism? Both? Neither? To find out, we're talking to Death Watch's very first customer. He followed in the footsteps of his father, a legendary adman, but found his path leading him into the dark corners of the American psyche. Welcome to *Dark Roast,* Coe Vessel."

From across my darkened office, Harup and Wren nodded and I leaned into the broadcast-quality microphone he had rigged up on my desk. "Good to be here, Jeremy."

"So first, I have to tell you, I'm fascinated by Death Watch."

"I was too, right from the—"

"It rejects life by risking its end. But it embraces life by celebrating the time that remains."

"That's a good point—"

"It's about selflessness but also self-destruction."

"I'm not self-destructive but—"

"It's the Sword of Damocles wrapped around your wrist instead of dangling over your head."

Nathan gave me a nod and I backed away from the microphone. Jeremy Wood was a solo artist spewing smarty-pants bebop and I needed to hang back like a sideman.

"I mean, from Timex to Rolex, there are watches at every price point, right? All the way up to the crème de la crème. A friend of mine who got rich in tech bought himself a Patek Philippe and after that he became intolerable, staring at it during dinner instead of talking. After a while he sold it, said he was crazy when he bought it. High on money. My first question—and it's a tough one in our country, in this time—are you crazy?"

I laughed. "Not at all."

"Then tell our listeners why you're the first person to buy—and wear—a watch that might kill you."

"I think it came down to this, Jeremy." I paused. Wren and I had gone through the list of questions over and over, like an actor learning lines, so I knew what to say. Or more accurately, what my persona would say. "My work took me all over the world but I wasn't appreciating any of it. I wasn't present. Not in my life. Not with the people I loved—my wife, my friends." Across the conference room, Harup lowered his eyes to his laptop. "I was just doing the same things over and over. I was alive but already dead—"

"Like a zombie."

"Exactly."

"So you paid fifty thousand bucks for Death Watch?"

"As soon as I heard about it."

"That's a lot of money," Wood said.

"People pay much more for less."

"Very true. We're in the end-time. The ones who hate to see the old ways go are still buying stuff like mad."

"They are." If only one of them would just go ahead and buy Death Watch, already.

"To fill the hollowness," Wood said. "Is that how you felt, Coe? Hollow? Disappointed? Is that why you bought Death Watch?"

"Yes," I said, going full New Nihilist. "I don't think anyone's life goes the way they thought it would."

"Agreed. Way too random. And this watch takes chance to a whole new level. Listeners, if you've been hiding upstate under a rock, I'll summarize. This watch could kill you at any moment. Only an algorithm knows for sure when—or to add to the mystery, *if*—its inner knives will emerge from the back of the watch and slit your wrist. Like *The Death of Marat* without the bathtub. Right, Coe?"

"Sure," I said.

"When I heard Watanabe's announcement, I was outraged at the audacity—the heartlessness, frankly—of a watch that could cause death. And I thought you must be an idiot for wearing it."

I said nothing, waited for the legendarily tetchy host to flay me with his savage wit.

"But then the more I thought about it, the more I realized it wasn't that different from being alive. You could smoke and drink yourself to death. An autonomous Tesla could run you over. You could have a genetic flaw. Inhale a deadly virus. Piss off the wrong cop in the wrong neighborhood with the wrong skin color. Point is, we're all at risk. All the time."

"Exactly," I said. "Whether we want to admit it or not, we could die at any moment."

"Rather morbid, isn't that?"

"I'd say realistic."

"Retort noted, *Mister Death*. For listeners who just tuned in, I'm on the phone with Coe Vessel, the New York advertising scion who's now wearing the first Cassius Seven. Also known by the catchy name Death Watch. It's a watch that might kill him. So how long have you been wearing the watch?"

"Couple of days now." It wasn't true, of course. The glowing red number on my watch was deep in double digits. We had created a parallel narrative, one that was true enough for advertising.

"Do you feel different?"

"I do, Jeremy," I said. "I really do. It's right there on my wrist from the moment I wake up to when I fall asleep at night, reminding me to live."

"Most people don't need to be reminded to live."

"But some do. More and more, I think."

"My producer tells me that Death Watch is already starting to get a lot of online buzz."

Wren, our buzz-creator, looked up from her laptop and smiled. "It really is."

"Some people are saying it's ridiculous. Others say it's dangerous. *A deeply disturbing sign of the spread of hopelessness in our compromised world.* So say the pearl-clutchers at the *Times.*"

"People say a lot of things. Mostly because they're scared. They don't want to think about death."

"What do you say to them?"

"The more you fear death, the more it rules your life."

"*Touché!*"

"If they think Death Watch is ridiculous, then they shouldn't buy it. If they think it's dangerous, they shouldn't put it on. If they think it's disturbing—well, it is."

"Final question. Who should buy Death Watch?"

Wren held up her hand like a stage director and I paused until she lowered her hand. "Anyone who wants to be set free from the world as it is."

She checked our script but that line wasn't there.

Jeremy said nothing. I had triggered a moment of silence from a big talker. "Well, to be honest, that might include me," he said, quietly. "I've got liver disease. I've lost faith in democracy, in activism, in our country. My parents and brothers are all dead. My cat Rosa died a few weeks ago. Named after Rosa Luxembourg."

"Not downplaying your loss, Jeremy," I said. "But you're not alone. People are more aware of mortality than ever. Maybe Death Watch is the answer to the question that we're all afraid to ask."

"Which is?"

"When am I going to die?"

"The Big One, yes. Unanswerable."

"We are all mortal. We need to savor the time that we have. And fill it with love, not desperate striving. I think that's what Watanabe's saying with Death Watch."

Wood took an audible breath. "Yes, life and death. *Quand même,* as the French put it so succinctly. Listeners—call in and tell us if you're ready to Buy Now and possibly Die Now. Are you brave enough to wear Death Watch? To admit you're mortal? Our guest this morning, Coe Vessel, bought the first Death Watch. Will you be next?" Wood paused. "Looking forward to talking again, Coe. Should we be so lucky. And I hope that we are."

"I hope so too, Jeremy. I've listened to your show since I was a kid. Such an honor to have a chance to talk to you, finally."

Harup gave me his *sincerity makes me sick* look.

"Listeners, are you ready to shed the cloak of delusion and take on the burden of knowledge? Let's talk about it—here and now, on *Dark Roast.*"

Harup pantomimed slitting his throat with his hand and my headphones went silent. I slipped them off, rubbed my hot ears.

Wren gave me a thumbs up. I'd managed to win over Jeremy Wood—or at least avoid getting wounded by his rapier tongue.

"Nice job." Nathan cupped his hand to his ear. "Know what I hear?"

I said nothing. I knew a set-up when I heard one.

"I hear a lonely grad student, who goes to every 92nd Street Y lecture, trying to figure out how to scam fifty thousand dollars from his parents to buy his way out of misery."

I held up my limp index finger in a gesture we called the Lazy Finger—as if we couldn't be bothered to give each other the actual finger.

"It was a really good first interview," Wren said. "So don't be a dick, Nathan." She handed me a page of notes in her meticulous handwriting.

Nathan looked over at Harup, monitoring the web traffic to the Death Watch e-commerce site, which Watanabe's crew was cleverly hosting in Belarus. "Any action?"

Harup shrugged. *Dark Roast* radio listeners probably hadn't even heard of the dark web. Death Watch had generated plenty of buzz, but so far it wasn't converting into sales.

"Attention Team Death," Nathan said. "We have seven days left to make a sale. Or we're out."

My phone rang and I clicked it on before I checked who it was. This caller wasn't saying anything, just breathing. Had one of Vanessa's haters managed to track me down?

"*Who is this?*"

"What are you doing, Coe?"

Alta's voice sounded shaky and icy. It was the middle of the night in Darmstadt.

I said nothing, just sat down at the kitchen table. I had meant to warn her when the Death Watch campaign was in full swing. Now she had caught wind of it.

"Do you believe all that stuff you said on the radio this morning?"

"How'd you hear about that?"

"My father listens to NPR on the way into work. He's really worried about you. So am I. Did you mean what you said?"

"About what?"

"Being so unhappy."

I thought for a moment, selected a justifiable lie. "Just an act."

"It's bad enough that you're wearing that stupid watch. Now you're trying to trick other people into putting it on."

"The watch isn't real. Told you that before." I knew nothing would comfort Alta, but I had to try. "The experiment will be over in a few weeks. Watanabe will have his moment. We'll get paid."

"The world will know you as the liar who sold Death Watch. I hope you're proud of yourself. Because I'm not."

I stared at the ceiling and said nothing. Over and over, year after year, I had failed to meet Alta's expectations—some unstated, others obvious—leaving her disappointed and raw. I botched the Zazzy buy-out offer. I didn't follow Zeno's grand plan of building a dream apartment. I wasn't able to provide the kind of extraordinary life a Van Schuyler might have expected. And then there was the harder truth; I was much better at creating ads than nurturing a life—mine, Alta's, anyone's.

"Coe?"

"What?"

"Do you need to be reminded to live, like you said?"

I thought for a moment. "I do."

"Really? I know our life isn't perfect right now. But don't you want to be alive? Don't you care about me, your friends, anyone, anything?"

I pressed my eyes closed. "Look, Death Watch isn't some kind of Rorschach test that reveals your inner feelings about life. Whatever I say about it is just ad copy, pretty little words that seem like they might convince people to do something destructive and stupid—like buy a watch that might kill them."

I could hear Alta breathing, knew that what I was saying wasn't making her happy.

"It's just a campaign. It'll be over soon."

"I love you. You know that. But what's wrong with you? That's what I can't figure out. Can you?"

I had no real answer, so I quoted the Magic 8-Ball. "Signs point to *no.*"

"You can't always hide behind being clever and funny, you know."

"So far, so good."

"We're going to deal with the real work when I get back," she said.

"I know."

Alta was talking about the very unfunny business of sorting out whether to keep coasting through life together or to spin off and go our separate ways.

"Not looking forward to it."

"It's like you said on the radio." Alta spoke quietly. "The more you fear something, the more it rules your life."

I said nothing, just shook my head. Having my own words circle back to haunt me was like getting bitten by my own dog, if I had one.

"Change is nothing to be afraid of, Coe."

Being alone was, I thought, but didn't say, because Alta wasn't alone.

She had Zeno.

THE SHIP

We wandered through the bright, white-walled gallery like spies, looking for a potential buyer for Death Watch, or at least an insight that might lead us to one. My father-in-law's annual summer fundraiser, *Body of Work,* brought together two unlikely tribes—high-end surgeons and physicians from city hospitals mixing with artists and collectors. Wren was chatting up a pinstripe-suited man over near the bar. Harup and Vanessa were drifting through the gallery, an unlikely couple getting lots of long looks during their rare public appearance. She was wearing her auburn wig, a tight black dress and high heels.

Nathan sidled up to me. "Who's that with Harup?"

"Vanessa." I held off on telling Nathan more.

"Is she his girlfriend?"

"Kind of. It's complicated. There's a fiduciary angle."

Nathan shrugged. "There's always a fiduciary angle." He wandered off toward a cluster of fans around a famous German artist—angular and pale, clad in black techwear that looked like it came from a 3D printer.

Robert spotted me from across the room and slipped through the crowd, stopping to smile at friends, exchange a few words, put his hand on a shoulder, kiss a wife on the cheek, say something clever that left them all laughing. Mixing easily with any crowd was just one of the many admirable qualities of Robert Van Schuyler, my tall, relentlessly kind father-in-law.

"Having fun?"

"Great night," I said.

"Been checking the silent auction slips." Robert's eyes lit up a bit. "Better than I thought. We'll hit our goal."

"Congrats." We clinked glasses.

The auction helped fund his nonprofit, Surgical Outreach, which sent a regular stream of doctors to perform heroic surgeries in East Africa—diagnosing curable diseases, removing tumors, saving thousands of lives.

He nodded at my wrist. "That's the infamous watch, is it?"

"It is." I held Death Watch up for a closer look.

"Looks normal," he said. "The banality of evil and all that. An expensive watch that might kill you? What's the point, Coe?"

"It's an experiment."

"By that Watanabe fellow? I heard him on the radio, too. My more behavioral cohorts would classify him as a megalomaniac."

"I just think of him as high-art narcissist."

"Narcissists think the world revolves around them. Megalomaniacs think they control the levers and knobs that can change the world. Important distinction."

"Point taken."

He leaned closer. "Anyway, Alta tells me the whole thing's a joke."

I looked around the room, crowded with people looking at art, talking about art, placing bids on art. "Let's just call it an art project with sociological implications."

"Not lethal, then?"

"Not lethal, but also not an easy sell." I told Robert the secret about Watanabe's experiment—and our campaign. Death Watch was a joke that needed to sound serious.

"I can understand why you're having trouble selling it," he said. "In my professional experience, people don't really want to die," Robert said. "In fact, they tend to be grateful when we manage to save their lives." He nodded toward a couple standing near a painting of the full moon rising. "See that man in the tan jacket? Had a major heart event a year ago. We opened him up, rerouted his plumbing, and patched him back together. Doing great. Now he's probably one of our biggest donors. It all worked out for the best for him. And us."

He put his hand on my shoulder. "It'll work out for you, too. You'll sell lots of watches and remind the world to not take life for granted, which is a lesson most people need to hear."

"Thanks." Confident and comforting, Robert could say *I'm afraid it's terminal* and keep a patient smiling.

"Glad you're not going to die in the near future. We like having you around the shack."

The *shack* was the Van Schuyler family's Cape Cod getaway, a rambling summer house high on the cliffs of North Truro. They had left it unrenovated as a haven from modernity. The closet shelves were lined with beach-splayed paperbacks and literary journals, kitchen cabinets stocked with cheap gin, guest room dresser drawers a veritable museum of WASPy summerwear—madras swimsuits, Nantucket pants, and well-worn T-shirts from Yale and Bowdoin.

"Will we see you sometime this summer?"

"Hope so."

"I mean, if your watch doesn't kill you first." He winked. "Got to work the crowd." He pointed across the gallery. "Be sure to check out the picture over there. I donated it to the cause. Bloom is of my favorite painters. You'll see why."

Having talked to enough guests, I walked over to the large, murky, paint-slathered painting, which showed a half-dissected cadaver on a slab. Its vivid, meaty colors seemed repulsive at first, but then the iridescent ribcage transformed into the remnants of a ship's hull, the decaying flesh into waves. The image reminded me of the rotted beams of the centuries-old wooden merchant ships that surfaced from the muck of the Hudson after storms.

I read the information sheet beneath the painting. THE SHIP, 1943, HYMAN BLOOM. Bloom, a Boston painter, was fascinated by morgues and slaughterhouses, which led some to see his work as morbid. But a quote from a critic pointed out how the viewer's *repugnance at the death and decay always gave way to reveal the indestructibility of the spirit.*

Staring at the painting for a moment, I wasn't sure I believed the critic. When my powerful father died, his spirit had evaporated, leaving nothing but memories and file cabinets full of browning ad clippings, growing more dated by the year. I gave Bloom's painting a long last look, wanting to remember it, wondering what it would be like to believe in the infinite instead of the instant. I smiled at the small irony that a painter exploring spiritual indestructibility had such a fleeting name, *bloom*—wilting and fading, dying and drying.

I knew I should regroup with Team Death, but I lingered in front of the painting, captivated. A waiter sailed by with a tray of hors d'oeuvres. After an hour of talking I was hungry, so I took a marble-sized mozzarella ball on a toothpick and tossed it back.

The mozzarella ball lodged in my throat. I tried to cough but my body just convulsed. No air. Nothing. Panicked, I rushed toward the restroom, scared and embarrassed and wanting to get away from crowd. In the mirror over the sink, I saw my red face, terrified eyes.

Choking to death. How fucking stupid.

I tried to cough. Nothing. The bright bathroom started to spin slowly and fade to gray. I pushed my body against the sink, as if I could save myself, but I couldn't. My body slumped and I held on to the sink like a life raft as I gave one last soundless exhale that did nothing.

Strong arms lifted me from behind and I saw Harup standing behind me in the bathroom mirror. He nodded calmly, then squeezed, hard.

Nothing.

He shifted my body slightly and squeezed again.

Nothing again.

Harup wrapped his arms more tightly around me and pulled his balled fist hard below my ribs. The mozzarella ball flew out and splatted on the mirror.

Harup put me down on my feet and leaned down to look me in the eye.

I'm okay, I managed to say. He reached down to turn on the water and washed his hands like a furtive bird. As the mozzarella ball slid down the mirror Harup shuddered and rushed out the door before I could thank him.

I stood at the bathroom sink, splashing cold water on my face and cleaning the cheese off the mirror with a paper towel, wiping away the evidence. In the mirror I saw a disheveled, crazed man breathing hard to stay alive. If it took wearing Death Watch to make other people feel this way—thankful for every new minute, lucky to be able to breathe, to feel cold water on my hands—then they should buy one.

And I should be able to find a way to sell them one.

Out in the gallery, the crowd was gathered around Robert, who was announcing the silent auction winners and auctioning off a few of the higher-end paintings.

Nathan walked over, Wren behind him. "Been looking for you."

"You look kinda fucked up," Wren said.

"I'm okay." I nodded, not wanting to tell the embarrassing tale of escaping death by artisanal cheese ball.

Harup and Vanessa joined us and Team Death was complete. Vanessa looked bored. An art auction must seem remarkably tame to her. I smiled at Harup but he gave absolutely no sign that he'd just saved my life.

"What have we learned?" Nathan asked. "Wren?"

She checked her notes on her phone. "The doctors I talked to said they'd heard of Death Watch, which is good—we're getting traction. And they said there was no way in hell they or any of their friends would ever buy something so stupid. Which is bad. One of them said something about how he was trained to save lives, not end them. Said maybe we should try lawyers, there were plenty of extra ones. They laughed at that. One guy asked if I wanted a drink. Another said he quote dug Asian chicks unquote. He also tried to grope my ass."

"Fun night," Nathan said. "Coe?"

"Talked to a lot of artists. Lots of complaining about the decline of the art market, greedy dealers, and how expensive studio space was in the city. Everyone said they hated Watanabe. Lots of debate about whether he was even an artist. They didn't have anything close to fifty thousand dollars to spend. Said when the price dropped to fifty dollars they might pick one up because Death Watch looked cool."

Nathan sighed. "*Shit.* Anything else?"

"I think we need to amp up the *appreciation of life* angle," I said, inspired by my scrape with death. "Like every morning they wake up is a bonus day, a gift. They could have died, but they didn't."

"What you're saying is we need someone who's just the right level of miserable," Wren added. "If they're nihilistic or whatever, they'll be pissed that Death Watch doesn't kill them right away and end their suffering."

"Exactly," I said. "They need to be miserable-ish but willing to reach for an antidote, even if it might kill them."

"More important than that, they have to be able to come up with 50k quick like a bunny," Nathan said. "Clock's ticking, pun intended. Remember all those potential buyers we came up with back in the office? Now we know who we're really looking for."

"Someone who's kinda miserable and really rich," Wren said.

Vanessa stepped closer, smiled. "And crazy enough to risk it all."

I took off my suitcoat, poured a whiskey, and sat at the dining room table, my ears ringing from the voices in the crowded gallery. The night may have been a complete bust for Death Watch, but it was always good to see Robert, the drinks were free, and Team Death took home an important insight—our would-be customers were societal unicorns.

That said, I had faith that the right early adopters would pull others along.

After the first sip of whiskey, I remembered talking with one of the other guests at the Okutama Institute, a Danish art dealer. Martin something. Even after the Death Watch demonstration—the shredded apple and eviscerated rabbit—he had smiled and said he would have no problem finding buyers. "Even if the watch is real?" I had asked him. "Especially if it's real," he said, explaining that Death Watch matched the dark fatalism of Danes.

I rushed over to my backpack and dug through it until I found the stack of business cards guests had handed me. I tossed them on the dining room table one after the next.

Here was his card, on heavy paper stock with his name and information embossed in an elegant typeface. Garamond, if I had to guess. Martin Sørgen, at Rare Elements, a gallery in Copenhagen. I opened my laptop and wrote a quick email, linking him to my *Dark Roast* interview and telling him in no uncertain terms what we needed—a customer, fast.

I sent the email and took a deep drink of whiskey.

My email bounced back almost immediately. I checked the address, which was fine. Then I searched for Martin Sørgen, art dealer. Nothing came up. I searched for his gallery. There was no Rare Elements in Copenhagen.

I picked up another card and searched, found that there was no Renata Stein at *Artforum*, though I sat next to her in the conference room, remembered her red notebook, her smoky perfume.

Another card, and another, then another.

There was no Niels De Vries, editor of *Het Moderne Horloge* in Amsterdam.

No Christopher Osborne, English watch aficionado.

I searched for the defiant Frenchwoman, remembering how deftly she had ridiculed Watanabe's experiment. There was no Madame Helena Déprit at Chanel, or anywhere else in the fashion world.

I searched for the Okutama Institute and found no website, no mention of it. I remembered the quiet trails, delicate gardens and koi pond, my cedar-scented suite, the conference room with its low stage.

"Fuck."

I closed my eyes and gave a low moan as the truth came into painful focus. I had been played masterfully by an elaborate con.

When we picked you. I heard Yohji's voice again, so nonchalant. I had been invited to Tokyo to audition, not to pitch. Would I be impulsive enough to put on Death Watch? Did I want the account and its plush billings enough to risk death? I had stumbled into Watanabe's sociology experiment, not recognizing the double-blind machinery running behind it. As its first subject, I was coddled and complimented then gaslit and manipulated.

Watanabe already knew that I could be the ideal first customer for Death Watch. I'd been researched and targeted. Were there even other agencies in the wings, waiting to try out for a lead role in Watanabe's latest and most audacious production? It seemed unlikely.

I was born to play the part.

That unsettling moment in the "Okutama Institute" conference room when the final pitch turned into an instant party? I realized now what Watanabe and his cohorts were celebrating. *Fortunately, the world is thick with fools,* he had said to the woman who played Madame Déprit so convincingly.

I had won the role of fool—their fool.

GETTING EVEN

I WAS TOO EMBARRASSED TO CALL NATHAN OR TEXT HARUP after I realized how I had been fooled in Tokyo. I wanted to call Alta but it was four in the morning in Darmstadt and I knew what she would say—*when in doubt, get out.* It was one of her many matter-of-fact truisms, instructive but not necessarily helpful. Extracting myself from Death Watch—the campaign and the watch—wasn't as easy as it might seem to her.

Vanessa sat on the blue couch in a severe black dress, almost funereal except it was low-cut and looked like it was made out of pleather.

I rushed into the living room, still holding the stack of business cards. "Need your help figuring something out."

"A regular's about to call," she said. "We'll talk after."

She nodded toward the guest chair. "Enjoy the show—should be a good one."

"Who is he?"

"Gordon. Owns a bunch of spas and healing centers in California that turn rich people's bogus health problems into bags of money. Calls himself a *mantrapreneur.*"

I sat in the chair and tried to relax, but my mind kept circling around how stupid it was to get scammed by Watanabe and his crew.

Vanessa took a careful look at herself on her phone, touching up her dark red lipstick. Her laptop started making the familiar *bloop* of an incoming Skype call. *"Hi ho, hi ho, it's off to work I go,"* Vanessa said softly as she settled into the blue couch and faced the webcam.

Tonight's client appeared on the laptop. Up close, wearing a white T-shirt, Gordon looked younger than Phillip and seemed less sad and more confident, at least as confident as a man in the thrall of a findom goddess could be.

Their intricate verbal parrying distracted me from my Tokyo

trap. I watched a new version of Vanessa, not the one I knew, or the one from her session with Phillip. This Vanessa seemed haughty but accessible. She was still in complete control, but she treated Gordon with studied indifference instead of outright scorn.

"I'll give you a hundred dollars per button," he said.

"What?"

"On your dress. To undo them. More to take it all off."

"Save it for your cam girls," Vanessa said. "Send me $500 to *not* take off my dress. Right now. You know you can't ask for anything."

Gordon smiled, pecked away at his phone.

Vanessa's phone pinged. She picked it up to see that he had paid, then dropped it like a filthy rag.

In that lull, Gordon leaned forward, his face looming like a sweat-veneered moon. He was breathing so loudly that I could hear it.

Vanessa looked back at the laptop screen at Gordon, caught like a night creature in headlights.

"Are you touching yourself, Gordon?"

"No."

"Are you lying?"

"Yes."

"You know what you have to do, then."

"Yes." He shrugged like a naughty little schoolboy.

"Then let go of your useless dick and do it."

Gordon stuck out his tongue, pinched it between two fingers, and pulled.

She shrugged, unimpressed. "Harder."

He squirmed.

"Now bite."

He did.

"Harder."

He pinched his eyes closed and bit down.

"*Harder.*"

Gordon's pale face glistened with sweat. He quit biting and moved closer to his webcam, revealing the bite marks in his tongue, the rivulet of blood that flowed from its tip.

I winced, but Vanessa's expression stayed neutral. "Now taste it."

He closed his mouth and worked his lips for a moment, savoring.

"That's what lying tastes like, Gordon. Would you like to do that again?"

He shook his head slowly. Whatever desire had driven him before seemed spent.

Vanessa gave a sly smile. "You just came, didn't you? When you bit your tongue hard enough, your sad dick got hard and you came."

Gordon said nothing.

"Couldn't help it." When he spoke, a little blood dripped from the corner of his mouth. He turned to the side and spat blood like a lizard. "Sorry."

"You know I hate that word." She bent forward, as if aiming her body at Gordon, shifting from ambivalence to intensity.

Gordon smiled, ready for more.

Vanessa looked directly at the webcam, her eyes narrow and glinting. "We're done, Gordon. Done for good. You broke the rules. Now you're out."

"Wait, but—"

She strode forward to shut off Skype and the webcam.

I stood up from the guest chair and walked to the blue couch, where Vanessa sat tapping furiously on her phone.

"I'm completely blocking that asshole."

She tossed her phone on the floor.

"When a regular strays, they turn into bad dogs." Vanessa pulled off her wig and sat on the edge of the couch, still quaking with anger. I walked into the kitchen and poured us each a glass of Maçon from the fridge—a crisp white seemed likely to pair well with blood and deception.

I handed Vanessa a glass and sat on the couch.

"The tongue thing? *Ouch.*"

"He may need someone with more of a sadistic streak." She took a long drink of wine. "Wants physical discomfort along with his financial pain. And that was mild. There's also this thing with his scrotum and a—"

I held up my hands. "Do NOT need to know. What happens next?"

"I'll ghost him for a few weeks, then give him a little opening to come crawling back through. They usually do. If he drifts, it's not because of me, it's because he needs someone else," she said.

"Must be some lunar phase thing happening tonight," I said. "Everything's messed up."

"Tell me about it."

"I will."

I drank the rest of my wine, poured us more, and told her about the Okutama Institute, how my time in Tokyo was orchestrated and monitored. I showed her the business cards, told her that everyone I met had been playing a role, and playing it well. I told her how my three pitches now seemed like acts in a perverse play, each intended to wear me down and make me doubt my work.

She leaned forward, eyes widening. "That's some next-level scammer shit. And a lot of work." She pointed at the couch, the darkened lights, the webcam. "To get a client to do what I want, all I have to is dress up and do my bit. Why did they go to so much trouble?"

"For this." I held up my left wrist and Death Watch glimmered in the dim living room. "They knew I was the right guy to rep Death Watch. And every day they nudged me toward putting it on because they knew I would."

"Because you're impulsive," she said.

"Right. And they knew we really needed the account." I shook my head. "Looking back, there were so many times when I should have seen through the whole thing."

"I'm getting you the universal antidote."

"To what?"

"Everything—that's why it's universal." Vanessa rushed out of the living room and into the kitchen.

Left alone, my thoughts rushed back to Tokyo. Would a more suspicious person, like Nathan, have seen through the whole setup? What if, after all their careful manipulation, I hadn't put on the watch? Would the engineers have held me down and strapped it on me?

A sinking feeling stopped the questions. Maybe the Death Watch campaign was just performance art and I was slated to be its only customer—a foolish American willing to do anything for money. Maybe Watanabe just wanted to see how far I would go, how many interviews I'd give. Then he'd reveal the hoax, show how I was gaslit by a scam that happened in a place that didn't exist, with people who were just names on business cards.

He would teach the world a lesson: *Don't be like Coe Vessel.* Glib and heedless. It made my head hurt to think of it.

Vanessa came back holding a very old bottle. She brushed away the dust with her hand, then pulled out the cork and poured us each a glass of greenish-gold liquid.

"To forgetting," she said. We raised our glasses and drank the sweet, weird liquor in them.

"Whoa, what is this?"

"Absinthe. The real stuff. Not the new kind."

I squinted at the bottle's faded label—ABSINTHE ROBETTE.

"Had a French client years ago who liked me to dress up like a French showgirl circa 1880—striped tights, frilly red silk skirt, black corset. This bottle was part of the old-timey scenario he liked to play out. He had this thing he liked to do with my—"

I held up my hand. "Enough."

Vanessa refilled our glasses. "Right. Fuck the past," she said.

"Fuck. The. Past."

We drank. She refilled.

"Forward ever, backward never," I said, my glass raised.

We drank again, then more until the dusty bottle was empty.

We sprawled on the blue couch for hours, Vanessa at one end, me at the other—like coy college kids keeping desire at bay. She smoked a cigarette and it smelled so good I asked for one. I hadn't smoked in years and she laughed as I fumbled with the matches.

"That stuff works."

"What?"

"The antidote. Almost completely forgot that I was fooled,

tricked—"

"Fucked," she said.

"Well, I wouldn't—"

"Quit being so nice, Coe. You got fucked by those guys in Tokyo. Fucked hard. Fucked badly."

Vanessa summoned up the disturbing image of Watanabe in full rut.

"When you get fucked, you have to get paid." She held her wavering finger in the air, as if explaining arithmetic to a slow child. "When you get fucked *harder*, you get paid *more*."

"So that's the way the word works, I mean, the world works?"

"Yes. That's why you need me to help you."

"Help me what?"

Vanessa's smile broadened. "Get even."

HIGH FASHION

"What do you think of these?" Yohji held up a pair of enormous black pants to his skinny legs.

"Just buy half of them." When I demanded that Yohji see me while he was still in New York, he asked me to meet him at Comme des Garçons. Now I was involved in a prolonged street fashion show starring him.

Yohji rolled his eyes. "So small-town, Coe."

"I live in New York."

"Fashion is a state of mind."

My state of mind was approaching murderous. We had been in the store for more than an hour as Yohji debated wardrobe selections. All I could think about was how he had lied to me.

"We'll go to Rick's next."

"Who's Rick?"

Another eye roll. "Rick Owens. The fall line is already in. They're holding some pieces for me."

We walked out of the silver portal that led from Comme des Garçons and into the summer heat rising from Chelsea in shimmering waves. Yohji was struggling to carry his haul. I reached over and took his bags like a fashion Sherpa.

He smiled. "Thanks, bro."

Bro, hardly. Unless we were Cain and Abel.

Yohji shook his arms and straightened his outfit, a T-shirt printed to look like chainmail, a black jacket patterned with the moon in all its phases, tight burnt-umber pants, and black sneakers that looked normal but were probably vintage.

Rejuvenated, he marched toward Soho while I lagged behind. As we were about to walk under the High Line, Yohji looked up and broke into a grin. "Cool."

He vaulted up the metal staircase and I trudged behind him.

I caught up to him near a stand of bamboo. The High Line was crowded with summer tourists holding selfie sticks and iced coffees, taking photos or just staring at their phones in a social-media stupor. As we dodged the meandering walkers I posed the question all New Yorkers ask during the summer invasion: *Why don't tourists know how to walk?*

Yohji shuddered at the sight of cargo shorts and taut T-shirts barely restraining belly fat. "I just saw a girl in a camo cami."

We drifted over to the less-crowded side of the walkway, looking down at 23rd Street as unfashionable people flowed past us like a river around two stones.

"Let's get out of here and go to some galleries." Yohji headed toward the metal staircase. "Might do you good to see some real art. You know, expand your world."

"Fuck you." I said it old-style, the voice my father taught me, freighted with enough anger to keep creeps at bay and loud enough that tourists turned to watch us.

Yohji stopped. "So *agro*."

I held up my left wrist. "You know why I'm here. And it isn't to see art."

Yohji looked confused. "Something about questions, right?"

"Here's one. Why did you lie to me?"

Yohji bristled. "About what?"

"The Okutama Institute, for starters. And everyone there."

Yohji shrugged. "Oh, *that!*"

"Why did you do it?"

He gave his big grin. "Because it was fun?"

"Better."

"Because Watanabe really wanted you to be the spokesman for Death Watch. He knew you were some kind of advertising renegade, like your father."

"Why go to all that trouble?"

"Would you have put on the watch if we hadn't made it seem like the only thing to do, Coe Vessel?" Yohji said my name with the stolid inflection of his slow-talking father.

"No."

"Then it wasn't a lie. It was a strategy. A winning strategy." He gave a guileless smile.

"In Tokyo you said you'd send me a code so I could take off

the watch. Then in the launch meeting you said there wasn't one."

Yohji shrugged. "I say a lot of things."

"Which is true?"

"Both?"

"Not possible." I reached into one of the shopping bags, pulled out Yohji's layered black pants from Comme des Garçons, and held them over the railing. "Is Death Watch real? You have a minute."

"What do you mean by *real*?"

"Can it actually kill people?"

Yohji just shook his head. "I told you already."

"Then remind me. Because I'm worried."

"About what?"

"That bit about the seven knives."

"That worries you?" Yohji waved to dispel my petty concerns. "Then just don't try to take the watch off."

I dropped Yohji's thousand-dollar pants over the railing, the black fabric kiting in the gentle breeze then fluttering down. I made the sound of an airplane diving as they circled, then gave a final *ka-boom!* when they landed in a gray puddle.

"Shit!" Yohji slapped his hands to his cheeks, eyes wide in anime astonishment.

The tourists perked up. Finally, some New York attitude.

I pulled out his ten-foot lime green scarf decorated with plastic toys.

Yohji took a step toward me. "Please, not that."

"Back off." I held up the scarf, which cost two grand and some change. "Unless you're going to tell me the truth."

He paused, eyes half closed, biting his lower lip.

I tossed the scarf over the railing.

"NO!"

I looked down. A woman in a black leather jacket picked up the scarf from the sidewalk, glanced up at us, then hustled toward the subway.

"I love that scarf."

"Then go buy another one."

"There are only seven in the world." Yohji bent over from the weight of his staggering loss.

I reached in the bag and pulled out a black and gray jacket made out of strips of delicately hand-knotted silk. I had to admit, this piece was really beautiful. "So is the watch real or not?"

"Quit being cruel."

"To your clothes?"

"To me."

"Then quit lying." I held the jacket over the railing.

Yohji gave a garbled scream and dropped to his knees.

I dropped the jacket down to the gritty street, where it fluttered into eager hands—people love a bargain.

"Last chance for the truth." I hoisted his still-stuffed silver garment bag and held it over the railing.

Below us, a small crowd had gathered on the street, waiting like sharks for chum.

I straightened one finger that held the bag, then another.

Yohji rose, dark eyes glimmering in the summer sun. "OKAY."

I lifted the bag back over the railing and hung it on a low-hanging birch limb. The sharks dispersed.

We sat on two benches, facing each other. Yohji stared at the ground, gathered his thoughts.

"The watch is completely real," he said, slowly. "They're going to start going off at random and killing people."

My stomach plummeted.

"Kidding!" Yohji looked up and smiled. "That's just what Watanabe told me to say to you."

"Why?"

"Because for the whole Death Watch thing to work, everyone needs to think it's real, *duh*."

"But is it?"

Yohji paused. I reached toward his garment bag.

"Okay, okay." He held up his hands in surrender. "The watch does have seven knives in it. That's so it'll seem very, very real if someone takes a close look."

"But it won't go off."

Yohji shook his head. "Right."

I held up my left arm. "That means I can get this watch cut

off now?"

"*Mmmmmmmm*, well, no." Yohji held out his hands, palms up. "Like I said, it has to stay on. Customers can't just change their minds and cut the band. They have to be *all in*, even you. We warn buyers online. In the packaging. There's even a warning etched right on the clasp." He pointed at my wrist. "You can read it yourself. Removal Equals Death."

"I thought it was just more of Watanabe's hype."

"It's not. There's a dead man's switch."

"*What?*"

"Sounds worse than it is. Makes the watch go off if someone cuts the band."

"So the watch works?"

Yohji shrugged. "Only if you cut the band."

"Then everyone has to wear Death Watch forever?"

"Of course not." Yohji seemed annoyed at my questions. "The engineers are super-smart. They'll tell people how to deactivate it or cancel it or something."

"When?"

"When the experiment's over. Anyway, your watch is different. A really early prototype. The engineers told me it was basically just a watch. But they also said you shouldn't try to take it off."

I watched the tourists trudge beneath the summer sun. None of them had to worry that their watch might kill them.

"You're not really helping."

Yohji crossed over to my bench and sat next to me. "It's simple, Coe. All you have to do is play along. Pretend that it's all completely real, just like the rest of us." He lowered his voice to a conspiratorial whisper. "You'll be the guy who convinced the world to buy Death Watch. You'll be famous, more famous than Vince Vessel."

Yohji's eyes opened wide, then blinked fast, amazed at the possibility of a son outdistancing his father.

"Death Watch is going to be huge." Yohji threw his thin arms open wide. "We'll sell a ton of watches."

"But none of them are going to go off and kill people. Not me, not anyone?"

Yohji lowered his arms, looked me straight in the eye. "*No,* Coe Vessel. I promise. You have my word of honor."

"For what it's worth."

"Hey, that's mean."

"Mean is fooling me for a week in Tokyo. Wearing me down until I did something I shouldn't have."

"It was Watanabe's idea. All about the performance art."

"Didn't appreciate being part of the act," I said. "Neither will the people wearing the watch, when Watanabe tells them it's a hoax. No one likes being fooled."

Yohji's face brightened. "But we'll teach the world a lesson."

"Maybe."

"For now, you better start selling watches," he said. "Only a few days left."

"I know, I know."

"Doesn't matter, we've got Zazzy waiting in the wings. Love those guys. So cool."

That, I didn't know.

Yohji gave a respectful bow, then unhooked his suit bag from the birch limb and walked into the river of tourists, which swallowed him up like a bright leaf sinking in murky water.

SLEEPING DOGS

Clayton's Hardware was a throwback to the 1950's, which was probably the last time anyone cleaned the windows, filled with a pyramid of sun-faded cans of paint. I stopped on Rivington Street and stared into the store where I'd been so many times with my father then without him, with Alta then without her.

My father loved New York holdouts like Clayton's. He saved the place from bankruptcy during a downturn with *Clayton's Waitin,* a *pro bono* ad campaign that put a portrait of a younger Clayton—short gray hair, pink Irish skin, honest green eyes—on billboards all along the West Side Highway.

Need it fixed? Clayton's waitin'.

Need it fast? Clayton's waitin'.

Need advice? Clayton's waitin'.

The radio spots featured an impossible-to-forget jingle that I was still humming decades later. The campaign worked, the store survived, and the Vessel family became hardware royalty.

The door chimed softly when I walked in the store, empty on a summer afternoon. The sun glinted off the amber floorboards, polished like the deck of a clipper ship, the smell of lemon oil sending me back in time. The shelves were crowded with paint, mousetraps (humane and not), nails, picture-hanging wire, batteries, smoke detectors, plumbing supplies, and pretty much anything else a city dweller could need.

Clayton appeared from the back of the store, smiling when he saw me. "Well look what the cat dragged in. Hey, buddy boy."

"Hey, Clayton."

He settled into his usual place, an old-style lawyer's chair behind the cluttered wooden table that served as the check-out desk. The Sherwin-Williams calendar on the wall behind him was more than a decade old. "You're looking kinda rocky."

"Got a lot going on." I had walked straight to Clayton's from my High Line showdown with Yohji, which left me wanting a more rational opinion.

"How's Alta? Haven't seen her around."

"Doing good. Working a lot in Germany." I hadn't seen much of Alta either, but Clayton didn't need to know that.

"And you?"

"Went to Tokyo and got a new watch." I held up my wrist.

"Heard all about that famous watch, buddy boy. *You're trending,* like they say now, even here. Everyone's worried about you. Tell me this is one of those adman stunts like Vince used to pull."

"No, it's the real deal." I was tempted to tell Clayton the truth but he was a legendary gossip. He liked to tell me about celebrities and actors who came in the store, how Alec Baldwin preferred dark gray grout to hide bathtub mold and Lenny Kravitz smelled like vitamins.

"Imagine that," he said. "A watch that can kill you. What'll they think of next?"

"Good question."

"And you're okay with it?"

"I have to be." I held out my arm. "But I'd like to be able to take it off sometimes."

Clayton leaned forward to take a closer look. "Can't you just unfasten it like a normal watch?" He reached for the band and I pulled my arm back.

"It's not normal—or that easy." I told him about the *dead man's switch.*

"That's messed up, son."

I nodded. Messed up was just the beginning.

Clayton stared at the shining watch face, then turned my hand over to see the red number glowing on the band. He rummaged in a desk drawer and found a magnifying glass, focused it on the clasp.

"Removal equals death. Then there's a skull and crossbones. Did you read this?"

"Yeah. But I'm not sure I believe it."

He let go of my arm, put down the magnifying glass, and turned quiet for a moment as he considered the task at hand.

"Know what knob and tube wiring is?" His chair gave a loud

squeal as he sat back down.

I shook my head. I wasn't a handyman, far from it.

"Used to be the way apartments were wired. From like the 1880's until about 1930. Electricians wrapped copper wire around these ceramic knobs they nailed inside the walls." Clayton illustrated the procedure with his hands. "Then they threaded the wires through these ceramic tubes through floor joists and wall studs. *Knob* and *tube*, get it? Anyway, it kept the wires tight."

Dad always thought of Clayton as a hardware savant who, in a perfect world, would have had his own reality show, featuring the real artists of New York—Vietnamese floor guys, Portuguese painters, Irish carpenters. But my mind was too jangled to appreciate his brief history of wiring.

"You're probably wondering why the hell I'm talking about wires."

"I was."

"Hold on, I'll get to the point in a minute." Clayton said nothing, then found the conversational thread. "So over time, the rubber wrapping around the wiring started to rot. As long as you didn't mess with it, it was stable. But once someone started tinkering with it—*boom*, the wires started shorting out. Smoldering inside walls and basements. All hell broke loose. Fires all over Manhattan until they changed the building codes."

"So what're you saying?"

"I can't tell what's going on inside this thing." He pointed at the watch. "The band looks like it's titanium, so it wouldn't be easy to cut off with bolt cutters. Might mess up your wrist or set off the watch. That blinking number looks kinda like—"

"Like a bomb?"

"Yeah, like in one of those thrillers when the numbers start counting down until—"

"It blows up?"

"Wasn't going to say it, but yeah, that."

"The numbers go up, actually."

"Maybe that's good. One last thing. There's a wire woven into the mesh of the watchband. Different metal." He tilted a magnifying lamp toward me and turned it on. I held my watch under the light and looked through the glass. A slightly darker metal meandered through the titanium band.

"Never noticed that."

He clicked off the light, moved the lamp out of the way. "Looks like the kind of thing you don't want to cut. Could be the dead man's switch they told you about."

"Can you just cut around it?"

"Wouldn't want to nick it and let those knives slash you up." Clayton held up his right hand and pointed to the missing tip of his index finger. "I've had my share of damage. This one's from a run-in with a circular saw." He held up his left hand and pointed to a long welt seared across its palm. "Grabbed a live wire that a storm knocked down in my daughter's backyard." He put his hands back on his desk. "Everyone gets their share of scars."

"They do." I ran through my own catalog of stitches and road rash, most from my skateboarding teens and being dumb in the kitchen.

"Difference is, they're accidents." Clayton gave me a hard, disapproving stare, one that channeled my father's steely gray eyes.

"You can't cut it off?"

"I could, but I won't. Not taking any chances with the son of Vince. I'd like for you to stick around longer than he did."

"I'd like that, too," I said.

"Then why the hell did you put that watch on in the first place?"

It was a hard question, one I couldn't answer.

Clayton stood and put his hand on my shoulder. "Don't worry so much, buddy boy. It's just a watch. Eventually the battery will give out and it'll probably fall off. Like I was saying about knob and tube, sometimes it makes sense to leave the problem alone instead of tinkering with it, just let sleeping dogs lie. That's what I'd do."

So would I, because I didn't have a choice.

MOMINATRIX

"RAPIDLY APPROACHING ZERO HOUR," Nathan said. "It's Friday night. If we don't sell a watch by midnight, all of this was a waste of time." He swept his hand over the conference table, covered with laptops and hard drives, takeout containers and coffee cups—the debris of Team Death. "It means Zazzy swoops in and gets the account."

"If we can't sell Death Watch, they can't," I said.

"You might be kind of biased about that."

"Zazzy would just slap together some clickbait that attracts millions of eyeballs but doesn't sell anything."

"Maybe they'll get an influencer."

"We tried that, but influencers tend to want to stay alive," Wren said. "No one gives you cool swag when you're dead."

Nathan stood and paced the room.

"You know how it works," he shouted. "If we lose this account, everyone will know. We'll look seriously bad. It'll be back to B2B bullshit for all of us. Optimized manufacturing processes! Breakthroughs in industrial gaskets! Solar lighting for prison parking lots!"

I raised my hand to stop Nathan's pacing. "You know who does all that boring B2B work? That would be me, Wren, and Harup. We want this account even more than you do."

Nathan sat back down and picked up his iPhone. Clients were emailing, news breaking. There were special discounts available. Friends liked his posts. He looked up, refreshed by dopamine. "Sorry, didn't mean to shout. The agency matters a lot to me, you all know that."

"Means a lot to me, too." Wren said quietly. "So quit being a dick, please."

"Okay, okay," he said. "More ideas?"

No one said anything.

"I mean, I could buy a couple of watches on credit," Nathan

said. "We all could. And disguise our names."

Harup shook his head, Wren, too.

"We talked about that," I said. "I mean, it's the most obvious solution. Buy your way out. Like when CEOs order ten thousand copies of their book to get it on the bestseller list. But once we do that, it's a whole new game."

"And not a good one," Wren said.

"OK, strike that one."

"We're mining the site traffic," Wren said. "Going after repeat visitors who might be on the fence. Can we give them a discount to give them a nudge?"

Nathan stared at the ceiling. "The contract says no discounting."

"Did you even read that contract before you signed it?" I asked.

"Yes, of course. I just didn't think we'd have a hard time selling one."

"Of course it's hard, maybe impossible." I wasn't giving up yet, but we were just hours away from our deadline. "No one ever woke up and said *I sure could use a watch that might kill me.*"

"You sounded a lot more confident a couple of weeks ago."

"That was before the launch."

"Meaning?"

"Since launch, we've been getting tons of media attention. But it's going to take more time for our message to filter through to the right people."

"Because?"

"They're outsiders."

"Then let's do one last push on social, all channels." Nathan pointed at Wren. "Plenty of outsiders there."

"We don't have to," Wren said. "It's pushing itself. Total buzzfest."

"What're they saying?"

"Half say Death Watch is insane and cruel. The rest think it's inevitable and genius. But it's just churn. No conversions."

"Hey, I know. We could ping those return visitors." Nathan pointed at Harup. "And remind them that they could be among the first buyers. Call them something. *The Elite*, the something. Make it sound exclusive."

The *Die*-ciples? hehehe fuk yeh

Harup opened his mouth in a silent laugh.

Nathan shook his head. "Okay, not that."

Wren brightened. "Maybe Yohji will give us another week. Can't hurt to ask."

"I don't think so," I said.

"Why not?"

"I threw his fancy new clothes off the High Line." I told them the abbreviated version of my Yohji showdown. Wren laughed at the absurdity. Nathan did not.

"*Shit*, Coe." Nathan looked up at the ceiling, as if a deity hovered there. "You know Yohji's our client, right?"

I nodded.

"You should have been buying him clothes, not trashing them."

I was about to explain when Harup's phone bripped. He turned it toward me.

Get here, now. Bring Coe.

I was sweating and winded after running from the subway, but Harup seemed unfazed, as usual. He gave Vanessa a casual nod as we rushed in her apartment.

She waved us toward the guest area, where there were two folding chairs waiting. The pillowy lights were blazing, webcam blinking.

"Sit down, got less than a minute." Vanessa sounded nervous.

Harup picked up one of the chairs and moved it as far away from the other as he could, then sat down as if waiting for a movie to begin.

I walked to the blue couch, where Vanessa was settling in for whatever was next. She was wearing a cream-colored blouse buttoned and tied high at the neck, and a gold cross necklace. Her skirt was long and pleated; her dirty-blonde wig frosted gray.

"Why're you dressed like Mrs. Drollinger?"

"Who?"

"My fifth-grade teacher."

"I contain multitudes," she said. "No time to explain. Just watch. If it gets too weird, leave quietly."

"Anything else?"

"Wish me luck."

"For what?"

"You'll see."

"Good luck?" From what I could tell, Vanessa didn't really need luck; she had power.

As I took my seat, Skype *blooped* and a close-up of a pair of glistening, puckered lips appeared on the laptop screen.

"Babyboy needs milk," a high voice squealed.

"We're not doing that, Babyboy," Vanessa said firmly.

The puckered mouth backed away and we could see that it belonged to a man with greasy brown hair split down the middle and the shadow of a beard. His face was pale and his dark eyes looked smudged underneath, like he never slept. When he smiled his face opened up and he suddenly looked very familiar from in-flight movies.

"Isn't that—"

Harup held up his hand, palm toward me, nodded.

"Why not? Why not?" Babyboy turned pouty, petulant.

"Because you're the runt of the litter." Vanessa said. "Why would I waste my precious milk on you."

"*Fuck yes*!" Babyboy turned into Actorman, with the LA-inflected voice I remembered from *Interstitial, Lost on Mars,* and a couple more.

"That's fucking cherry, Vanessa, I'm the runt of the litter. *Nice.* Best Mominatrix ever."

"Don't ever fucking call me that again. Pay me. Now."

He picked up his phone and tapped it. Vanessa's phone pinged with what I assumed was some of the *fin* of findom.

"You don't deserve any milk," she said. "I'll feed your brother. But not you. Your brother's smarter. And a better actor."

Her phone pinged again, then again.

"You shouldn't have any toys, either."

"That's right," said Babyboy, back in character. "My brother should get all the good stuff."

Babyboy turned and pulled a small, dark painting from the wall. He gripped the frame with both hands and twisted it until it buckled and the canvas tore, and threw it on the ground.

"Oh, that's very bad, Babyboy. You're a bad little baby, busting up his toys. Babyboy needs to be better."

"He does," said Actorman, in a low, shaking voice. "I need to be a lot fucking better, Vanessa. Get the demons out."

She smiled. "No can do. Too many."

"Yeah, for sure." Actorman stood and wandered off. He wore a rumpled black T-shirt and baggy gray sweatpants that ended in pale, splotchy ankles.

"What's going on?"

Harup shrugged.

"Smoking crack," Vanessa whispered in the lull. "So retro."

Actorman was back, eyes red, shaking a little less.

"Babyboy needs."

"Yes, you do. You need something."

"What?"

"You need milk, don't you?"

"Yeth. Yeth. Yeth."

"If I give you milk, will you do what I tell you to do?"

"Shit, Vanessa, really?" Actorman seemed floored by the offer. "You never—"

"Tonight's special. And so are you."

"*Ooooooo.*" Babyboy lowered his face into his hands, his nails dark crescents, as if he had dug a hole in the yard with his hands. "*Ooooooo.*"

"Remember that shiny watch I told you about, Babyboy?"

His red-rimmed eyes opened wide.

"That watch will make you better. You have to buy one. Now. And put it on the moment you get it."

"*K*, hang on." Actorman took out his iPhone and tapped at it furiously. "Done," he said, as if he had just ordered a value-pack of Bounty.

Harup checked his phone, swiped a couple of screens. He nodded. An impulse buy from a crack-addled famous actor was still a first sale.

"Good, Babyboy. You're so good. Do you want your milk now?" Vanessa started to untie the bow at her throat.

"*Yeth. Fuck yes, Vanessa!*" The hybrid creature—half Babyboy, half Actorman—pounded his fists on the black-leather arms of his Barcelona chair.

Vanessa stopped untying her bow. "You need to do one more thing, Babyboy."

"What?" Actorman said. "I bought the watch like you told me to."

"Shut the fuck up," Vanessa said, pointing at the webcam. "I want Babyboy."

Actorman held up his hands in surrender and Babyboy reappeared. "*Yeth?*"

"You need to text your other manbaby friends and tell them to buy Death Watch, too." Vanessa shot a look our direction and all we could do was shake our heads at her audacity. She had already made the sale. Now she was shooting for over-quota.

Actorman messed with his phone, then muted Skype and called someone. He disappeared for a moment then came back, eyes even more blurry. "My brother's buying a watch. And telling his friends." He shook his head slowly. "Got a lot more of them than I do."

"Babyboy? Babyboy?" She seemed to be trying to summon him out of the failing husk of Actorman.

He lowered his head in his hands. "Yeah, okay, *yeth*."

Vanessa stood up from the couch, pulled her blouse down, and freed a pale breast from her grandmotherly white padded bra, revealing a wide areola and flat nipple. Vanessa walked slowly toward the webcam, as if in a trance, rubbing the nipple to raise it, then offering it up to the webcam, to Babyboy.

"Take, drink," she said. "You're thirsty, Babyboy. Drink. This is my tit. This is my milk."

He looked up. "*Yeth*. So thirsty."

He rose from his chair and the screen filled with his puckered mouth. He moaned and slurped, as if drinking it might cure all that sickened him.

Vanessa pinched her dry nipple; there was no milk, no easy antidote. She drifted closer to the webcam. "There's more," she said softly. "I'll save it for you, Babyboy."

Vanessa reached down and shut off the webcam and lights, dropping the room into darkness. She paced around the living room, elated but shaking.

"You okay?"

She shook her head and sat on the couch, her body shuddering.

Harup strode toward the kitchen. I sat next to Vanessa, rubbing her back through the slippery polyester blouse.

"This shit is not easy," she said softly.

"You're amazing." Vanessa had soothed a manbaby with non-existent breast milk, hustled a famous actor on drugs, and closed a sale.

"Also, a mess," she said.

"You sold the first Death Watch."

Vanessa shook her head. "It's not always all about your watch." She sat up, rubbed her eyes, pulled off her wig and threw it into the shadows. "Jimmy's been my client since way before he got famous. Needed me to control him because he knew he couldn't do it himself."

"Right." I was just beginning to understand Vanessa's work.

"I gave him a fantasy he could use to get him through everything else. But I went too far tonight and gave him what he wanted."

"That's bad because?"

"Because no one should get what they want," Vanessa said, as if everyone knew it but me.

"He'll be okay, seems like. I mean, the last time I saw him he was walking on a red carpet next to Scarlett Johansson."

She shook her head slowly. "None of that matters to him."

"Buying Death Watch may end up being embarrassing when Watanabe's done," I said. "But it isn't going to kill him."

"He's doing a good job of that all by himself." Vanessa sat up, looked down and realized that her blouse was still undone, left breast out. She caught me staring.

"Always wondered what Mrs. Drollinger looked like naked."

"No free shows." She buttoned her blouse.

Harup came back with three water glasses and a bottle of Champagne. Even in the gloom, I could see that the substandard glassware disturbed him. An ugly font could ruin his morning.

"It's okay, Harup."

"More than okay," Vanessa said. "A good night for Team Death."

Harup sat on the other side of the couch, Vanessa between us, and handed the glasses around.

Vanessa raised her glass, took a sip, and gave a faint smile. "To Babyboy."

"No, to you."

Harup and I raised our glasses, to Vanessa, who brought us the perfect customer for Death Watch—rich, miserable, and willing to risk it all.

SCULLYWAGS

When Vanessa jumpstarted sales with Jimmy Vance—AKA Babyboy, brother of the more famous Niles Vance—she found our first cohort of buyers. The self-proclaimed Young Bums were New Nihilists, Hollywood chapter. They walked off film sets and quietly quit acting. They holed up in their beach houses, giving up on personal hygiene, doing drugs, sending out ominous tweets, and waiting for the end of the world. The lineage from James Dean and Robert Mitchum to Johnny Depp and Joaquin Phoenix led right to the Young Bums.

The Vance brothers and their friends started showing off Death Watch on TikTok, taking sales to another level. Word spread to the wannabes, status-seekers, and second liners—an apt New Orleans phrase that Vanessa taught me. These buyers craved attention as hard as the Young Bums and New Nihilists ached for destruction.

With early sales coming in, Team Death decided to take Death Watch higher and lower.

Higher led to a 10-page think piece in the *New York Review of Books*: "*Telling Time*: Is Death Watch the High-Art Harbinger of the End-time? Daniel Mendelsohn and Zadie Smith Join in Conversation." Higher drew Death Watch into the culture wars, with the we-want-the-freedom-to-do-anything crowd applauding it, and the we-have-to-protect-people-from-themselves contingent denouncing it. Higher meant coastal elites strapped on Death Watch and raised their clenched fists to show solidarity with the disenfranchised, who faced the constant threat of death in an unjust world. Never mind that the woke buyers paid $50,000 to experience that threat, which the truly vulnerable could feel for free.

Lower led to an enthusiastic endorsement from the NRA, which supported putting any weapon in the hands of (or on the wrists of) freedom-loving Americans. Lower led to rallies by the Faces of the Faithful, a splinter group of Catholic radicals who saw Death Watch as anti-life. Lower still led to insanely great product placement on *The Chair with Jake Scully* and an invitation from Jake himself to attend the game show's season finale.

A security guard ushered us from Times Square into the theater, already crammed with fans, who watched us, wondering what made us so special, as we took our places in a chained-off section to the side of the stage, protected by our own security guard. Walking next to me, Harup held his arms to his sides to avoid contagion.

"Why do they need so many guards?" I shouted in Wren's ear.

"You've never seen the show, have you?"

"Maybe once."

Wren smiled and settled into her orange plastic seat. Getting Death Watch on the show was all her doing, and she was thrumming with excitement. I sat next to her and Harup reluctantly lowered his black-clad skinny self into the terrifyingly ugly seat next to me. The security guard in our private section leaned forward and solemnly handed us each a fried chicken bucket printed with Jake Scully's leering face replacing solemn Colonel Sanders. The bucket was packed with cold cans of Budweiser.

I shook my head. "Not a beer guy."

"Take it," Wren shouted. "You'll need them."

We took our buckets of Bud and set them on the sticky cement floor between our feet. Harup gave me his *why are you doing this to me* look.

The crowd started to roar even louder, chanting. *Scully. Scully. Scully.*

Wren shoved her phone toward me, turned the volume up and stuffed a hot earbud in one of my ears. "LISTEN, THIS JUST HAPPENED."

She clicked and I saw video of a pale, black-haired woman in her twenties slipping Death Watch around her narrow wrist. She startled as the watch's band gripped her, then held up her tattooed arm so the world could admire her Death Watch, activated and ready to kill.

She leaned closer and spoke, words and princess filter sparkles trailing across the screen in front of her.

> **The fking world is garbage and doomed so all I want is someone beautiful to know me and love me while I die that's why I'm wearing this watch for you Cate Blanchett.**

We knew that fans were buying Death Watch to express slavish devotion to an unreachable celebrity crush. But this was some next-level shit. I shook my head in amazement.

Wren plucked the earbud out of my ear, and leaned closer. "Dozens more. Different idols. Same message." She gave a manic smile. "We're hitting a nerve."

Like a sloppy dentist, I thought, but didn't say.

The lights rose on stage and a spotlight zeroed in on a stumpy elfin man wearing thick glasses. Even among the unhinged Scullywags, his apoplectic face and stringy long hair stood out. The screams rose even higher.

"*Eww*, it's Roger the Lodger." Wren stuck out her tongue.

The elfin man waved the crowd down to a mere roar. "ARE YE FUCKING READY?"

"YES!"

"LOUDER. ARE YE READY?"

"FUCK YES!"

"ARE YE ARMED AND DANGEROUS?"

The crowd erupted, throwing cans of Bud at Roger, who scurried around the stage, picking up the burst cans to shower himself with beer and stuffing the rest in a gunnysack.

"He lives in the studio," Wren yelled in my ear. "They let him sleep under the seats and keep him stoked on beer and energy drinks like a modern-day geek."

"You seem to know a lot about this show."

Wren shrugged. "I eat pop culture for breakfast."

"Hate to see what's for lunch."

The spotlight shifted to the side and Jake Scully slid into the light—flame-red hair slicked up to a swirled soft-serve peak, dead green eyes, tight brown suit. He waved as he walked across the stage. Someone threw a can at Scully and he picked it up and threw it back, hard. He took no shit from his audience. When he got to Roger, Scully reached down to rub his troll's hair for luck, then picked him up and threw him headfirst into the audience, which caught him and passed him around like a beach ball.

A stagehand handed Scully a microphone. "This is it, friends, the final show of the season, where I find out how many of you bastards love me and how many hate me."

The crowd roared so loud my eardrums rattled.

"Love?" Scully thrust the microphone at the crowd and it erupted.

"Hate?" Even louder roaring sent Harup curling into the fetal position.

"Well fuck you, *Scullywags*." Scullywags were his fans, minions, frenemies—and meal ticket.

Scully walked across the stage to The Chair, a sinister black-leather lounge contraption that looked like something the Nazis would have come up with if they had invaded Design Within Reach. As he lowered himself into it, silver constraints slithered around his ankles and chest.

"Not used to actually being in the Chair." The Chair was usually filled by actors and musicians—all equally bruised by Scully's brutal questions and gleeful revelations of their misdeeds. But tonight was special, the finale.

Scully kept talking, mixing jokes and insults as the clock above him counted down. Viewers all over the world had been voting online for weeks to decide whether Scully, their crass but charismatic host, should put on Death Watch or not. Night after night, the votes streamed in, voting *thumbs-up* or *thumbs-down,* tallied above the Chair by red and green thumb icons on a massive digital screen.

His very own celebrity Judgment Day had finally arrived.

The vote tally blurred past four million as the clock counted down the last seconds. A loud bell clanged. Roger rattled the bars of his cage. A fusillade of Bud cans hit the stage.

"Now the moment you've all been waiting for." The crowd

cheered as an assistant dressed as a slutty nurse wheeled out a hospital gurney, stopped, and pulled off the sheet to reveal Death Watch on a low stand, glimmering in the studio lights.

The crowd roared.

"Best product placement ever," I said.

Wren beamed. She had sent a free watch to Scully and dared him to put it on.

"I honestly don't know what we're about to find out." Scully waved the crowd down into near silence. "All I know is I've put my fate in your hands—my audience, fans, and judges. I've entertained many of you, offended others. Now the moment of truth is upon me."

Fkng drama queen

"Just get on with it," Wren muttered.

Team Death leaned forward, eyes locked on the stage.

"Reveal the results!" Scully shut his bright green eyes and the Scullywags started screaming and shouting. Above him, numbers blurred under the two thumb icons. They stopped, revealing a winner by more than a million-vote margin.

Scully opened his eyes to see an enormous, throbbing thumbs-up. *Yes,* the world wanted Jake Scully to wear Death Watch.

"The people have spoken." Scully stared into the crowd, eyes sparkling as the slutty nurse handed Death Watch to him. He slipped it on, cringing as the band cinched tightly around his wrist.

"It's official," he said. "I'm going to die."

"News flash," I said. "You already were." That the watch wouldn't really kill him made his histrionics seem superfluous, at least to us. The rest of the audience turned ecstatic, locked in a *kill your idols* moment.

We took advantage of the roar to slip out of our seats, leaving our half-empty buckets of Budweiser to scavengers. Our private security guard escorted Team Death out a side entrance down to a dark Times Square alley seething with rats.

Not that different from inside the theater, we agreed.

From a few blocks down 57th Street, I could see the figures circling on the sidewalk in front of our apartment building. The clip of incels stalking around in front of Vanessa's old apartment surfaced in my mind. How could they have possibly found her?

I ducked into an alley and called Vanessa.

"Hey," I whispered. "Don't go outside."

"Why not?"

"They're here."

"Who?"

"*Incels.*"

"You mean those people out front?"

"Did you see them already? Did they see you?"

She laughed. "Those are your stalkers, not mine. Look closer."

"Can't, I'm three blocks away."

"They're the Faces of the Faithful," she said. "Whatever the hell that means."

I walked closer and saw their white robes, the watches painted on their faces, black hands set to midnight.

"They look kinda spooky," I said.

"Just a bunch of grandmas who don't like Death Watch."

"So they came to my apartment building to tell me that?"

"You're a public figure, like it or not. Saw you guys on *The Chair* tonight."

"Really?"

"Camera zoomed in on you when Scully put on the watch. You looked pretty happy."

"I was. I am."

"Well, now you're dealing with the downside of fame."

"Which is?"

"Freaks come to bug you," she said.

I said nothing.

"At least they're not here to kill you. Yet."

"Not funny."

"If you need help pushing your way through the church ladies, let me know." Vanessa laughed and her phone clicked off.

MULTITUDES

I DRANK COFFEE IN VANESSA'S KITCHEN while she finished up an early morning session with a Dutch client named Stijn, who was speed-talking his way into submission, word clusters separated by his high nervous laugh. Vanessa stayed almost silent, letting him wear himself out like a border collie in a small yard. Her clear, powerful voice calmed Stijn, slowed his racing mind.

A loud ping echoed in the living room as Stijn sent her money, then again as she told him to give her more. The session ended abruptly. There was never any need for good-byes; they'd all be back.

Vanessa walked in from the living room wearing a black bodysuit that shimmered in the sunlight.

"Morning, Cat Woman."

"Stijn likes the old-school look," she explained. "You should have seen what he was wearing."

"No thanks."

"Help me unzip this thing. It's impossible."

I tugged at the zipper at the top of her bodysuit but couldn't get it to move. "Leather?"

"Vintage vinyl."

I pulled harder and lowered the zipper down to reveal the sinuous curve of Vanessa's pale back. She walked into her bedroom, the body suit unfurled behind her like black wings.

I opened the cupboard and took down a mug with the Columbia Medical School insignia. The kitchen was directly across the hall from the bedroom and Vanessa had left the door open. She stood with her back to me, dust motes swarming in the amber morning sunlight. In the corner of my eye, I could see Vanessa peeling off her bodysuit, her skin marked by its seams. A tattooed arrow wrapped around one arm and a jagged white scar crossed her lower back.

I thought about her pale skin while I poured her a coffee. When

I glanced back toward the bedroom, the doorway was empty and I could hear her opening drawers, rummaging for clothes, getting dressed.

We sat together at the tiny kitchen table drinking coffee as cars honked down on the street, crowded with people rushing to work. Vanessa wore a black T-shirt and jeans now, no shoes, no wig.

Closeness muted our easy conversation. We were both relieved when my phone bripped on the table.

"It's Harup," I said, not reaching for it.

Vanessa shook her head. "Someday he'll talk again."

"When that happens, it better be good."

"Don't count on it."

New Watanabe thng jst dropped.

Watanabe had turned into a loose cannon, releasing unscripted videos on YouTube every week to fuel the firestorm of attention Death Watch was getting.

"We should watch this."

Vanessa drank her coffee, nodded.

I leaned forward and clicked on the link, propped my phone up against my coffee cup.

Watanabe appeared, all stringy hair and wan smile, staring into the camera like a hypnotist. Fame, or more accurately infamy, had done little to make Watanabe improve his personal hygiene or upgrade his wardrobe. In fact, he just looked more manic and frayed around the edges.

Vanessa gave a low laugh. "Too close to that camera, big fella. I can count the pores."

"Not a beauty contest."

"Apparently."

Watanabe put out his cigarette and began to speak.

"To the many of you who have purchased Death Watch, congratulations. We are heartened to see your number grow so rapidly. You have made a commitment to life, though many in the media would say the opposite." He lit another cigarette. Smoke filled the screen, then cleared.

"All great movements create a strong reaction. The world will eventually see the importance of the Cassius Seven."

"Just call it Death Watch," we said in unison.

"For now, we must accept that many will not comprehend the enormity of our project. But you do, brave people who wear the watch. You are not the faceless. You are the fearless. I will have more to say next week." The video ended. I turned my phone off.

"Aren't you supposed to be the spokesman or whatever?"

"Seems like he wants to do it." We hadn't created a monster; Watanabe was already fully formed before we met him. But we had given him a new platform, one that he was enjoying way too much.

Vanessa nodded, reached for her coffee. *"Desire is a reverse mirror.* A friend told me that when I was escorting and it stuck."

"Meaning?"

"Like if a client says he wants to have anal sex, a lot of times what it really means is that he wants to get fucked up the ass with a big strap-on."

Coffee sprayed out of my mouth.

"Sorry, shop talk."

I set my coffee cup on the table.

"When they switch, it's kind of beautiful," Vanessa said, smiling. "Watching someone get what they really want, even though they shouldn't."

"It's about asking for one thing but wanting the opposite?"

Vanessa nodded slowly.

"Watanabe said he wanted me to be the pitchman for Death Watch, but what he really wanted was to do it himself."

"Right. Duplicity is the *D* in every man's DNA."

"And all this time, I thought it stood for delusional."

"Or dickhead."

"Or that." My phone vibrated on the table again.

Nathan's looking 4 u get in here quik.

"And we were having such a good morning," Vanessa said.

"We were," I said, "and we will again."

"Yes, we will." Vanessa smiled.

Our morning together in the kitchen felt relaxed, our connection deeper. That said, I knew I should distrust easy familiarity. I had watched Vanessa with her clients and seen how she shifted effortlessly to become what they needed her to be. And I knew she could use her pro-grade knowledge of men's needs and weaknesses to scope out mine, then recalibrate herself to become exactly the Vanessa I needed—an accepting friend, one who saw me as better than I actually was.

Or maybe she was just keeping her lonely landlord intrigued and entertained so she could keep staying in her comfortable bolthole. Anything seemed possible.

I stood up, ready to leave.

"Wish you didn't have to go so soon." Vanessa set her coffee cup on the table. "Work always gets in the way, doesn't it?"

"It does," I said. "It definitely does."

MOMENTUM

I WALKED IN LATE TO OUR WEEKLY TEAM DEATH MEETING and took a seat. Nathan gave me his scolding look. I gave him the Lazy Finger. He smiled. We moved on.

Harup pulled up the chart showing sales over time and projected it on the screen. It looked like an escalating curve heading up a tall mountain.

"Great work, team." Nathan had been surprised when we managed to sell one Death Watch. Now he was astounded—we had sold more than two hundred.

Wren smiled, Harup didn't. Progress was boring.

Death Watch's star turn on Jake Scully's wrist amped up the white noise online. Death Watch was attracting the blaringly cocky, terminally disillusioned, and silently suicidal. Some wanted status, others relief. Everyone paid. Watanabe was making millions. The agency was on a roll—a fat roll of money.

"How much longer can this go on?" Nathan pulled up his project calendar on the screen. He tracked project milestones like a human spreadsheet. "It's almost the end of July. Are we going to be doing this through the summer? End of the year?"

No one said anything. It was Watanabe's experiment. No one else could decide when it was over.

"Coe?"

"I guess that's not mentioned in the contract?"

Nathan inhaled deeply. "No, it's not. Okay, any updates?"

"Let's see." Wren settled, checked her notes. "The Canadian government banned the sale of Death Watch this morning."

Harup rolled his eyes.

Gd luck ppl pay w crypto and its shipt from Belarus

Wren continued her media report. "An editorial in the *Washington Post* today denounced Watanabe as *an attention-seeking charlatan* while *Artforum* praised him as *a prescient artist willing to use his art to trigger dark insights into the human condition, no matter what the cost*. He'll like that last part."

"We haven't talked to him in more than a week," Nathan said. "Let's give him a call?"

"Why?" I had already seen enough Watanabe today.

"You know what they say. Keep your friends close, your clients closer."

Harup did his magic and a smiling, moon-faced Watanabe appeared on our screen.

"Team Death, hello!" He smiled like a goony kid, ran his fingers through his long black hair, streaked with gray. "Did you see my message this morning on YouTube?"

"We did. Brilliant." Everything Nathan said sounded sincere, especially when he was lying. It was a gift.

"Thank you so much." Watanabe smiled broadly. "Death Watch is getting very popular."

Nathan gave his client-friendly smile. "Yes, it is."

"The engineers are struggling to keep up with demand," Watanabe said in his low, slow voice. "I have them working overtime."

I pictured the engineers around the koi pond—their cigarettes, sly smiles, indifference. They didn't care. They just wanted money and now it was raining down on them.

"I am on NPR tomorrow, can you believe it? *Fresh Air with Terry Gross!*" His voice shifted to an *it's my tenth birthday and I just got a pony!* level of glee.

"Cool for you," I said. Wren kicked me under the table.

"I never received this much attention before. Even when I dumped tsunami debris on the Emperor's doorstep."

"Goes to show you," Nathan said.

"What does it show me?"

"The power of a brilliant idea."

Wren gave a tiny gagging noise at Nathan's false nod to the myth of male genius. I made a note to remind Nathan not to lean on *brilliant* so much.

"*Yesssssss*," Watanabe said, sucking on a ubiquitous cigarette. "There is nothing else like Death Watch. But I must ask you, Team

Death, how are you selling so many watches?"

Harup's lip curled as he texted.

Bcuz we're fkng good

"Down, bloodhound," Nathan whispered.

"Because Death Watch is the device for our time," I said.

"Like the Apple Watch was?"

"Right."

Watanabe laughed. "That watch enslaved its users by binding them tightly to their schedules and work. Ours sets them free to live. We should use that insight, Coe Vessel." In his Tokyo studio, Watanabe's big hand reached toward the screen and Skype went blank.

"Watanabe's gone so Hollywood," Wren said in the silence.

"Well, he sounds like a happy client," Nathan said.

"Like he's super high on money," Wren said.

Harup locked his eyes on mine and we shook our heads in sync, remembering software product managers who had turned into monsters after they moved ten thousand units. All we could do was hope Watanabe could contain his blossoming ego until he decided to tell the truth about his experiment. Until then, Team Death would keep pitching as hard as we could.

Harup gave a long, soundless yawn and stretched his long arms up in the air. His shirtsleeve rode up his arm revealing—.

"What the fuck?" Wren spotted it first. Then I saw it gleaming on Harup's left wrist.

He smiled, texted.

Wantd to b more like Coe

I rose out of my chair, eyes locked on Harup's wrist. "*No,* fuck no."

"You okay?" Nathan said, not standing.

My mind raced. I had lured strangers into putting on Death Watch without any worries at all. But Harup was like my weird little brother, who needed protecting, not tempting.

I managed to speak, finally. "What the hell is that?"

Harup pointed at Death Watch's matte silver face and then the titanium band, as if holding a product demonstration. He turned his wrist slightly to reveal the blinking red number *1*. Then he pinched the band and it opened. The watch slid from his wrist and into his waiting hand. He gave a beaming smile.

"How'd you do that?" Had Harup figured out how to take off Death Watch, a problem that even the legendary Clayton couldn't solve?

He tossed me the watch and I turned it over in my hand, felt its metallic heft, saw the serial number on the back.

"Where'd you get this?"

Bought it in Washington Sq. Guy had Rolexes 2. Any watch 50 bucks.

Wren grabbed the watch from me. "Cool, I love knock-offs."

Harup walked over and put his hand on my shoulder, a rare physical interaction.

Sry. Thought it wd be funy.

"It's not. Not at all."

Nathan looked concerned. "Is this good news?"

"Consider it flattery." Wren turned the fake watch over in her hand. The knock-off was realistic enough to pass as Death Watch from a distance, but at a fraction of the cost, with maximum end-time street cred and zero possibility of death. No one would know it was fake except the person who bought it.

Wren tossed the watch to Harup but he missed the catch. The watch hit the floor and the crystal popped off. But no deadly knives emerged.

Wren smiled. "You get what you pay for."

Nathan pointed at Harup. "Now that you made Coe almost *plotz*, maybe you could share what you've been working on."

Chk it out. New vid.

We settled in to watch Harup's latest Death Watch content play out on the screen at the far end of the conference room. First image—a familiar photo of me with my parents. I was thirteen, my mom on one side, Vince (in his prime) on the other. We were standing in Rockefeller Center during the Christmas season, bundled in long overcoats. I remembered it as a brief stop without gawking or skating; we didn't do that crap.

My mother faded, her image replaced by the date of her death from breast cancer, sending my heart skipping.

The screen shifted to a black-and-white photo of Robert Mapplethorpe a couple of years before he died. I knew the photo well; it had been on my office wall for decades. It showed Mapplethorpe sitting in a high-backed chair in a hotel room in Montreal in a *pro bono* public service campaign for AIDS awareness that BBDO was shooting. Looking like a sepulchral drum major, Mapplethorpe held up his cane with its silver death's head. My father, account exec on the project, stood behind him, hands on Mapplethorpe's narrow shoulders as he gazed into the camera with his thousand-yard stare. They had become unlikely friends.

Mapplethorpe faded, replaced by a fading *March 9, 1989*. My father lingered for a few more seconds, then *October 25, 2006* appeared and faded.

"*Shit,*" I said softly.

The next black-and-white photo showed the early Moriawase agency, with all of our copywriters, designers, production people gathered around. We looked so young and enthusiastic. Even Nathan was smiling. One by one, about half of our cohorts faded, replaced by their death dates. I was left standing, along with Nathan, Harup, and about half of the team. I hadn't realized how many had died, but Harup had done his homework. I closed my eyes for a moment and tried to think of some reason for not knowing what happened to all of them. There were no excuses except that we were like wolves—a pack, but not a family.

The decimated team was followed by the tagline: TAKE YOUR LIFE IN YOUR HANDS.

The final image was of me, standing out on 57th Street, my left arm held up to show off Death Watch. Photoshopped meticulously, the watch gleamed like unalloyed consumer longing. My face held a look of calm acceptance that took Wren about an hour to coax out of me during the photoshoot. The businessmen swirling around me were out of focus, like fish in a stream. The image faded to black and the call to action faded in.

DEATH WATCH—LOOK FOR IT ON THE DARK WEB.

"Incredible," I said, gutted but awed. Harup had mined my life, finding those who had faded, disappeared, died.

"Use it everywhere," Nathan said. "Social. Regular media. Everywhere. It's fantastic."

Harup began to text.

Stole it frm th opening of tht old show, *The Leftovers*.

"Good work." We stole, but gracefully, and from the right sources—high and low, never middle. As my father taught me: *Steal from the elite, borrow from the street.*

And also, th Drink By date on beer bottles.

There, the low bit.

The conference room windows reflected my shadow-self as I stood and paced around, staring down at Grand Street and wondering what my dead father would think of what I was doing. Maybe Alta was right, after the campaign was over, I'd be known forever as the liar who sold deadly watches that didn't work—not that different from a guy selling knock-offs in Washington Square.

My phone bripped and interrupted my gloomy vision of the future. I stared at the caller's name and wondered what else Zeno Zenakas could possibly want from me.

QUATORZE

I HAD WALKED BY HOTEL LOUIS XIV but had never set foot inside until Zeno asked me and what he called the "Moriawase thought leadership team" to join him for a late dinner at Quatorze, its venerable restaurant. Inside, it looked very pre-9/11—plush, flush, and oblivious to the reckoning on the horizon.

"*Whoa,*" Wren pointed at the renowned restaurant's walls, painted a familiar green. "I think they managed to match the exact color of money." The elaborate chandeliers, the gilt-edged chairs, even the tableware—it all seemed locked in amber.

Nathan nodded. "The Sun King would definitely approve."

We stood in the bar, the air thick with the familiar scent of whiskey and wine, reminiscent of my parents' Christmas parties. I nodded toward a bartender, wearing a black suit with an immaculate white shirt. "The bartenders are dressed better than we are."

"Speak for yourself." Nathan was wearing his *going to meet with the bankers* blue suit and striped rep tie, an outfit that made him look like Stephen Colbert's Jewish cousin. I wore my *universal creative* outfit—black jeans and a black jacket over a black T-shirt. Wren wore exactly what she wore every day in the summer—dark blue shorts, white tank top, denim jacket, black Converse sneakers. She carried it off with such unshakeable confidence that the diners turned and stared, assuming she was a celebrity so famous she didn't have to dress like one.

The head waiter signaled and led us briskly through the restaurant to the table of a true celebrity, Zeno Zenakas, looking exactly as I remembered. His wild mop of hair might have looked even a little less gray and his agile face a few years younger. Then again, age reversal was his business.

Zeno stood to give me a brotherly hug. He looked genuinely glad to see me, despite our awkward, shared connection—Alta. I'm sure he could explain the evolution of *our* marriage to *their* relationship. Everything happened for a reason in Zeno's universe.

I introduced Zeno to Wren and his powerful aura and considerable charisma already went to work. His smile was as irresistible and potentially counterfeit as a dollar waiting on the subway stairs.

No one could be faulted for being attracted to Zeno. Effortlessly elegant in a dark tailored suit, white shirt unbuttoned at the neck, he looked like a Clooney, maybe George's cousin visiting from Athens. Diners at the tables across the room were stealing glances and sneaking photos. Did they know who he was or just think he looked handsome AF? Didn't matter.

"Come, let us sit down together."

After some perfunctory chatter, Zeno opened his goatskin manbag and handed us each a crisp sheet of paper.

"Just a brief non-disclosure agreement." He shrugged. "Much of what I want to tell you tonight is proprietary."

Our table was far away from other guests for a reason.

We scrawled our signatures on the NDAs without reading them and handed them back; we knew they were worthless.

"First, I want to congratulate you on doing such a fantastic job." Zeno smiled broadly and we smiled back, not knowing what he was talking about.

"Everywhere, I find Death Watch. The radio. Online. In the *New York Times*. Such excellent press, how do you do it?"

I nodded at Wren. "Our Chief Awareness Officer is a genius."

"Awareness." Zeno leaned toward Wren. "Such a beautiful thing to be in charge of. You must be very, very talented."

Wren beamed as if Zeno had just handed her keys to a spacious pre-war apartment with excellent light. She couldn't even squeak out a *thank you*.

"And you, Nathan and Coe, you have continued to make Moriawase thrive through thick and thin." He said the last bit awkwardly, as if the phrase were unfamiliar to a Greek futurist. Alta had told me Zeno's origin story once after a bottle of white; he grew up in Paramus, New Jersey, not Peramos, Greece, as he claimed.

"I can't thank you enough for your fantastic work in the very beginning." To Zeno, the world began with the Infinity Project. "Brilliance always withstands the test of time."

We smiled but said nothing, remembering the branding project from back when the agency was young and Zeno was just beginning his life extension empire. I had named the company and its embryonic product, Xtensia. Harup developed the logo. Nathan helped get their business plan together.

None of us got paid.

"Let's order and then begin our discussion, shall we?"

Zeno opened the thick menu and began studying it like a scholar.

"Please feel free to have some wine." Zeno handed me the red leather binder. "I don't drink but you should partake, if you'd like."

I'd like. Having dinner with my wife's lover roiled my mind. I flipped through the binder to get to the reserve list.

Our waiter came and we ordered, a process that took longer for Zeno, who insisted on being coached through the origins and preparation of every ingredient in each dish. The waiter managed to not roll his eyes. If Zeno knew that he was behaving like a cultural cliché, he didn't let on. He combined elements from three entrees to come up with his special dinner. We ordered, then I added a magnum of Calon Ségur from the year we founded Moriawase. It seemed appropriate.

The waitress left the table and Zeno leaned forward, sweeping the thick hank of hair from in front of his dark eyes.

"You're probably wondering why I invited you to such an extravagant restaurant."

We did.

"There is something to celebrate. Not just your fascinating watch." He pointed at Death Watch on my wrist. "May I try it on?"

"Doesn't come off," I said.

"What happens if it does?"

"Seven knives come out of the case, pierce my wrist, and spin—spraying arterial blood all over this beautiful tablecloth until I bleed out and die on the floor of Quatorze."

"Then it *is* real."

Nathan leaned forward. "It's *very* real."

Zeno nodded, fooled by Nathan's faux sincerity. "I had to wonder. I mean, it seems rather foolish, this desire to rush death."

"As foolish as searching for the Fountain of Youth? Needling

Zeno was my guilty pleasure."

"That myth was used by Spanish imperialists to justify destruction." Zeno's voice turned edgy. "Our work is based on data and intended to promote longevity, not eternal life. But you know that, Coe."

The sommelier brought the wine to our table.

"A large bottle, yes?" Zeno looked surprised.

I smiled. "We're professionals."

The sommelier went through the elaborate ritual of opening the bottle, decanting the glimmering blood-red Bordeaux and pouring me a taste that I approved with a nod. He filled our glasses—except Zeno's, since he held his hand over it—before drifting away from our table.

We raised our glasses—three full, one empty—and took a long drink.

"Good?" Zeno didn't scold me about how wine was anti-longevity. Death Watch cut the legs out from under any criticism of my diet.

"It's awesome." Wren reached for the decanter.

Nathan pointed next to his plate. "Put that right here."

Zeno leaned forward now that the four of us were alone. "Think back when we first worked together." He nodded at Nathan, then me. "We had a grand plan back then," he said. "But the future has a life of its own. You cannot control it, you know."

His charming demeanor and carefully titrated Greek accent made Zeno's platitudes sound original and serious, like a great actor reading inane tweets. But was he talking about the plan to buy up a lot of apartments, the plan to pull Alta into his orbit, or some other plan that I didn't remember? Whose future couldn't be controlled—mine, hers, ours, theirs?

I calmed my swirling mind and waited for answers.

"Let's get to the heart of the matter, shall we?" Zeno took out his phone, swiped through his photos.

Was he looking for one of Alta, one that revealed how deeply in love they were? A selfie of them walking hand-in-hand through the Darmstadt botanical gardens? Huddled on a hotel balcony, sexually sated and smiling over a post-coital breakfast? I wasn't proud of how quickly my mind could spin out jealous scenarios.

Zeno found the photo he was looking for and turned his phone slowly toward me, his face locked on *serious.* I shut my eyes for a moment, then opened them to confront the painful truth.

The photo showed a spiky-quilled animal that looked like a rat-nosed porcupine peering up from its muddy pen.

Zeno turned the phone slowly from me to Nathan then Wren.

"The echidna," Zeno intoned, "is a remarkable animal."

"Definitely remarkable," Nathan said.

"*Eww,*" Wren added.

"The echidna an Australian marsupial with many fascinating qualities." Zeno stretched out one of his long fingers to tally its qualities. "It's one of the last surviving creatures of the order *monotremata.* It has the lowest body temperature of any similar creature on the planet. Its low metabolism lets it live a remarkable fifty years. Lucky for us, it hadn't been studied by pharmacologists until we came along."

If Zeno was a real client, I'd be taking notes. Instead, I refilled our wine glasses to the brim.

"We're harvesting the echidna's biogens for Xtensia. So far, we're seeing remarkable results in its ability to slow cellular degradation."

I sensed a caveat. "But?"

Zeno raised his hands, palms forward. "As I'm sure Alta has told you, the pace of drug development is glacial."

Zeno said Alta's name with no special emphasis or discernable emotion, as if she were just another co-worker.

Our salads arrived and Zeno tucked into his dandelion greens and raw sea urchins. It was like watching someone eat a plate of leaves and leeches. I looked away and tucked into my arugula and shaved parmesan salad. I thanked the universe for wine.

Wren pushed her glass over for more.

"Don't get me wrong," Zeno said, chewing while he talked. Gray bits of urchin dotted the white tablecloth. Despite his refined veneer, Zeno ate like a truck driver in a hurry to get back on the road. "Alta's doing a fantastic job with the heavy lifting in Darmstadt. But it's going to be years before we finish all the trials of

Xtensia, not to mention FDA approval."

I nodded. More chewing for Zeno, more wine for us.

"But there's another angle to the story that I want to talk to this team about. And this is why I asked you to sign an NDA. No one, and I mean *no one*, can hear what I'm about to tell you." Zeno laid his soft hand on top of mine. "Not even Alta knows of this news," he said. "So I must ask you, Coe, to promise me that you'll keep this secret."

"Yes." I slipped my hand out from under his. "I promise."

"Of course we will," Nathan said, adding an extra dose of credibility.

Zeno turned back to the three of us. "We found a secondary use for Xtensia as a *nutraceutical*." Zeno pronounced the word like a spell. "A pharmaceutical alternative. Over-the-counter and unregulated, like a dietary supplement." Zeno beamed. "No approval. No delays. Huge potential. A win-win-win."

A covey of waiters dressed in red smocks delivered our entrees in silence, bowed, and disappeared. Zeno's dinner consisted of a bed of greens and nuts topped with a beige dollop. Hummus? High-end tuna salad? I couldn't tell, didn't care. My plate held a couple dozen identical tortellini arranged in a circle, alternating with chanterelles, and dotted with green sauce. I looked around the table and saw that Nathan and Wren had equally stingy, geometric dinners.

I was getting ready to spear the first tortellini when Zeno turned his phone toward me again.

"Take a look at this. Do you know what it is?"

I squinted, saw what looked like a fleshy hand with four glistening, nubby fingers. "Uh, no."

Zeno slowly revolved the phone to the rest of the Moriawase team. He didn't wait for an answer.

"The echidna is quadraphallic. It has a four-headed penis. Remarkable!"

Wren dropped her fork. "TME," she said.

Zeno squinted.

"Too. Much. Echidna. Can't unsee that."

"Apologies." Zeno shut off his phone. "Along with longevity, the echidna is remarkably virile."

"Cool for the echidna." Wren eyed the veal sausages on her plate.

Zeno leaned forward. "I have a separate group in Miami developing a supplement that builds on a different subset of the echidna's biogens."

So far, nothing Zeno revealed seemed to require secrecy. The echidna wasn't proprietary, just repulsive.

Zeno anticipated my question. "Alta and the Darmstadt team know nothing about the Miami project," he said. "I need to keep it secret to avoid any internal confusion about our focus."

"Because?"

"The Xtensia supplement isn't about life extension," Zeno said. "It's remarkably effective at addressing a medical issue."

"Which is?" Nathan gave a look that said *I'm fascinated, tell me more.*

Zeno glanced around to make sure other diners weren't sneaking up on us to hear his secret. "ED."

"What?" Nathan leaned forward.

"Erectile dysfunction."

"Oh, that." Wren rolled her eyes.

"Xtensia." I smiled like a junior-high smartass. "At least the name still works."

"That's funny," Zeno said, not laughing.

Nathan and Wren stifled their laughter.

"Make jokes if you'd like, but it's a big issue for an aging population. We're not just restoring sexual function, we're rejuvenating confidence."

My mind flooded with a personalized Pornhub of ecstatic sex scenes starring Alta and Zeno. I shut it off.

"Tell us more," I said, with zero enthusiasm. The world did not need another dick drug. Men did not need more confidence.

"It's a $3 billion market. We should be able to capture at least 30 percent of it in three years." Zeno's eyes glinted with the possibility of millions of dollars rolling in from men eager to be as virile as a spiny marsupial with a four-headed penis. "Wendy, our project manager in Miami, took some early data and ran with it,"

Zeno said. "A true entrepreneur."

At the mention of Wendy, Zeno's face softened and he gave a knowing smile. Was Wendy his next lover? A beta site for his miracle supplement?

"Thanks to her, we should be launching a supplement within a year."

"Go Wendy," I said. "But why are you telling us all this?"

Zeno pushed aside his plate. "I want you three to know something, very important."

We leaned forward.

"I'd like for your team to create a campaign to launch my new supplement," he said. "It would mean the world to me to collaborate with you again."

Was this whole dinner about getting us to do more work for free? I gave Nathan the look that begged *can I have this one?*

He nodded.

"A fascinating opportunity," I said. "But I have to ask, would the project be *pro boner*?"

Wren sprayed wine out her nose. Nathan let out a rare, extremely loud laugh—a guffaw, even.

I held up my hand and waved to the rest of the restaurant, staring at us and wondering what drugs we were on. "I'll be here all week."

"Always very clever with words, you creatives," Zeno said when we had settled. "It's a great talent. One that I appreciate. But to answer your question, no, we fully expect to pay for excellent creative and a global campaign."

Silence from the Moriawase thought leadership team.

"Your project sounds remarkable." Nathan reverted his po-faced self again. "No doubt—your nutraceutical will be a success. But we're fully committed," he said, as if Team Death were Quatorze on Friday night.

Zeno looked surprised, as if he expected us to just start creating content at the table while we waited for dessert.

"I want to thank you for the great dinner." Nathan rose up from his chair and held his hand out to Zeno. "And for sharing your exciting news with us. But we have to get back to the agency."

"Got to get prep for an early call with Tokyo." Wren stood and gave Zeno a respectful nod.

I leaned over and shook the hand of my semi-nemesis. "Good to see you, Zeno. Thanks so much for dinner. And the wine."

"Wonderful to see you all." If Zeno realized he was being ditched, he didn't let on. "Please let me know if you reconsider."

"We certainly will," Nathan said.

The three of us left Zeno's table at a respectable pace until we were out on the sidewalk, when we broke into a full run, screaming like teenagers. We clumped on the next street corner, gasping.

"Four. Headed. Penis!" Wren managed to get out.

Nathan shoved me. "*Pro boner.*" The guffaw again, echoing down the empty streets of Tribeca.

"Two. Thousand. Dollar. Bottle. Of. Wine." I added, and we started running again, as if Zeno might be chasing us down with the check.

Bar Dog was warm and almost empty now that the midsummer doldrums had settled over Manhattan. We commandeered a table, texted Harup to meet us, and ordered three orders of *steak frites* and drinks all around to sate us after our doll-food dinner with Zeno. I put in an order for Harup's salty dog, scheduled it to arrive when he did.

I took out my phone.

"Are you telling Alta, or should I?" Nathan said, smiling.

"Already texting her, but thanks."

Wren looked shocked. "The NDA?"

"Secrets are for telling." I clicked SEND and some surprising news was on its way to Darmstadt. "Besides, no one shows us something that gross without consequences."

Wren shivered. "That ... thing. I keep seeing it."

Nathan stretched out four fingers and reached toward her.

She shoved him away. "You're triggering me!"

Our food arrived and we ate in a quiet frenzy.

We looked up when Harup sidled into the bar. Tracy delivered his salty dog. He studied his drink and found it up to his standards. Tracy smiled, fled.

My sleepy gaze stayed on the bar television, still watching even though the Yankees were already eight runs ahead of the Sox. Harup and I needed to talk about new creative for Death Watch, but even Team Death had to take a holiday.

When we finished our manic feeding, Wren and Nathan wandered off to the pinball machine in the far corner of the bar.

I opened my notebook and flipped through the pages, looking for content to feed the insatiable monster we had created. We had been trying new angles, tweaking the tone, pulling photos from Harup's mother lode of images. But it was getting harder to find new ways to convey Death Watch's brand promise—the life-affirming power of embracing death. I had to look further and further afield.

"Found a Twain quote that might work."

Harup texted from across the table.

Who dat?

"Got to be kidding."

Harup shrugged. He didn't do books.

I read. "*The fear of death follows from the fear of life. A man who lives fully is prepared to die at any time.*"

Sounds old.

"Because it *is* old," I said. "But everyone loves Mark Twain."

Harup gave me a look that said *not everyone.*

"Okay, okay. Just cut the first bit and use the last part." I reached over and scrawled in his notebook. How about *Live fully, but be prepared to die.* Death Watch."

Harup said nothing, which meant he wasn't going to do anything. I could hear my phone vibrating in my backpack. Harup's phone started bripping and vibrating on the bar. He turned it over. The screen flooded with alerts and texts.

He waved at the bartender, then snapped his fingers and

nodded at the television over the bar. Used to Harup's antics, the bartender tossed him the remote. He caught it and changed the station to CNN.

The newscasters looked concerned as the video showed a body covered with a yellow sheet on a brick sidewalk, police milling around, patrol car lights flashing blue. I read the chyron below them.

Dow up 128 points ... Boston man becomes first victim of the "Death Watch" ... more hot weather ahead...

"*No,*" I whispered. "*No no no.*"

Wren and Nathan rushed back to the table.

Harup turned up the volume and we watched the news, transfixed.

"Cassius Seven, also known as Death Watch, claimed its first victim tonight in Boston—a 32-year-old financial advisor who died early this evening in the city's tony Beacon Hill neighborhood."

"Shit." Nathan stared at the television. Wren kept her eyes on the tiled floor, unable to watch.

The newscaster paused as his co-anchor shook her head slowly in disbelief.

"Police haven't identified the victim, who was discovered just after 7 PM on a sidewalk near Boston Common. He was declared dead at the scene."

I gave an involuntary shiver.

The co-anchor picked up the story. "In its brief time on the market, Death Watch has become an Internet sensation," she said.

Wren burst into tears.

"Critics see it as a disturbing development in the evolution of technology." The newscast showed a photo of me, standing on 57th Street, holding my arm out, Death Watch gleaming on my wrist.

I wanted to run out of the bar but I had to keep watching.

The camera shifted back to the newscaster. "Death Watch was invented by the controversial Japanese artist Watanabe." The screen behind him shifted to video of an unsmiling Watanabe, holding his palm forward like a crazed shaman.

"As Death Watch claims its first victim in Boston," the newscaster continued, "local authorities are issuing a warning."

A Boston police captain came onscreen and mumbled about a completely avoidable tragedy, a vicious assault on public safety.

"We'll be bringing you more details as they become available." The newscaster gave a look that said *can you believe what the world's coming to?* Then they moved on to the next story.

We stood in a tight cluster, stunned, unable to talk.

Death Watch wasn't a hoax. It was very real.

It didn't kill someone. We did.

I looked at my wrist and saw a gleaming threat.

Wren put her arms around me and cried on my chest. Nathan just kept shaking his head *no.*

Harup texted.

Sht jst got supr real. We're in deep trble

Yes, we were.

AFTERMATH

"Get any sleep?" Nathan paced. No one answered. Harup looked like he had slept in the tech closet. Wren stared at her laptop with glazed eyes. I was still wearing last night's wrinkled clothes. I had spent a sleepless night in the first hotel I could find after staggering out of Bar Dog—not drunk, but burdened with fear and guilt. The brutal news from Boston proved that Death Watch wasn't a clever project; it was a deadly weapon, one that we had managed to sell to the world. Watanabe created the monster, but we brought it to life.

Last night, Death Watch killed someone. We killed someone. I killed someone. Now Team Death gathered in the conference room at dawn, wrestling with guilt as we struggled to figure out our next move.

"Anything new on the victim?"

"Boston police released his name a few minutes ago," said Wren. "James Lorber. Thirty-three years old."

Harup typed furiously on his laptop keyboard, calling up the late James Lorber. We stared at the conference room screen, filling up with his online life.

"Trinity College," Nathan said, deciphering the flood of photos, posts, news. "Camping in the White Mountains."

"In a bar with other smiling dudes," Wren said.

"Looks so normal," I added. James Lorber had uncombed straw-colored hair and blue, Nordic eyes. He seemed at ease, happy, surrounded by friends. I remembered the sheet-covered body on the streets of Boston.

Nathan kept reading details of the victim's life as Harup dug them up. "Married—wife's named Linda. Son's named Jackson. He's five years old. Jimmy Lorber worked at Merrill Lynch in Boston, then moved on to venture cap. Lived in Marblehead, Mass. $1.8 million house. No arrests. No court cases. No bankruptcies. All seems incredibly normal."

I shook my head. "Why would a guy like that buy Death Watch? Doesn't seem like a New Nihilist."

"Too early to know," Wren said.

"May never know." Nathan shrugged. "But that's not where we need to focus. We've got to get ahead of the story before clients start waking up and firing us."

My phone bripped. Everyone I knew was calling, as if I hadn't heard about what happened in Boston. But this call was different.

I slipped out of the conference room and stood in the empty workroom. I answered, heard nothing but silence.

"Hey," I said.

"Don't start acting like everything's going to be okay." Alta's voice was a tremulous mix of anger and fear.

I pressed my eyes closed.

"You promised me that the watch was fake, that no one would get hurt."

"They fooled me."

"You know who gets fooled?" Alta didn't wait. "Fools."

I said nothing.

"That awful watch killed someone. You get that, right?"

"Yes. Of course I do."

"You could be next."

I looked at Death Watch gleaming in the workroom lights. "My watch doesn't work."

"How do you know?"

"It's just a prototype. *A watch without a soul,* Watanabe called it." That I was safe while others weren't made me feel even more guilty.

"And you still trust them, after what happened?"

Alta didn't wait for an answer. "You have to do something, Coe. My father said he can cut it off, he's got a—"

"Hold on." I explained the dead man's switch.

"You can't cut it off?"

"No. That's probably what happened in Boston. Yohji said it was the only way the watch could have activated."

"You talked to Yohji?"

"We called him right after we heard. He was just as shocked

as we were."

"You know what's shocking? That you still listen to him."

"It's going to be okay, really."

"You don't know that," Alta shouted. She paused and settled. "Tell me you don't want that watch to kill you."

"I don't."

"You sure? Your interviews, they—"

"They what?"

"Sounded like you're okay with dying."

"I'm not."

"You said wearing the watch makes you feel more alive."

"I said a lot of things."

"Don't let the watch kill you—my father can help. I know he can." Alta always thought her father had the answer. "You have to go see him."

"I'm in a meeting. I'll call him after."

"No, you won't. He's expecting you in his office at eleven this morning."

I paused, reached for an excuse, couldn't find one. "Okay, I'll be there."

"And—"

I waited, listened to Alta breathing.

"That text you sent me last night. The one about Xtensia. That was just you trying to be funny, right?"

I paused, pressed my eyes closed. Death Watch killed someone hours ago, news that overshadowed all else, including the pharma-drama at the Infinity Project. "Why don't you ask Zeno? Or Wendy."

Alta's phone clicked off.

I slipped back into the conference room and into my chair. Nathan looked crazed. He'd been running his fingers through his hair, leaving it in a nervous tangle. "What about the fallout on social?"

Harup shook his head slowly.

Supr bad. Hatestorm.

"Hating Watanabe?"

Harup shook his head, pointed at me.

"The pitchman always gets blamed," Nathan said.

"Didn't want to do it, remember?"

Nathan waved his hand in front of him. "Too late for that." He gave me a hard glance. "We have to cover our butts and get out of this mess—now."

"Get out? We killed someone," I said. "It's our fault."

"Wrong. It's Watanabe's fault. Or the engineers. They didn't warn people the watch was dangerous."

"It's called Death Watch," Wren said. "It's got warnings all over it," she said. "In the packaging. And right on the watch."

"Okay, okay." Nathan paced faster. "But it's like ... like blaming a corner bodega for selling cigarettes when it's the tobacco company's fault. Watanabe came up with the idea. We thought the watch wouldn't kill anyone."

Harup and Wren shook their heads. Nathan's furious blamestorming left us unconvinced.

"Be honest," I said. "We just fooled ourselves into thinking it wouldn't kill."

Nathan's eyes narrowed. "Because?"

"Because we heard what we wanted to hear. Because we wanted the money."

Nathan stood up and his chair bashed against the wall. "We *needed* the money. You came back from Tokyo and told us it wouldn't work. That it was a joke."

"Never said it was a joke."

"Joke, hoax, project, experiment, whatever. Now it's a huge lawsuit waiting to happen. The only way forward is to pin the blame on Watanabe and get out."

"No." I stood on the other side of the conference table. "We helped create this mess, now we have to help clean it up."

"Like an oil spill," Wren said. "But with blood."

I pressed my eyes closed and saw the news report, stuck on permanent repeat in my mind—the cops milling around, the body covered with a sheet.

"We're not doing that." Nathan said. "We need to step away

from the whole disaster."

"Meaning?"

Nathan stopped pacing and gave me an even stare. "I talked with Bruce and Norm already."

"Really?" I knew our lawyers as an overdressed, unfun presence at our holiday parties.

"They say you should go on furlough."

"Furlough?"

"Just stay kind of hidden for a few months or so until this whole shitshow blows over. Then we can reevaluate."

Harup slammed his laptop.

U suck.

"You don't have to worry about paying our bills and meeting payroll, do you? All you have to do is be creative and weird. Grow the fuck up, Harup. All of you." Nathan waved his arms spastically, then sat back down and held his head in his hands as if it were about to wobble off.

"I'm leaving," I said. "But I'm not going on furlough."

Nathan sat up. "Leave now and you're fired."

Stunned silence.

"Really? You're going to fire your partner? After twenty years?" I stood up and my chair slammed against the wall. "You can fire me for stealing or doing shitty work, Nathan. But you can't fire me for wanting to stop more people from getting killed by a disaster that's our fault, whether you want to admit it or not."

I shoved my notebook and laptop in my backpack. "Death Watch killed someone. Now we have to destroy it. If anyone wants to help me, fine."

Nathan said nothing, just stared down at the table as if it were an unsolvable puzzle.

I walked out of the conference room, pausing in the workroom to take a last look at the place where I had spent much of my life—working, daydreaming, and occasionally sleeping on the floor when we had a tough deadline. Then I kept going, shoving the glass doors open and walking out of Moriawase.

I heard footsteps running after me as I walked toward the stairs.

"Where are you going?" Wren looked at me as if I was leaving the planet.

I tried to smile. "Got a doctor's appointment."

DO NO HARM

ALTA CAME FROM UPPER EAST SIDE ROYALTY, the hard-working, do-good side of an enduring milk-white monarchy. As if her father Robert's humanitarian efforts weren't enough, her mother, Eustis, ran Haven House, a shelter for women escaping abusive relationships, and had taken in several foster children. Alta's grandfather's name could be found carved into the donors wall at the Metropolitan Museum and the Frick. Her Dutch ancestors, merchants and early arrivals in New Amsterdam, were memorialized with Van Schuyler Street. Alta never told me about it, of course. I found it when walking around the Seaport one night.

I had never been to my father-in-law's private practice, nestled among plastic surgeons and fertility clinics on a rarefied stretch of Park Avenue. I waited in his walnut-paneled office, its shelves lined with books on Greek history, Robert's passion. He had wanted to name his only daughter Athena—goddess of wisdom, handicraft, and warfare—but opted for Alta, less freighted with expectations.

On his bookshelf sat a silver-framed photo from last summer on the Cape, showing the extended Van Schuyler family, my forced grin next to Alta's more natural smile. She was with her clan; I didn't have one.

The door to the examining room opened and broke me out of my reverie. Robert ushered out a patient who looked familiar. His specialty was discreet mezzanine healthcare for the famous. Along with the requisite diplomas (Columbia, Harvard Medical), his walls held signed photos of a former governor, a renowned cellist, Al Pacino, and many others.

Robert waved me into the examining room and soon I was wearing a flimsy blue hospital johnny and perching on a cold steel examining table. The examining room seemed to come from another time, with its black and white tiled floor and row of glass-fronted cabinets. With his longish hair gone elegantly gray, owlish eyebrows, and piercing blue eyes, Robert could be a history professor, the life he probably would have preferred. My father would have lumped Robert with *those silver-spoon Harvard guys,* which would have been a reductive, inaccurate call.

"Welcome to my lair."

"Good to be here."

"Really? Alta said you only came under pressure."

"I'm definitely under pressure."

"So I hear. Let's have a look."

I held out my left arm and he leaned forward to take a first look at Death Watch, examining its bezel as if it held an answer. "You know, from the outside, this looks pretty much like a Geist."

"What's that?"

"German watch, expensive and collectible. Fancy friends of mine wear them. Can't say I understand the attraction. Surgeons never wear watches. Germs, blood." He ran his graceful fingers over the watchband gripping my wrist.

"Not coming off without a fight, is it?"

I shook my head.

Robert opened several cabinets before he found what he was looking for—a small silver tool with a dime-sized wheel at one end and an electric cord at the other, which he plugged into a wall socket.

"Diamond saw," he said. "We use it to cut off ingrown wedding rings and the occasional set of handcuffs with misplaced keys."

I gave Robert a questioning look.

"Carnal, not criminal." He shrugged and pressed a button to start the saw, setting the wheel at the tip spinning with a high-pitched buzz. "The simplest solution would be to cut the watchband with it, carefully of course."

I pulled my arm away. "Don't touch it. Really. It might go off."

He set the saw carefully on the counter. "Last time we talked, you told me the watch wasn't lethal. Then last night I saw what happened in Boston. So which is it?"

"It *can* be lethal."

"What do you mean?"

"It doesn't just kill people at random. But it can get set off." I explained the dead man's switch, pointed out the thin wire running through the band.

"So you still can't take off the watch without it killing you. Like a loaded gun with a sensitive trigger."

"Right. It's clear that the watch can't come off. It's etched on the band. "The guy in Boston—"

"The victim, you mean."

"Yes. We think was trying to take his watch off when it killed him."

"Isn't there some way to just disable it?"

"No tech bro has figured out how to hack it yet."

"Alta said you're wearing some kind of special prototype."

"I'm not sure what that means anymore."

"Seems prudent to get it off your wrist."

I nodded.

Robert took a pen from his lab coat pocket. "Put your left hand there, please." He pointed to the examining table.

I pressed down and felt the cool metal beneath my palm.

Robert traced a confident line across the top of my hand with an indigo-colored pen—the same kind butchers used, I couldn't help but notice. He continued the line from my ring finger down to my outer wrist, capped his butcher pen, and set it on the steel counter.

"You're not actually going to *cut* anything today, right?"

"Of course not, just an initial consultation."

Robert's smile put me at ease; the long blue line on my hand did not.

"Alfonse d'Issan, a French Army field surgeon came up a procedure that may solve your very particular problem. It's named after him—the D'Issan procedure. Hasn't been used much since World War I."

"Why not?"

"It's used to treat a very specific type of wound. French soldiers tended to get a lot of hand lacerations in trench warfare, during hand-to-hand combat," he said. "To inflict maximum damage, German front-line troops dipped their bayonets in their field latrines before battle."

"Gross," I said.

"Very. The wounds had to be treated immediately, before infection set in, but it was often too late. In the past, field surgeons simply amputated the entire hand. But D'Issan devised a method that preserved two fingers and the thumb, giving survivors some remaining functionality. There were so many D'Issan procedures performed that the streets of Paris were filled with three-fingered beggars after the war. Their hands were referred to as *les serre de la guerre.*"

I didn't like the sound of that, even in French. "Which means?"

"Talons of war."

Robert traced the blue line with his finger. "We'll cut here, sever the tendons, and remove the outer two fingers—the metacarpal bones and the phalanges. We'll leave most of the carpal bones." He turned my hand over as if he was folding a napkin. "Then we'll pull the flap of skin from the back of your hand over and stitch it together neatly, so that infernal watch can slip over your—"

"Talon?"

"Yes, that. Then the watch can be disposed of like a tumor or bullet. Or anything else that might have killed you but didn't."

"I don't want to have a talon, Robert."

"Neither did the soldiers. But D'Issan's procedure was the best option available to solve a dire situation. Maybe yours, too."

"Sounds so simple."

"Not really. It's rather complicated given all the nerves and blood vessels in your hand. Not to mention the ulnar artery in your wrist. It's a major one. So you need to consider the surgery, carefully, then let me know. The sooner the better, it would seem."

I nodded. "Have you done it before, the procedure?"

"Of course not."

"How do you know about it?"

"When Alta told me what you had gotten yourself into, I did some research in the surgical library."

"Thank you," I said, knowing it wasn't enough.

"Just trying to save you from yourself." Robert gave a tight smile. "In case you didn't notice, I don't have a son. So you'll have to do." Robert gave a curt nod that told me he had reached the outer edge of his emotional frontier and it was time to retreat into more comfortable territory. "You can get dressed now."

As I shed the awkward johnny and put on my clothes, Robert turned discreetly to peer through the blinds at a wind-whipped ginkgo, its leaves silvered by the bright sun.

"I find your whole situation fascinating, Coe," he said quietly. "Fascinating and terrible. You see, at first, we let the gods boss us around. Fates and furies, Zeus and Athena and all that. The Enlightenment passed the torch to man—scholars and tyrants, kings and popes. Now technology rules us—iPhones and Alexa, VR and AI. Giving an expensive but inanimate watch control over your fate is simply the illogical conclusion. I can't imagine what might come next, can you?"

"No, I can't." I tucked in my shirt.

"We'll leave that to the next generation." Robert turned from the window.

"I have to ask you about something."

"Sure." I slipped my shoes on.

"You mentioned that wearing the watch makes you feel free."

"It does." That was my story and I was sticking to it, even now.

"I never really thought of you as depressed. Are you?"

"No, just weighed down, like anyone else."

"By what?"

"Uncertainty."

"About?"

"The future. Mine. Alta's. The world's."

Robert squinted at my inept generalization.

"Rising oceans, roasting temperatures, constant noise. How we've monetized everything we can possibly sell, polarized everything else." My litany started slow, but now the words started blurting out. "How no experience feels real anymore—just filtered and retouched, edited and tagged. How we create curated versions of ourselves until we don't know who we really are. How our entire species is sleepwalking toward oblivion. How survival doesn't seem like a possibility. How time doesn't feel like it's passing anymore, just running out."

My rant stunned Robert into silence.

I took a deep breath, settled. "You taught me that great Greek word. The one for uncertainty."

Robert nodded. "*Acatalepsia?*"

"Right. That's exactly what I've been feeling—that nothing can be known for certain anymore. Every time I see Death Watch on my wrist, it reminds me that there's only one thing that's certain. We're all going to die someday, probably sooner than we think."

Robert went silent for a moment. "I have fifteen good years left, maybe twenty if I'm lucky," he said. "I know for certain that I'm going to die, Coe. I just don't particularly want to be reminded of it."

"So, you're in denial, then?"

He smiled. "Let's just call it *delayed acceptance of reality.*"

"Is there a Greek word for that?"

"Probably, but I don't know it." He put his hand on my shoulder. "Listen, we've spent a lot of time together over the years. I like you. I respect your enthusiasm. Your sense of humor makes family gatherings much more tolerable, as does your heavy hand with the gin bottle. I sense we have a lot more to talk about. I don't want you to die before your time, Coe. I'm sure Alta doesn't either. And plenty of others."

"My watch isn't going to go off."

"You sure?"

"It's just a prototype."

"You're safe?"

"I think so." I couldn't help but wonder if my Death Watch prototype, serial #0001, was as neutered as it seemed. That said, cutting off two fingers just in case seemed foolishly cautious.

"You think so?"

"Is the risk worth whatever you claim to get from wearing it? Particularly now?"

I said nothing. Much as I respected Robert, our lives were so different that we might as well be from different species. Any insights I could pass along would be out of context the moment he heard them. And then there was the disparity of our work. His actually saved lives, while mine, apparently, ended them.

Robert peeled off his green rubber examination gloves and

tossed them into the trash. "If you decide you want to move ahead, I can do the D'Issan procedure. But it's a non-standard intervention, so I'll have to get approval from hospital, which takes time. So decide soon."

I nodded, knew I wouldn't.

"You'd be in the hospital for a day at most. Then you'll be home. Free from all this Death Watch nonsense. How does that sound?"

It sounded pretty good.

After my appointment with Robert, I wandered aimlessly for hours, letting the thrumming city push Death Watch to the back of my mind. When I finally got home, it was late and the Faces of the Faithful were swarming in front of our building like ghouls. In the hot night, the clocks painted on their faces smeared and dripped.

Glenn nodded as I slipped in through the side entrance into the lobby. "Saw you on the news."

"Thanks," I said, then realized how ridiculous that sounded. But by then I was already in the elevator.

Vanessa opened the door to the apartment, her eyes narrow and bloodshot, and shoved me away.

"You told me it didn't work."

"Didn't know."

"Fuck you and your stupid watch." She slammed the door.

"Need to talk."

"We don't," she shouted. "Go. The. Fuck. Away."

Down the hall I could see Mrs. Aronson peering out of her half-open door.

"I can explain."

Silence. Then the lock clicked and the door drifted open. I followed Vanessa into the living room, where she sat heavily on the blue couch.

"I've done terrible things to all kinds of men." She shook her head. "But I never killed one."

I sat next to her. "You didn't kill anyone."

"Made some of my best clients buy your stupid watch."

"I convinced hundreds of people to buy it."

"Those were strangers. I *know* my clients. They love me." Vanessa glanced at me, spotted my confusion. "Yes, they pay me. But they love me, too. And they trust me."

"They bought the watch knowing it might kill them. Everyone did."

"I talked to some clients after that guy in Boston died."

"And?"

"They don't care. That's the weird thing. They're okay with Death Watch. I'm the only one who's upset—and I'm their dominatrix." She shook her head at the absurdity.

"Look, they're not going die."

"Someone already did."

"Could have been an accident."

"How do you know that?"

"There's a dead man's switch."

"A switch that kills men?"

"Not exactly." I explained how the dead man's switch kept people from just getting their watch cut off.

"Well that's fucked up."

"It is, but if they leave the watch alone, they'll be okay."

"What if they want to take it off?"

"There may be a way."

When I started to tell Vanessa about the D'Issan procedure she held her hand out to stop me. "You're going to let them do that to you?"

"Not sure, but maybe."

"Don't tell me more." She gave an uncontrolled quiver.

"You're squeamish?"

"Told you I'm not a sadist."

She got up from the blue couch and I followed her into the kitchen, where she poured us each glass of white. We sat at the breakfast table, gray light filtering through the window that looked out on the airshaft.

"And I'm not cruel," she said. "You should know that by now."

"But you make men do terrible things with their tongues,

scrotums—"

"It's what they want, Coe. I don't make them do anything."

"You take their money and make them feel like there's never enough they can give you. That's kind of cruel, isn't it?"

"No, not at all." Vanessa took a sip of wine, then another, and put her glass down. "It's just a fantasy. When the money runs out, the act ends. Everyone is okay. They heal. They get the desire out of their system and move on. They make more money. And no one actually gets hurt because it isn't real."

"You make it seem real."

"That's just what I do. It's my work. But none of it's real. Desire, power, money—none of it. They're just systems of control men came up after they were done hunting and gathering."

Vanessa shook her head at the inanity of it all, then gripped my shoulders and held me just inches away, her eyes reddened, gaze intense. "But your stupid watch is real, Coe. Very fucking real. Real enough to kill. Death? That's real."

"And inevitable."

"Yes, but it should happen when it's supposed to. Not when Watanabe decides. He's not the Fates. He's a moon-faced fuck on a power trip."

Hard to argue with that.

Vanessa let go of my shoulders. "I don't want anyone else to die. Not my clients. Not you. Not anyone."

"No," I said. "Not anyone."

She reached out and held my hand, rubbing it gently with her thumb. "Can't even think about you getting a couple of your fingers cut off."

"Neither can I."

Vanessa gave a quiver again. "You don't deserve that."

"Thank you."

"You don't have to thank me."

"I know." But to be cared about, who wouldn't be thankful?

"Don't have that operation yet," she said. "Wait and see what really happened in Boston."

"We might be able to find out."

"How?"

"Got a black dress?"

Vanessa let go of my hand. "Lots of 'em."

"One that isn't made out of vinyl?"

"Don't be a smartass. I have real clothes, too. Why?"

"We're going to a funeral."

MYTH OF INFINITE NOTHINGNESS

We rode the early-morning Acela in silence, carrying unreconciled guilt with us on the train north to Boston. A short cab ride took us to an imposing granite church in Brookline, where a somber, gray-haired usher greeted us at the door and handed us a program bearing James Lorber's smiling face, sending a plummet of guilt washing over me. Several days had passed and his tragic death was still in the news—and in my thoughts almost every waking moment.

We took a seat in the very back row of the packed church and listened to the quiet introductory hymns echoing from the pipe organ in the upper galley. The church smelled of incense and stone. Around us, women started to rustle through their purses for tissues as the service began.

The minister climbed slowly to the pulpit and stared somberly into the crowd for a long time before speaking. I checked the program and found his name: Father Thomas Callahan.

"I have a sermon I give when a younger member of the parish passes before their time." Father Callahan held up a piece of paper and showed it to the mourners, who packed every pew of the Church of the Holy Father. He set the paper aside. "But I'm not going to read that one today. Because this is no ordinary funeral service. And Jimmy Lorber was no ordinary member of our parish."

Vanessa gripped my hand.

"Jimmy Lorber joined our parish when he and his wife Linda moved to Boston for his work." Father Callahan nodded toward a dark-veiled woman in the front row. "Linda is here with us today, grieving, as we all are." He gave the widow a long look and shook his head. "We've missed you since you moved up to Marblehead. I'm truly sorry that you're returning to the Church of the Holy Father under these mournful circumstances."

My stomach twisted as Linda put her arm around a squirming

young boy. I knew James Lorber had a wife and child, of course. But these were just words. Seeing his family made the enormity of what had happened to James Lorber—and what we had done to him—painfully real. It made me hate Watanabe even more for creating something so deadly and devious, then going silent to avoid facing the outrage.

Dark sunglasses hid my reddened eyes, bloodshot from fitful sleep and nightmares that seemed to have been curated by Hieronymus Bosch. A dark blue blazer, white shirt, and black-and-indigo striped tie completed my disguise, chosen by Vanessa to keep me unnoticed.

Father Callahan looked out over the mourners, gray eyes flashing. "Jimmy Lorber was a special man who lived a godly life and met a senseless death." His gray eyes seemed to find me among the crowd.

"He recognizes me," I whispered in Vanessa's ear.

"Don't get weird on me," she whispered.

"No, Jimmy didn't have a rare disease or a heart attack. He wasn't the victim of a crime. He didn't have an unfortunate accident." Father Callahan paused. "He gave in to a seductive myth peddled by ruthless amoralists."

I swallowed. That would be us.

"The Myth of Infinite Nothingness is not new, of course. It's common among the faithless seeking a way to explain their inability to believe. But new betrayers of the faith use all the tools of the modern era to take infinite nothingness to unimaginable heights."

Father Callahan paused to quell his rising anger.

"These devious salesmen of the so-called New Nihilism have managed to convince thousands of people, including our beloved Jimmy Lorber, that there's nothing after life ends. Therefore, we have nothing to hope for, to live for."

At the mention of Lorber's name, Father Callahan nodded toward a dim nave to the right of the pulpit. In the smoky distant reaches of the cathedral, a coffin waited on a low dais.

"The Myth of Infinite Nothingness is simple and seductive. Why believe in anything if everything means nothing? If all we have is what we *do*, not what we *believe*? If the tangible triumphs over the transcendent? This myth has found a new expression in the abomination known as Death Watch." He paused. "*Death. Watch.* Take in the absurdity. A watch, can you imagine that? The simple gift that many of us give to our fathers or pass on to our sons. Now perverted into a fiendish machine against Man. And God."

Behind my sunglasses, I pressed my eyes closed.

"Every day alive on this wondrous earth is a gift. Make no mistake about it. But God gives us much more than days. More than life. More than death."

The organ faded in softly, sending out thrumming celestial notes.

"As sure as this church is made of granite and those windows are made of glass, I'm sure that there is a heaven, and that Jimmy Lorber is in it now, waiting for us to join him. We'll get there in our own time. Lifted up by our belief, by our faith in God the Father." Father Callahan paused for a moment and stared into the audience from the pulpit, gray eyes bright with anger and sadness. "Now please stand and join our voices in Hymn number 204, *Sing Praise to God Who Reigns Above.*"

As the congregation stood slowly, Vanessa gripped my hand, not letting me slip away.

We watched the crowd filter toward the front of the church as the choir sang from a balcony above us. One row after the next joined the line moving toward Father Callahan.

"What's going on?" I whispered.

"Communion. It's a funeral mass."

"Right."

"The part with the wafer and the wine. The body and blood of Christ."

"Oh." I could only think of James Lorber's blood pooled on a sidewalk. "Do I have to do it?"

"Supposed to be for people who've been baptized. Were you?"

"Don't think so. How do you know all this stuff?"

"Went to Catholic girl's school." This detail simply added to Vanessa's cluster of complications.

The gray-haired usher who had been summoning the Catholics to communion stood at the end of our aisle. The believers stood, clasped their hands in front of them, and gazed at the ground with humility as they trudged toward the front of the church. Only Vanessa and I were left, still sitting in the pew.

The usher coughed and wiggled his fingers, signaling us to rise.

"We're not—"

Vanessa took my arm and we rose together to join the line.

"Why don't we just slip out the back?" I took off my sunglasses, ridiculous in the dim church.

"People will notice."

"No they won't."

I shuffled forward, dreading being in the front of the whole congregation, confronting Father Callahan, the Fighting Father as he was known in Boston. I had Googled him between hymns, found that he had spent his life working for social justice.

"Just let him put the wafer on your tongue, then take a sip of wine. Nothing to it."

I nodded, kept walking, eyes down, hands clasped, hoping no one would recognize me. The choir hit a verse with the line *cast each false idol from its throne*. What was Watanabe but a false idol? And me. And any man, pretty much.

Now we were just feet away from the railing where people knelt for the sacrament. And not much further from the open casket of James Lorber, the saintly young man I had helped kill. If there was a God and he was watching me, this might be the moment to smote me.

Vanessa and I knelt at the railing, hands forward, palms up.

Father Callahan approached and pressed a wafer gently into my palm. "This is the body of Christ," he said softly, then moved on. I looked over at Vanessa and followed her lead, putting the wafer on my tongue.

The body of Christ stuck on the roof of my mouth.

The communion helper, who appeared to be about the same vintage as the usher, walked slowly down the railing, bearing a trembling silver chalice in both hands. When her turn came,

Vanessa leaned forward and took a graceful sip. I tried to do the same, but felt the cool lip of the chalice hit my nose instead of my lips, splashing about a pint of Christ's blood down my shirt. Oblivious, the chalice-bearer tottered down the railing.

We stood and Vanessa stared at my white shirt, marked by a vivid red blotch that made me look like the Japanese flag.

"Just button your coat," Vanessa whispered. But the blotch was too big to hide.

The receiving line continued into the dim nave, without any way to escape. James Lorber's grieving widow, Linda, stood a few feet in front of the coffin, hugging those she knew, shaking hands with strangers. She stood with other family members—James Lorber's brothers, I assumed. Young but exhausted, they looked like college football players just back from a tough away game.

Vanessa went through the line smoothly, looking suitably upset but not attracting any attention. As I stood in front of Linda, I decided to say something instead of just shaking her hand.

"I'm so very sorry," I said.

She squinted, leaned toward me. Her reddened eyes flicked down to the wine stain on my shirt.

I kept walking, head down.

In my wake I heard the brothers whispering.

I paused at the open casket and looked down at the body of James Lorber in a blue pinstriped suit, white shirt, and deep green tie. A red Holy Bible rested next to him where his left hand used to be.

His face looked like a waxen mask of peace, eyes pressed closed. Had been trying to cut off Death Watch somehow, driven by desperate second thoughts, in the minutes before his death? Or had the watch just gone off on its own? Irrationally, I thought we might find out how James Lorber died by coming to his funeral. But the only one who could answer that question was lying still and silent in front of me.

A firm hand grasped my elbow.

"We have to get out, now," Vanessa whispered. "They're talking about you." She nodded toward the cluster of Lorber brothers shooting glances our way.

We walked slowly down the dim side aisle of the church, past stained-glass windows of Saint Sebastian pierced by arrows, Jesus walking across the waves, and Mother Mary kneeling over her son's lifeless body. We pushed gently against the thick wooden door, heavy as stone, then stepped outside into the fading afternoon to find the steps of the church crowded with dozens of news crews.

They sprang into action when they saw that the funeral mass was over.

Vanessa grabbed my hand as I tried to put my sunglasses on and they clattered down the stairs.

"Just keep going," I said. "Get to the street and jump in a cab."

I held Vanessa's hand and we pushed past the reporters and microphones, cameras and lights, heads down, looking like we were too deep in grief to talk, hoping no one had recognized me.

On the Acela, several drinks south of Boston, Vanessa handed me her phone. DEATH WATCH PITCHMAN FLEES BOSTON VICTIM'S FUNERAL. It was the top story on the *Boston Herald* website.

"We weren't really fleeing," I said.

"Yes, we were."

She pointed at the photo, which showed me hustling down the church steps, my hand raised against the media onslaught, hair disheveled, shirt wine-splashed. It looked like a bouncer had just thrown me out of a pub. I read the short article, which quoted relatives of James Lorber, who said they didn't know who I was or they would have confronted me.

"Confronted me?"

"In Boston, I think that means kick your ass."

I kept reading. Just below the article, breaking news flashed in red. The headline stopped me cold—heart, mind, soul, all.

Death Watch Claims Second Victim in San Francisco.

"No!" The passengers across the aisle from us gave me the *keep it down* look. But I couldn't.

THE BRUTAL TRUTH

"I didn't know that Death Watch was actually deadly. Its creators—the artist Watanabe and his son, Yohji—told me that it was just an experiment, one that wouldn't harm anyone. Watanabe wanted to prove that people would buy anything. Selling death, or the potential of it, seemed like an intriguing challenge, one that I took on myself, not as part of my agency."

I shifted forward before continuing. Vanessa told me to pretend the camera was a friend I was very glad to see again. Harup made a gagging noise at that advice, but I took it. Vanessa knew more about connecting with strangers than any of us.

"The latest news, however, has revealed the brutal truth," I said. "The creators of the watch lied to me. The watch kills. It has claimed two victims so far and it seems certain that there will be more. All I can say at this moment is that I'm so deeply sorry for the damage Death Watch has caused, and I'll do whatever I can to stop it. To the families of the victims, I can only offer apologies, not answers. Those must come from Watanabe. To anyone considering buying Death Watch, I can only say *don't*. Seek out other solutions for your unhappiness, your despair. Not this."

I held my arm toward the camera for a moment and Harup focused in on Death Watch, glimmering like a shiny gun. "If I had it to do over, I would never have put Death Watch on my wrist. May you learn from my mistake."

"That's it." Wren held up her hand, Harup stopped filming, and I stood up from the blue couch.

Vanessa handed me a glass of water and I drank it. Harup carried his camera into Vanessa's bathroom, repurposed now as his tech cave, to start editing.

"That was okay." Wren held out our carefully constructed script, now covered with notes. "We'll need to get better at cranking these out," she said. "This one took, what—"

I checked Death Watch, realized the irony. "About four hours."

"No redos next time. Got to be ready."

"Right."

"We need to back off from the guilt and ramp up the anger," Vanessa said.

"I get your point," Wren said, "but anger looks defensive and bad." She turned to me. "Try to inspire other people to get angry at Watanabe."

"Okay."

"But I have to warn you, it's going to get nasty."

Of course it would. I was an easy target—a pitchman betrayed by his own product. Vanessa and Wren walked out of the living room together, fleshing out my new persona, the penitent.

The latest iteration of Team Death had regrouped in Vanessa's apartment, meeting at night so Wren and Harup could sneak over from Moriawase after work without Nathan noticing. During long nights in the living room, we struggled to figure out how to destroy the monster we'd unleashed. My *mea culpa* video was our first salvo in The Brutal Truth, our new campaign, intended to counter Watanabe, who had reemerged after a brief silence to spew a new barrage of high-art deathspeak.

I would be revisiting all of the media outlets where I had promoted Death Watch so recently, admitting that I was a fool and that people were dying because of my foolishness. If we could stop Death Watch, I might be redeemed for my role in bringing it to the world. But Vanessa was right, I would have to bend the blame—and anger—back to Watanabe and his team.

Vanessa walked back into the living room, holding her phone out. "It's for you," she said, puzzled.

"Who is it?"

"Glenn from downstairs."

I took the phone. "Hey, Glenn. How'd you know I was up here?"

"Uh, I'm the doorman?" he said. "It's part of my job?" He paused. "Look, Alta just showed up from LaGuardia. Lots of bags, loaned her the luggage cart. She's on her way up. Thought I should let you know."

"To our apartment?"

"Yeah. I didn't tell her where you really were," Glenn said. "That's not part of my job."

Alta stood in the living room next to her gleaming German luggage—a gift from Zeno—supposedly made from the same aluminum as Lufthansa jets.

I walked in, acted surprised. "You're back!"

"Where were you?"

"Just got off work," I said. "Grabbed some dinner."

"The Mexican place?"

"Of course."

"Thought you'd be home. Wanted to surprise you."

"You did. You definitely did."

We put our arms around each other and kissed. I felt her body shaking.

I kissed her neck, breathed her scent, so familiar, whispered in her ear. "You usually tell me when you're coming home." Alta's return used to be celebratory—a chance to return to our pre-Zeno life, if only for a few days. I'd get a special bottle from Sherry-Lehmann and have dinner waiting.

"Left Darmstadt in a hurry."

I said nothing, not exactly sure what she meant.

She pulled away from me, grabbed my left hand, and took her first look at Death Watch. "I don't want you to die."

"Already talked to your father. He's getting me scheduled to—"

"Have that horrible operation." She held my fingers tightly. "I don't want you to lose any fingers."

"I'll take proactive loss of fingers over potential loss of life."

She shook her head. "I don't like this, not at all." Alta wanted definitive answers, primary colors, clean solutions.

"I don't either. That's why we're trying to stop the whole—"

"Experiment?"

"Disaster." I explained Team Death, how Harup, Wren, and I were trying to stop Death Watch. I didn't mention Vanessa.

Alta quieted for a moment and stood in the living room, still shaking.

"Drank too much coffee on the plane. Couldn't sleep. Do we have any wine? I'd like some wine. Have to tell you some things. Some wine first would be good."

I took her hand and we walked into the kitchen, where I opened a cold bottle of Sancerre, Alta's favorite, and poured her a full glass.

We sat to the kitchen table. "I..." She took a long sip.

I waited.

After the first glass, she settled down to her calmer self. "Darmstadt was a huge mistake."

"Darmstadt is a city in central Germany."

"I mean the Infinity Project. Xtensia. All of it."

"So you quit?"

"Of course I quit. I'm mortified to be part of it. Should start blowing up in a few days. I sent around some emails to the trade press before Zeno had my account shut off. They'll have a field day with this one—a life extension drug that's actually about, you know—"

"Extending dicks?"

"If you hadn't told me, I probably wouldn't have found out for months, maybe years."

"That's why I told you," I said, then asked the tough question. "And Zeno?"

"You're probably thinking what an idiot I was to get involved with Zeno."

"I'm not thinking that."

"You know how Zeno is. I got pulled in. I even thought I loved him, can you believe it? He told me I was the only one for him, that we would be together forever, that there was so much more ahead—how stupid could I be to believe something so cliché?" She paused, gulped her wine. "It's so over."

"Darmstadt?"

"Zeno."

I refilled her glass.

"I talked to Wendy, the woman you told me about, and it turns out he was saying the same things to her. And to another woman in Research. And probably a dozen more. It's like he collects trusting women. We could MeToo him into the Stone Age but I just want to get as far away from him as possible."

She shut her eyes, shook her head slowly. "Zeno and I were, you know—"

"Fucking?"

"Right."

"You can't control desire," I said, passing on some of Vanessa's wisdom. "It just happens, like gravity. You didn't do anything wrong. You just need to forget about it."

She shook her head. "I thought you'd be furious. I was so embarrassed I didn't even want to come home. And you have every right to—"

"No, I don't."

"When I first told you about Zeno, you were furious."

"That was a long time ago. Now it doesn't seem like something I should get angry about."

"Are you drunk?" Alta looked puzzled. "You used to overreact to everything."

I pointed at my glass, still full from the first pour.

"Then what?"

I shifted my left arm on the kitchen table to reveal Death Watch.

"Kind of puts other problems in perspective, doesn't it?"

I nodded.

"I should have been with you in Tokyo. I could've stopped you."

Alta was right; she saved me from my worst impulses. "But you weren't."

She stood and gave me a look that seemed infinitely sad, or maybe it was just international-arrival bleariness amplified by white wine. "I should be alone tonight, I think," she said. "I'll stay in the upstairs apartment. It's still empty, right?"

Wren and Harup would be gone by now, but Vanessa was beginning her long night on the blue couch, delving into her clients' desires, lives—and investment portfolios.

"Well, if you want." I gambled, knowing that if I said *no*, Alta would insist.

Alta drifted out of the kitchen and walked unsteadily toward her luggage. But the urge to punish herself faded. Or maybe she remembered the smell of the Langerstein's apartment. She swiveled and walked back toward me, rested her forehead on my chest. "I'm so tired. All that coffee finally wore off. And I miss our bed."

"I happen to know where it is."

I took her hand and led her into the bedroom, helped take her clothes off. She was almost asleep by the time she lay between the time-softened linen sheets. Years of business travel made her a quick, deep sleeper. I stayed wide awake for hours, watching her, wondering whether she was really here to stay.

We woke in the middle of the night when Alta's wine wore off and she pushed closer to me, falling back into the same position we had slept in for so many years—my arms around her from behind, chest against her shoulder blades, our legs bent, the soles of her feet resting on the top of mine. She pressed back harder from the waist to tell me what she wanted. I stretched and stroked her gently, fingertips guided by her low murmurs. More awake now, she pressed closer and turning urgent. I slipped inside her from behind and we moved in rhythm, so familiar, as if nothing had happened between then and now.

Alta came a little and cried, from happiness or exhaustion or regret—I couldn't tell. I just held her and kissed the back of her neck until she fell asleep again.

In the dark bedroom, the red number on the band glowed like the exit light in a theater. Death Watch had been on my wrist for 82 days now.

"Wake up!" Alta tugged on my T-shirt. I opened my eyes slowly, still lost in a dream, and smelled coffee. It was a little after seven in the morning and Alta was already dressed and concerned.

"Someone broke into the upstairs apartment." She spoke softly, as if the intruder was listening.

"What?"

"Woke up early. Heard voices when I was in the kitchen. Walked upstairs and listened. You told me the last tenants had moved out. But there are definitely people in there."

I nodded.

"There was a woman. She seemed kind of angry. And a guy speaking really fast. He sounded Dutch."

Vanessa started her mornings with European clients. "That's Stijn."

Alta squinted. "How do you know him?"

"I don't, he lives in Utrecht."

"And the woman?"

"That's Vanessa."

"You know her?"

"She's our new tenant."

"Why didn't you tell me?"

I smiled. "Wanted to surprise you?"

"Vanessa and Stijn aren't medical students, are they?"

"No," I said, "they're not medical students." I got out of bed and walked toward the shower. "You'll like Vanessa. Super-smart. Friend of Harup's. Long story."

"Tell me."

I held up my hand to pause Alta's relentless vitality. "Give me a few minutes to wake up and drink some coffee. Then we'll go upstairs."

"Got a key?"

"It's always unlocked." For someone in hiding, Vanessa wasn't very vigilant.

I tried to make a lot of noise opening the door to give Vanessa some warning. "Hey! It's us."

"*Us*?" Vanessa called from the living room.

"Alta's here."

Silence. Team Death wasn't used to surprise visitors.

I led Alta quickly past the bathroom full of racks of costumes to the living room scattered with last night's Team Death debris—laptops open, whiteboard scrawled with notes, takeout coffee cups on the floor.

Her face twisted in confusion when she saw Harup sitting on the blue couch, drinking a coffee.

"Harup?"

He stood and gave a jittery wave and splashed coffee on the rug.

"What're you doing here?"

His smile froze and his dark eyes pinged around the room, looking everywhere but at Alta.

"This is where we're destroying Death Watch." I pointed at the laptops and the whiteboard. "Kind of like our office. Harup is our tech guy."

Harup nodded and got up from the blue couch and perched on a windowsill.

Vanessa walked into the living room, strode across the floor, looked Alta in the eye, and shook her hand firmly, like a co-worker. "I'm Vanessa. Good to meet you, Alta—finally."

"Good to meet you, too," Alta said. "Finally?"

"Coe talks about you all the time."

Alta looked at me and I nodded. "All the time."

"You're the new tenant?"

"I am. And I've been working with these guys."

True enough, but too vague for my precise wife. "You've been doing—"

"Consulting." Vanessa pulled an appropriate persona from her multitudes. "Been doing some situational analysis. And some crisis management."

Jesus, where did Vanessa get it from? Her look—red online wig, tight black skirt, cream-colored top with hints of a burgundy bra showing through—didn't exactly scream McKinsey. But it was better than a vintage vinyl catsuit.

"When did all ... all this start?" She looked around the apartment, which Vanessa—and now Team Death—had colonized so brazenly.

"Right after the first watch went off," I said. "Nathan didn't want to try to stop Death Watch, but I had to. So I left."

"You left the agency?" Alta stared at me as if I had just told her I was selling heroin on a playground. "You didn't tell me."

"Officially, I'm on furlough. But now Nathan's threatening to sue me for reputational damage. I'm guessing I won't be going back."

Alta shook her head at the news about Moriawase, the center of our lives for so many years. "It's probably a good move. You always did the work. Nathan just made it harder."

Harup gave a solemn nod.

"People aren't still buying Death Watch, are they?"

"They are," I said.

"Can't you stop it?"

"We're trying as hard as we can," I said. "But we're struggling against the momentum we managed to create back at the agency." *Struggling to kill the sacrilegious calf we had nurtured* was the real answer.

Vanessa walked over to the whiteboard and read Wren's meticulous handwriting—MEA CULPA, BRUTAL TRUTH, then a big question mark.

Alta took it all in—the blue couch in the living room, the redecorated apartment, the debris from long nights of work.

Vanessa tilted her head. "Don't you work for big pharma?"

"Did."

"And now?"

"Not sure," Alta said.

"We'll try to keep it quiet up here," I said. "But stopping Death Watch is a lot of work."

Alta went silent. Maybe she was thinking about her big office in Darmstadt with its view of the Luisenplatz, whiteboard covered with clinical trial schedules. Maybe she was missing Zeno or her work; both had meant so much to her and now they were gone. Maybe she realized that working to stop Death Watch wasn't that different from trying to extend life.

Alta looked up and shook her head, as if agreeing with an internal memo.

She smiled at me, without a job and (soon) a couple of fingers.

She looked over at Harup, a puzzle too baffling to solve.
She turned to Vanessa, our enigmatic new tenant.
"If it's okay with all of you," Alta said. "I'd like to help out."

FREEDOM

"Death Watch is living up to its name, killing those who wear it at a rate of about one a week. We've seen the horrifying photos, read the shocking news. Now we'll hear from the man who sold Death Watch to the world. At first he thought it was a hoax. Now the joke's on him. And he may just die laughing. Welcome back to *Dark Roast,* Coe Vessel."

"Good to be back, Jeremy."

"Last time you were on the show, you acted like Death Watch was very real, right?"

Harup held the boom microphone at the right distance from my lips. Wren, Vanessa, and Alta were all leaning forward on the blue couch, watching my latest interview. "Yes, that's right."

"Now you're telling the world that you had been hoodwinked into thinking that it didn't work, that it was just more arty agit-prop from the legendary Watanabe, now in hiding. Am I right?"

"You are."

"But you didn't tell me that at the time, did you?"

"I—"

"No, you didn't. I'll tell you what you said about the watch. Quote. *It's right there on my wrist from the moment I wake up to when I fall asleep at night, reminding me to live.* Unquote. So you were lying to me, right?"

"I lied to everybody. For the project to work, people had to think Death Watch was real."

"But *ha ha,* it actually is real. Six people dead so far."

I closed my eyes and shook my head. Harup kicked me to bring me back. "There are no words."

"There are plenty of words—more than a million in English. Give it a try, Coe."

I paused. I would have written something, but I knew it would sound like I was reading from a teleprompter. "There isn't a moment in the day when I don't think about the victims, Jeremy.

The guilt is overwhelming. Staggering. I quit my job so I can spend all my time trying to stop people from buying the watch."

"It isn't working, is it? I mean, from what I've read, sales just keep going up."

"A lot of the buyers are probably just collectors."

"You don't know that for sure, do you?"

"No, not really."

"You said that the ideal buyer for the watch was *anyone who wants to be set free from the world as it is.* That line stuck with me because I'm sure there were plenty of people who fit the bill."

"Right, there are."

"Even after seeing what happens when the watch goes off? I mean, I watched a security video that caught that Atlanta victim—"

"Todd McLaughlin."

"Yes, him. Awful isn't it?"

"Beyond awful." The video showed McLaughlin writhing on the ground in an underground parking lot, trying to stop the blood spurting from his wrist, with no one near to help him.

"That may happen to you, right?"

"Right."

"But unlike everyone else, you put on Death Watch thinking it would never work."

"That's right. I made a terrible mistake."

"You're the only one who was surprised to find out that the watch worked. Maybe all the people who buy the watch don't care, Coe, they just want *to be set free.* What do you say to them?"

"If they feel that way, there are other ways to be free."

"Like what? Psychotherapy? Meds? Meditation? Yoga? All of the above?"

"Whatever works."

"Did anyone who bought Death Watch have buyer's remorse or second thoughts."

"Maybe. But we haven't heard from them."

"Then why are you here, Coe? It's America, land of the free. Let the people buy what they want. I think that's in the Constitution, right? Maybe it'll make them feel better about living—until it kills them, of course. Why try to stop them?"

I said nothing for a moment, wished the interview was over. But Jeremy kept the sarcasm coming.

"Do you hate freedom?"

"No, but I hate Watanabe for lying to me. I never would have gotten involved if I knew that Death Watch was real."

"Well, too bad for you. But think about the people you lied to. Things got a lot worse for them, didn't they? After all, you convinced them with your highly effective propaganda—"

"I'd call it advertising."

"Same thing. Once they strapped Death Watch on their wrists, they weren't just mortal anymore. They were painfully mortal. Vulnerable as lambs with a vicious lion ready to bite their wrists at any moment. And you put them there in unnecessary peril. All because they believed your lies."

I looked over at the couch. From Wren's flat expression, I could tell I was bombing. Jeremy Wood was conducting an inquisition of one.

"Yes, I lied, Jeremy. To you and to everyone else. I pitched Death Watch because I thought it couldn't hurt anyone. I told a good story, that's what advertising does. Now I know that the only way to stop Death Watch is to tell another story. This one's true. I don't want anyone else to die, or for their families and friends to suffer. I'll do anything to stop Watanabe."

I could hear Jeremy breathing during a long pause. "Well, good luck to you, Coe Vessel. Thanks for being honest, at least half of the time."

I stared ahead, blankly.

"Listeners, do you believe what you just heard from this amoral adman? Or is it just another chapter of a cruel hoax being played on the vulnerable by high-art hooligans? You New Nihilists out there? Are you ready to die for your beliefs or lack thereof? Let's talk about it—here on *Dark Roast*."

Harup nodded and my headphones went silent. I slipped them off, sat on the folding chair, sweat trailing down my sides.

"*Shit.*"

Vanessa and Alta sat silently on the couch, stunned by my pummeling.

"We need something better."

"I looked over at Wren, sitting on the floor, notebook in hand. "Better than what?"

"Better than the truth."

BLOODLETTING

TEAM DEATH—NOW A PARTY OF FIVE—gathered in Vanessa's living room to watch Watanabe's latest message to the world. "Cassius Seven has spoken in Boston, San Francisco, Atlanta, Chicago, and Montreal. It will speak again elsewhere very soon." He paused. "Now the world is listening."

"Watanabe's going full megalomaniac," Wren said. But he was more than that. He was a murderer on his way to becoming a mass murderer.

"The end of the Holocene, the era that saw the dominance of our species, is upon us," he said, voice rising with every word. "For centuries, we controlled our earthly empire and our future. No longer. The rising seas cannot be stopped. Nor the rise of cruelty and inequity. The brave participants who wear Cassius Seven are making a bold statement about the world. They're reclaiming their lives from malicious systems and their human factotums. They're escaping the inevitable by claiming it for themselves."

Watanabe leaned forward and we could see a thin trail of sweat running down his neck. Harup looked away.

"To those who wear the watch that some have called Death Watch, we salute you. You are redeeming the modern world through the ancient act of intentional sacrifice. Your selfless bloodletting may save us. To those who criticize us, take a look around you, see the cruelty that dominates the world—and join us."

Watanabe's creased, unsmiling face faded out. His voice seemed even more vehement, as if he were emboldened by Death Watch's rising death toll.

"He's just talking to himself," said Alta, sitting next to Vanessa on the blue couch.

"Every man's in his own echo chamber," Vanessa said.

"But every time Watanabe shows up, he sells a ton of watches," I said. "Someone's listening to him."

Harup slammed his laptop closed and rushed to his tech cave.

"What's up with Harup?" Alta said.

"Got *all the feels,"* Wren said.

Wrestling with guilt, for Harup, meant self-harm via bad diet. His tech cave was cluttered with greasy takeout food bins and soda cans. Some sinners flagellated themselves with whips; Harup ate fish sandwiches and onion curls, washed down with Diet Dr. Pepper.

"Harup, come back," I shouted. "We have to figure this out."

He walked into the living room and lowered himself heavily down on the floor. Wren sat next to him, close but not too close.

Vanessa pointed at each of us. "All of you have to drop the guilt. It's not your fault."

"We killed people," Wren said.

"No, you didn't," Vanessa said. "Watanabe made the watch and told you it was fake. People made the choice to buy it, thinking it was real. You just made some really good ads."

"She's right," Alta said. "Guilt isn't going to stop watches from going off. It's not going to stop more people from buying them."

I stood and paced the living room, windows dim in fading evening light. Alta's pragmatic mind never ceased to amaze and annoy me. "What will?"

"Some kind of breakthrough idea that destroys Death Watch," Alta said. "A magic bullet."

Wren brightened. "We'll shoot Watanabe with a magic bullet!"

"Exactly."

We sat in silence, trying to come up with ideas that were magic.

We were still thinking when the Skype alert went off. Harup checked to see who was calling.

Fukn Watanabe!

I took the open laptop from Harup and accepted Watanabe's call. His grizzled face and dark, unfathomable eyes appeared on the screen from wherever he was hiding—rumors put him everywhere from South Korea to Serbia.

"Did you see my latest video, Coe Vessel?"

"No," I lied. "Why would I want to watch that? No one cares

what you have to say anymore."

"Or you." He shrugged, gave a wan smile. "But we have to say it, don't we?"

Wren rolled her eyes.

"What are you doing, Coe Vessel?" Watanabe sounded sad, like a disappointed father. "Trying to stop something you helped start. It's like you're at war with yourself."

"I'm done with Death Watch."

Watanabe laughed. "How can you say that? Just look at your wrist."

"What you're doing is evil, you know that don't you?"

"Of course!" Watanabe gave a broad smile. "I've created an unimaginably horrible device that the world can't seem to get enough of."

"A device that kills people."

"No, they're killing themselves. I'm simply presenting them with the opportunity to escape."

"And getting rich."

"It's true. We'll sell our two thousandth watch soon. We're making millions, from what I hear."

"From the misery of others."

"We didn't make them miserable. The world did that. In any case, there is no stopping it. We have set the wheels in motion. They keep turning no matter what. The experiment goes on and on."

Watanabe looked to the side and said something in Japanese. "Too bad that you are no longer with us, Coe Vessel. You did a very good job. A shame that your old-fashioned morality keeps you from continuing." He looked to the side again. "Yohji also wants to say something."

Watanabe's face left the screen, replaced by his smiling son.

"Hey, Coe. It's me!" Yohji waved as if he were on vacation in the Caymans instead of on the run. He wore a vintage T-shirt bearing the blood-red image of Patty Hearst as gun-toting Tania, radicalized mascot of the Symbionese Liberation Army. "We had quite a time together," he said. "Excellent working with you. Remember hanging at your cool office in New York? Walking on the High

Line? It was all so super-fun."

I wondered if Yohji had a clothes rack where his soul should be.

"You and your father have a lot of explaining to do."

Yohji gave an even broader grin. "We don't have to explain. Everything we do is valid, Coe Vessel. People may not like it. But as artists, we have the right to do it."

"Even when people start dying?"

Yohji shrugged, looked off-camera and laughed at something Watanabe said. "People die all the time. It's part of the natural order."

"And you're okay helping them along?"

"Of course! It's good to be helpful."

"I'm done." I reached to cut Yohji off.

"Wait! How about instead of trying to stop Death Watch, you should just enjoy your life." Yohji smiled. "Because when you wear our watch, *minutes become hours, hours become days.*" He was quoting me from an interview I did with *Asahi Shimbun.*

"I said that when I didn't think the watch worked."

"Now it's even more true!"

Yohji smiled inanely and the screen went black.

Alta and I took a long walk through Central Park after the call, trying to make sense of it. Could Watanabe and Yohji still be in charge? We agreed that it seemed unlikely. No matter where he was hiding, Watanabe dwelled in high-art Valhalla and Yohji was more about looks than logistics.

"My bet's on the engineers," I said. "From what I saw in Tokyo, they seemed pretty clever and greedy."

"That's not enough."

"They're getting a lot of attention." There had been plenty of media airtime given to the technological audacity of the world's first deadly accessory. "I mean, it's an innovation. A terrible one, but still."

"Innovations. Inventions. Artworks. Creations." She looked off to the side of the path, into the darkening underbrush. "All just different ways for men to think they're special, to say *look at me, tell me how smart I am.*"

"Like Zeno?" I said, before I had a chance to stop myself.

Alta looked right at me, her eyes narrowing. "I don't want to talk about him, ever." She started walking faster as if to escape the mention of his name.

I caught up to her, walked by her side.

"Shouldn't have said that."

"I was wondering why you were so forgiving," she said. "But now I think I know. You were *shtupping* Vanessa."

"Is that German?"

"Yiddish, I think. It means you've been—"

"Fucking?" Alta went to great lengths to avoid uttering the f-word.

"That."

"Well, I haven't," I said. "We haven't."

"Not sure I believe you."

"Then ask her. No need for Yiddish. Vanessa's not shy."

"No, she's not. And she's not a consultant, either. She's a sex worker."

I stopped walking. "*What*, really? That's just crazy talk."

"Don't be funny, Coe. We had a great talk yesterday. I asked her what she really did and she told me. Now it all makes perfect sense."

"What does?"

"I've seen what you two are like together. You're close."

I considered a convenient lie but decided against it. "We are."

"You went to Boston with her."

"*Jesus*, it wasn't a date. We went to a funeral."

"Why?"

"To try to find out how James Lorber died."

"I can tell you that. His stupid watch killed him."

"Would've taken you but you weren't around."

"No, I wasn't." Alta settled, kept walking. "You know, I wouldn't blame you for wanting to get even with me for ... for Darmstadt."

"A revenge fuck? You know that's not the way I'm wired."

A charged silence descended on us. We were veering into connubial quicksand.

"We should head home," Alta said.

"So you can quiz Vanessa about *shtupping*? You're in for an earful."

"No, because we need to get back to work." Work was Alta's go-to substitute for emotions.

We walked quietly back down the winding path we had taken, the park darkening around us.

"Didn't mean to sound suspicious," Alta said as we walked through the entrance. "It's just that Vanessa seems very ... I mean, even I feel it."

"Seems very what?"

"Seductive. Powerful."

"Doesn't just seem that way," I said. "She is."

We walked down 57th Street towards home. The office buildings along our street had changed since we first moved here, growing tall and glassy. But the pink-and-blue sky in the west just after sunset stayed the same.

Up ahead, I saw the white figures marching in a circle in front of our building.

"*Shit*. Forgot it was Sunday."

Alta saw spooky robes, more than a little Klan-like, faces painted to look like watches, black hands set a few minutes before midnight. "Who are they?"

"Faces of the Faithful." I explained their unique objections—that Death Watch's promoters, including me, were playing God, and conducting post-birth abortions that killed innocents.

"In what world does that make any sense?" asked my rational wife.

"Ours."

As we walked closer, the clot of white-faced protestors in front of our building fell into battle formation.

"Hey, hey, kill anyone today?" One of the Faithful chanted.

I took Alta's arm and we tried to blow past them.

We passed a woman who looked a lot like my grandmother.

"James Lorber. James Lorber. James Lorber."

I stopped, stilled by her mantra, which brought me back to Lorber's funeral, the scent of incense and stone. "I'm sorry about James Lorber. About all of them. I made a mistake. Now I'm trying to stop it. Don't you know that?"

"False god," the grandmother said. "False god. False god."

"We're going to fucking destroy you," a pale guy added.

He raised his protest sign and brought it down on my shoulder. Others joined in. We fell to the ground. I scrambled toward Alta and covered her body while the Faithful kicked us, beat us with their signs. The pale guy crawled over to us and tried to pull Death Watch from my wrist.

"Fuck off." I couldn't get my arms free from the tumble of bodies.

Alta flailed at the clawing man, giving him a hard kick in the throat, an accidental bar-fight move that left him gasping for breath.

Tear gas sprayed over all of us as the police arrived.

"Clear out, clowns. You're done for today."

I looked up. There were no cops, no tear gas. Just Glenn with a fire extinguisher, spraying away the Faithful like wasps from a nest. He lifted the gasping man by his belt and tossed him toward the retreating crowd.

I stood, brushed myself off, and took Alta's hand to pull her up from the street, covered with signs and crushed pamphlets (SINNERS, YOUR TIME HAS COME!).

"Get inside, you two, fast." Glenn waved us into the entryway and locked the door behind him. Most of the Faithful faded down 57th Street, with a few stragglers knocking over trash cans as they retreated.

"Real freak show out there, huh?" Glenn took his place behind the doorman desk. "You okay?"

"I think so," I said. We inspected each other. Except for long scratches on our arms and dirt on our clothes, we seemed unscathed.

"You know, the Faithful started out okay," Glenn said. "They gave me bake sale stuff so I wouldn't call the cops."

"Like what?" Dessert was Alta's secret weakness.

"Chocolate chip cookies. Ginger cookies, too. Angel-food cake with almond icing, or maybe it was marzipan. Also, popcorn balls—who makes those anymore? And pineapple upside-down cake, which I got to say, is my favorite."

Alta nodded; those were pretty good reasons to put up with protestors.

"But now I'm seeing interlopers among the church ladies. Younger dudes. Angry and alone. Stomping around. Like that guy who was trying to steal your watch."

"He'd have to cut off my arm to get it."

"To get a watch worth fifty grand," Glenn said. "People are desperate."

They were. That's why they were still buying Death Watch.

"I'm calling the cops next time I see a Face of the Faithful anywhere near our building."

"Thanks, Glenn. Your Christmas bonus is going to be huge."

"If you're still around to give it to me."

"Not funny."

"Didn't say it was. Just a fact, Mr. Vessel. We're all short-timers.

Couldn't argue with that.

"Got to *carpe* the damn *diem*."

Or that.

We took the elevator to the eighth floor and stumbled through the unlocked door into Team Death HQ. Vanessa and Wren looked concerned. Harup wandered off to his tech cave when he saw that we were still alive.

Vanessa put her arms around me, then Alta, who tightened up at first, but let her shoulders drop. "Sounded like a riot down there. We were worried about you."

Vanessa noticed scratches on our arms, hands. "Human scratches and bites are the worst, believe me," she said, leading us out of the living room. "Got a first aid kit in the kitchen."

Alta smiled. She wanted to be cared for, tended. So did I. So did everyone.

ASPHÁLEIA

"THERE'S STILL SIGNIFICANT RISK INVOLVED." Robert sat behind his desk, a thick sheath of multicolored forms between us. "You know that, don't you?"

I nodded too quickly. We were just beginning our pre-op discussion and I was already nervous.

"Every surgery has some risk, but the D'Issan procedure is—"

"Is what?"

"Untested. Risky."

"That doesn't sound particularly encouraging."

"I'm not encouraging you—I'm informing you," Robert said. "That's why I asked you to come back in." He stood up and turned around to face his bookshelf. "The concern we have, meaning the surgical team and hospital administration, is that the procedure may activate the watch."

"I'll be in an operating room. If it goes off, can't they just tie a tourniquet around my wrist or something?"

"That would be possible if it just severed your hand neatly." Robert turned back to me and pressed his fingertips on his desktop. "But that's not what really happens when the watch goes off."

"What do you mean?"

He pushed a file folder toward me. "I've been in touch with the hospitals that treated some of the Death Watch victims—in Boston, Los Angeles, and Chicago. They sent some forensic images."

I reached for the folder and Robert gripped my wrist, the one without Death Watch on it. "I've never treated soldiers on the battlefield," he said, "but my colleagues who have say this looks very familiar." He let go. "Fair warning, right?"

I nodded and opened the folder, saw an image of a thin man, lying on his back on a gurney, face pixelated, lower body covered with a bloody sheet. Clumps of bloody gauze decorated the floor like rose petals. In the next photo, the sheet was folded back to reveal his left arm, shredded up to the elbow, ripped into bright red chunks of flesh and glistening white bone—like a victim in a zombie film. A wave of nausea swept over me but I managed to stop myself from rushing into the examining room to throw up my morning coffee.

I closed the folder.

"From what the other doctors say, the watch doesn't just plunge knives into the wrist and spin them. It uses the gap between the ulna and radius bones to travel up to the elbow, knives shredding everything in their path. Like an animal gnawing a bone."

I remembered Watanabe's demonstration, the instantaneous conversion of a white rabbit into a crimson aerosol. "Why would it do that?"

"Thought you might know."

I shook my head. The insidious design of Death Watch was the domain of the engineers.

"I suppose it's to ensure that the watch kills the unfortunate person wearing it," Robert said. "Bleeding out would happen much more quickly from an injury that traumatic, even in a clinical setting. Can't just slap on a tourniquet on dendritic bleeding, as it's called. We're lining up a second team, one that's ready to deal with a major bleed-out."

I shook my head to clear it.

"This isn't good news," Robert said. "But I wanted you to know what we're up against."

"Thanks."

"All I can promise is we'll do the best we can."

When Robert first told me about the D'Issan procedure, it had sounded like a safe, old-fashioned way to escape my certain fate. Now it seemed like uncharted territory.

"We're lining up the surgical team," Robert said. "You're on the schedule for the week after Labor Day."

"That's soon." Even after all that had happened, I couldn't shake my belief that my watch was different, not deadly—and that desperate measures wouldn't be necessary.

"Overwhelming, isn't it?"

"What?"

"Realizing that you're mortal."

I nodded, tried to come up with a few short, evocative sentences, like an ad for mortality. "It's like trying to imagine winter in the middle of summer. I know it's going to come, but I don't feel it. It doesn't seem real."

Robert leaned back in his chair. "Here's what I tell my patients when they get that stunned look. *The possibility of death can only be considered when all other options disappear.* Most of them are older, of course. You've got a very good shot at living to be old, too. So don't give in to despair quite yet." He nodded at the stack of papers. "Meanwhile, start signing."

I worked through the waivers and permissions, filling in all my information, signing and initialing.

"You're lucky you have good health insurance. If you didn't, the procedure would cost you—"

"An arm and a leg?" I gave a wry smile.

Robert paused, not amused. "It would cost much more than the watch."

He took down one of his books, copied something onto a prescription pad, and folded the piece of paper. When I finished the forms, he slipped it across the table to me.

"Another ancient Greek word for you." He smiled.

I opened the piece of paper, read what was written on it. ASPHÁLEIA

"Which means?"

Robert read from his book. "Security, surety, certainty. As in, I'm certain the procedure will go well, and sure that you're going to be fine."

I refolded the paper and put it carefully in my pocket. Who couldn't use some certainty?

The strategy meeting was already underway when I got back from my appointment with Robert.

I sat in a folding chair next to Harup in what used to be Vanessa's guest area. Alta and Vanessa were sitting on the blue couch, nose-down on their laptops, while Wren stood at the whiteboard, adding the names and locations of the latest victims in her meticulous script. I shut my eyes, shook my head.

"Sales?" Alta asked.

Harup looked up, checked his phone. He could still access all the Death Watch data.

up 9% frm last week

Wren added the latest figure to our chart, which showed sales growing steadily since Watanabe launched Death Watch, then spiking when it claimed its first victim.

"I know I keep asking this, but why are people still buying the watch?" Alta's question was rational but unanswerable. "More deaths, more sales." She shook her head, frustrated.

"Our campaign reached the people we targeted," I said. "And it's doing what we said it would—building demand."

"Well, what we're doing now isn't working at all." Alta joined Wren at the whiteboard, drew a square, and divided it into four boxes. She labeled the upper left quadrant of the square MEDIA ASSAULT. "Your story isn't getting any traction. People have trouble believing someone who already lied to them."

Wren and I looked at each other. Always the brutal voice of reason, Alta was right.

Alta wrote TECHNOLOGY ATTACK in the next quadrant and pointed at Harup.

"You've been working to destroy Watanabe and his team online. Trying to interrupt his supply chain. Disrupt his e-commerce."

Harup nodded.

"But he's still able to sell watches—and people still buy them."

Harup's face fell like he'd just been given a failing grade on his homework.

Fukn crypto's hrd to beat

"Then try malware, DDOS attacks, anything, right?"

She wrote LEGAL ENTANGLEMENT in the third quadrant.

"What Watanabe is doing is illegal, of course. He's just slipping through because of international jurisdiction issues. I've been trying to get the families of the victims together for a class-action lawsuit. They're furious at Watanabe and his crew. They think Death Watch is evil. But they're still too stunned to do anything."

The final quadrant was blank. "Remember this?"

"Magic bullet?" Wren said.

"Right. We still don't have one, do we?"

Silence from Team Death. Like most creative teams, we were strong on ideas and weak on execution. And in this case, execution took on a whole new meaning. We needed to stop Death Watch and its horrifyingly steady flow of victims by any means necessary. And if that meant finding the illusive magic bullet, we had to look harder.

"Hey," Vanessa said.

Alta perked up. "Idea?"

"Another victim." Vanessa looked up from her laptop. "In Los Angeles this morning."

Wren stood, got ready to add another name to the list.

"Shit." Vanessa shook her head.

"What?"

"It's that loudmouth TV show guy, the one with the chair."

"Jake Scully?" Wren dropped her marker. "You sure?"

"Says here that *TV personality Jake Scully was found dead in his car in West Hollywood this morning,"* Vanessa said. *"Though the exact cause of death has not been identified, Scully was known to be wearing Death Watch, the controversial device that continues to claim victims."*

Harup tapped away on his phone, diving into Searchland.

Scullywags r saying he bled to death. They're pissed. Trending. Prolly don't read wht theyre saying.

Wren sat on the floor. "I sent him that watch. Got him to wear it."

"We didn't think it worked," I said. "And his fans told him to wear it, remember?"

"No guilt, sister." Vanessa moved closer and wrapped her arms around Wren. "Remember, Watanabe invented Death Watch. Scully put it on. Don't blame yourself. You were just the messenger."

Wren nodded, then lowered her head on Vanessa's shoulder.

Guilt was almost as hard to get rid of as Death Watch.

MAGIC BULLET

THE STRANGER WORE A BLACK SKIRT and pale blue blouse, walked confidently down the sidewalk on high heels. She kept her eyes directly on me, standing in front of our apartment building taking a break from Team Death.

"Hey," she shouted. "Coe Vessel, right?"

An unmasked Face of the Faithful? A reporter? I couldn't tell. As she walked closer, she stretched up her left arm. The sleeve of her blouse drifted lower to reveal a gleaming watch.

She wasn't a stalker; she was a customer.

We met on the sidewalk, both keeping our distance.

I nodded. She was in her late twenties, straight blonde hair, remarkably unremarkable—a Businesswoman of Midtown.

"Alison Flynn." She paused, touched her hair, focused. "I need your help."

"What kind of help?"

She pushed her arm close to me and I could read the number of days she'd been wearing it tallied on the band—9. She tapped one of her shiny black shoes on the sidewalk as she waited for me to say something.

"Real or knock-off?"

"Real," she said.

"Thought only men were buying Death Watch."

"My boss bought one. Jerry was always flashing it during meetings to remind the team how tough he was, how none of the rest of them had the balls to wear a watch that would kill them."

I corrected her. "That *could* kill them."

"Whatever. Given how many of them are going off, seems like they all will, doesn't it?"

I couldn't argue with that.

"So you bought Death Watch to impress your boss?"

"I was sick of his bullshit. Wanted Jerry to know he wasn't that tough or that special. Wanted everyone else—particularly the cocky young guys—to know that I was tough. That was my mistake, trying to be as dickish as they were." She gave a quick shake of her head. "Never lower yourself to their level, Alison."

"And?"

"They fired me, quick. Said I was endangering my co-workers."

"How?"

"If the watch went off they'd be traumatized. Something like that. And they might sue. Truth is, Jerry just wanted me gone because I was getting more attention."

"He wasn't the only kid on the block with a dangerous new toy."

"Yes, that."

"Did they fire him, too?"

"Not a chance. I worked in the pit, jammed in with all the other junior analysts. He had a corner office and didn't deal with his team that much. Wasn't as dangerous. At least that was the way HR spun it."

"Well, that sucks for you."

"Oh, it more than sucks. When they fired me, they cancelled my VISA card, the one I used to buy Death Watch. Thought I could just pay off it off over a long time but now the full balance is due. I need to get the watch off fast so I can sell it—"

"You know it doesn't come off, right?" I started to tell her about the dead man's switch but she waved me down.

"I know, I know. Did my research before I bought it. Read the warnings. But I figure that there has to be a way out. Panic rooms, software apps, video games—there's always some kind of backdoor. And I thought you might know where it is."

I held out my arm. "If there was a secret way to take off the watch, I would have already done it—and told everyone else how to do it."

Alison paused. "Well maybe you could get me in touch with the chain-smoking art douche who invented it."

"Watanabe?"

"Right."

"He's in hiding. I don't have anything to do with him anymore."

She looked at me as if what I was saying was incomprehensible.

"YOU made me buy the watch," she said, loud enough that other people on the sidewalk turned to see what was going on. "YOU made it sound like it would make me appreciate life. But it doesn't. Everything in my life has FUCKED UP since I put it on. I don't have a job. I'm in debt to the bank I used to work for. No one will hire me—why train a new employee who might DIE at any moment and also FREAK OUT all her co-workers?"

She stopped, closed her eyes, breathing hard. "Alison, you're so fucked," she said softly.

"Okay, there's one way out that I know of."

"Tell me. I've got to get this watch off."

"It's pretty disturbing."

Alison held up her arm. "I'm wearing Death Watch, remember? I'm okay with disturbing."

I explained the D'Issan procedure without going into too many gory details—but not making it sound easy.

"Which fingers?" she asked at the end.

I pointed.

"If I get married, I'll have to wear the ring on the other hand?"

"I guess so." I hadn't thought of that. "I'm scheduled to have the procedure in a couple of weeks. Gives you time to think about it."

"And make sure you don't die, right?"

Alison was a chilly realist. "Right."

"How much does it cost?"

"I don't know exactly," I said. "But more than the watch."

"More than FIFTY THOUSAND DOLLARS?" Alison bent over, crumpling almost to her knees.

"It's a complicated procedure, and it's elective surgery."

She stood back up, eyed me warily. "Wait a minute, if something's going to kill you, shouldn't that count as an emergency?"

"It's not deadly. Just potentially deadly. And we put it on ourselves."

"You did," she said. "I bought mine because you made it sound so good."

I shook my head. "You put it on because you had a point to make with your boss."

"Okay, fair enough." She pinched her eyes closed. "I take responsibility. You're twenty-nine, Alison. Time to stop blaming everyone else. Okay."

She turned quiet, staring west toward the Hudson.

"It'll work out," I said. "Your health insurance probably covers most of it."

"*Uhh,* here's the other way that I'm completely fucked. They canceled my insurance when I got fired."

If Alison wasn't a New Nihilist before, she just joined the team.

"I'm not ignoring your situation, which is terrible," I said. "But I have to ask—do you think there are other people who feel like they made a mistake?"

"Sure, there must be plenty of people who wish they hadn't put on Death Watch. Buyer's remorse, whatever you want to call it. They want a way out. And someone they trust to help them get rid of the watch."

I smiled, looked up at the summer sky, robin's egg blue and fading. If I were a true believer I might claim that Alison's sudden appearance was pre-ordained. I might have fallen to my knees and thanked a deity. But I didn't. Like so much of my life, this moment was just incredibly lucky.

"Thanks, Alison," I said.

"For what?"

"A magic bullet."

SURGICAL OUTREACH

"THE LAST TIME YOU WERE ON THE SHOW, you sat right there and told us that wearing Death Watch was enhancing your life."

"That's right." I had returned to the white-leather guest chair on the bright set of *Andy and Bev in the Morning.*

Bev leaned over the host's desk, so close I could smell her musky perfume. "Is it just another lie you're here to tell us, Coe?"

Vanessa had warned me about the show's power dynamic, designed to put guests off-balance. Tiny Bev was a former prosecutor, tough and difficult. Ursine Andy was soft and sensitive as a nature poet.

"No," I said. "I've got some news."

"News?" Bev said. "Here's what we've been seeing in the news."

Photos of the victims appeared one after the next on the screen behind us, each identified by name before fading. In the photos, the victims were smiling, standing on beaches, huddled with friends at bars. Their singular lives were all cut short by Death Watch.

"They look so normal, so alive." Andy's face twisted like he just tasted something very bitter.

"It's horrible." Bev shook her head, put on her black-rimmed glasses. "Still wearing your watch, I see." She pointed at my wrist.

"It doesn't come off."

"Well, *boo-hoo,* Coe." Bev's smile morphed into a sneer. "You made your choice and it turned out to be wrong. Wasn't art. It was death you were putting on."

Here we go, I thought.

"You made your mistake and now you have to live with it." Bev stabbed a finger at me. "But you inspired lots of other people to make the same terrible mistake. That's wrong, very wrong. What do you have to say to them?"

"I'm here to say that there's a way out."

"Really?" Bev looked confused; the producers hadn't clued her in about the latest Death Watch news.

"Yes." Andy signaled the producer, who started airing the video clip behind us. It showed Robert sitting behind his desk, wearing a lab coat over a gray suit, pale blue eyes staring directly into the camera, projecting total WASP surgeon credibility. His title scrolled onto the screen. DR. ROBERT VAN SCHUYLER, HEAD OF NEUROLOGICAL SURGERY, NEW YORK PRESBYTERIAN HOSPITAL.

"Good morning. I'm Dr. Robert Van Schuyler, here to announce that next week, we'll be attempting to surgically remove Death Watch from a patient. It's a complicated surgery known as the D'Issan procedure. It involves removing two fingers and their associated tendons."

Andy looked away.

The screen flashed with an old-school medical illustration of the D'Issan procedure in bloodless black and white.

Robert returned. "As far as we know, it hasn't been performed in almost a hundred years. But if this first procedure is successful, we'll offer it to anyone wearing Death Watch who wants to live free from its threat. For free."

Alta and I had convinced Robert to be our magic bullet, one that rebranded Team Death as Good Samaritans, of a sort. We could reach out to find others like Alison, who regretted their decision to strap Death Watch around their wrist. They were like bridge jumpers who leapt with enthusiasm but on the way toward the gray water realized they shouldn't have. We could pull them all back—for free.

"As a doctor sworn to *do no harm*, I feel obligated help stop the damage that Death Watch inflicts."

Heavily edited photos of destroyed arms and severed hands flashed by on the screen. The audience groaned.

"My nonprofit organization, Surgical Outreach, is coordinating and funding this effort. Anyone who is wearing Death Watch and wants out, for whatever reason, can contact us directly."

His beloved nonprofit organization's info appeared.

"If you'd like to contribute to Surgical Outreach, your donation is completely tax-deductible—and much-appreciated." Robert gave a carefully arranged smile, one that suggested he had a bit of pitchman in him. Then his image faded.

Bev twisted her mouth. There wasn't much snide to say about free surgery that could save people from a horrific death.

"Wait a sec," she said. "You told people what Death Watch was all about. It wasn't called Shiny Watch or Fancy Watch."

The studio audience laughed.

"Right, all of our ads made it clear that the watch could be deadly. And that it couldn't be taken off once it went on. There were warnings on the packaging and even on the watch."

"So you weren't trying to trick them into dying," Bev said. "Wasn't false advertising."

"It was great advertising," Andy added. "Those videos? Intense. Really intense. Anyone who bought Death Watch had to know what it was all about."

"They did." I didn't need to point out that I was the only person who didn't know the score. The campaign wasn't about me anymore. It was about unshackling the Alisons of the world, who just wanted to be set free.

"So maybe a lot of people who bought it are okay with it," Bev said, revving up a little. "Maybe they like the idea of sudden death, maybe they even get off on it. What about them?"

"They made their choice," I said. "If they're okay with the fact that their life could end at any moment, then that's fine. But I want to be free. And I think there are probably a lot of other people who feel the same way."

"Free to be disfigured," Bev said.

"For now, that's the only way out," I said. "But we're hopeful that there may be a way to neutralize the watch so that no one needs to have surgery. There's a crowd-sourced team of technologists working on it, but so far, the results aren't good."

"What do you mean?"

"They've exposed the watch to high levels of radiation, magnetism, pressure, you name it. But the watch still works."

"Takes a licking, keeps on ticking," Andy said, offering up an old Timex slogan lodged somewhere in his long-term memory.

"Right, that."

Andy put his hand on my shoulder. "You'll be the first to get this procedure?"

"Since World War I."

"The surgery looks awful," Andy shuddered. "You're so brave to take one for the team."

Hardly. The team wouldn't be here if I hadn't leapt before I looked, hadn't tempted others to jump with me.

OVER THE TOP

We worked late in Team Death HQ despite the hot, damp end-of-summer air, which our tired air conditioner didn't cool, just stirred. We had our magic bullet now. The D'Issan procedure undercut Death Watch's power by offering a way out to those who wanted it. But Team Death was still working hard to stop the flow of new customers. As Vanessa put it, *better to not get the tattoo in the first place then to have to get it burned off.*

Over on the blue couch, Vanessa was helping Alta track the litigation she'd set in motion, including a new lawsuit in Germany. Robert was right. Death Watch's titanium case and watch face design was a direct knock-off of the Nomos, the signature watch from Geist, a high-end German watchmaker that protected its brand with a cadre of vicious intellectual property lawyers. As Alta put it, *no one wanted a team of German lawyers on their tail.*

Her class action suit was moving ahead. She was suing government officials in Minsk to stop shipments of Death Watch. She was setting up conference calls with Japanese authorities to hunt down the engineers. All with the help of Vanessa.

Harup was coordinating cyberattacks on Death Watch's supply chain from his tech room, but for now he sat out on the fire escape, headphones on, flipping through a book about UFOs. Just being around Alta's boundless energy left him even more listless.

Wren was drinking coffee in the kitchen when I came in, opening the mail.

"Anything good?"

I opened an envelope and read for a moment. "Sure, check it out." I handed her the letter.

"What is it?"

"Another screenwriter pitching us. Wants to make a film about Team Death."

Wren started reading. "Oh, this is rich. *Thanks to a quirky team of misfits, Death Watch soon becomes a cultural phenomenon, attracting global attention and outrage. Then the watches start going off, killing their owners—and an elaborate stunt becomes a life-and-death nightmare. As time runs out, Vessel takes to the world stage via all media to send an urgent warning. Can our unlikely hero stop the watch once it's out in the world? Or will Death Watch kill him first?"*

Wren laughed for a long time.

"What?"

"We're not misfits. And a film about you would be really boring, Coe. All you do is talk."

I plucked the letter from her hand and dropped it in the trash. "A documentary filmmaker from France wants to film me getting my hand cut in half. Would you find that more interesting?"

"Maybe. You going to let them?"

"No." I didn't want the world to watch my hand turn into a talon.

Wren stood, turned serious. "Almost forgot. Nathan told me to thank you."

"For what?"

"Not mentioning the agency. Making it sound like the whole Death Watch thing was your fault."

"Well, it was."

"Not really," Wren said. "We all made it happen. Anyway, he said you should call him. You know, to talk about ending your furlough."

"Really?"

"Sure, I mean, after your talon thing heals."

Done with me, Wren walked out of the kitchen.

I still loved Moriawase, probably the same way parents still manage to love a demanding child who has taken up most of their time, stolen their youth, drained their bank accounts, and destroyed their brains. But I couldn't imagine going back to work with Nathan. I just wanted to get Death Watch off my wrist so I could be free to imagine whatever was next.

I walked back into the living room, where Wren kept updates on the whiteboard. Online buzz about Death Watch had shifted after Wren posted edited video clips from our Skype calls with Watanabe, making him seem pathetic and venal, not visionary.

Not even the most desperate nihilist wanted to sacrifice their life for a greedy artist.

Online postings of unboxings and devotional donnings of Death Watch stopped cold. The allure of Death Watch had dropped to the point that buying it seemed stupid instead of brave. We were amazed that anyone would still buy Death Watch, except for canny collectors to resell the watches for a profit once the project imploded.

Standing in front of the whiteboard, I sensed that the decline in interest in Death Watch wasn't entirely due to our work. The world had just moved on to other atrocious ideas. Death Watch was just another cautionary tale of technology gone very awry. Viral attention doesn't last. Cults fade. Death Watch was becoming old news.

Harup waved us toward his laptop.

Fkn Watanabe!

In his latest online pop-up video, Watanabe's face glistened in harsh light, as if lit by an oncoming car.

"Makeup, hair, and wardrobe. Please report to set," Vanessa intoned.

"That's funny," Alta said, not laughing.

"I am speaking to you far from my home." Watanabe spoke quietly, as if someone was sleeping in the next room. "Those who question my intentions have hounded me, my family. Some members of my team are in custody. Others are unable to cross international borders. My lawyers are receiving many spurious lawsuits."

Vanessa gave Alta an exaggerated high five. *Go Team Death!*

"But still, Death Watch continues," Watanabe said. "We are selling more than ever."

Harup shook his head at this desperate lie.

"Others have told me that I should stop my experiment now."

I raised my hand. "That would be me."

"But I don't listen to the advice of fools."

I raised my hand again. "Also me."

"I listen only to the artistic spirit that compels me to create. No one can stop the great wave that I have set in motion. Death

Watch will continue to rise, to gather energy, and to sweep across the globe, shocking the complacent and culling the brave. Medical science cannot stop metaphysical exploration."

"What a dickhead," Wren said.

"Those who attempt to undermine my finest work will fail. We are on the right side of history. Fires, floods, political insurrections, the acceptance of evil—we are witnessing the death of the world as we know it. Death Watch is an escape hatch. Step through it."

We shrugged. Nothing Watanabe could say was that shocking anymore. Like the Great and Powerful Oz, he was just flipping switches and levers that did little more than create noise and flashing lights.

Watanabe reached out, opened the familiar black box, and held Death Watch up to the camera. He slipped it around his wrist and held his arm up, fist clenched.

"Join us!"

The screen went black.

"Did he just do what I think he did?" I said.

Wren was still staring at the blank screen, stunned.

Mbe it's a knock-off.

"No," I said. "He's gone over the top."

"Guzzling his own Kool-Aid," Vanessa said.

Watanabe's desperate move proved that he was willing to be destroyed by his own monstrous creation—the only thing that might stop him.

Seeing Watanabe always made me crave fresh air. While the other rejoiced in Watanabe's downfall, I slipped out of Team Death HQ.

I walked down the back stairs and through the lobby, past Glenn, asleep at his desk. Outside, the cool night took me in. I sat on the warm cement steps of our building, the last ugly apartment building on West 57th Street. The long summer was ending, the autumn wind sneaking in, but the night still felt burstingly alive.

Later in the fall, Harup, Wren, and I were planning on starting up our boutique agency, tentatively called the Talon Agency, though Three Finger Discount was also in the running. *Putting the digits in digital advertising*. The finger puns from Harup were constant and not particularly appreciated. Our new agency would work with smaller clients that sold products that weren't deadly.

It would be a lot of work, but we'd have a chance to start over again with a fresh slate—and no megalomaniacs on the client list, ever.

When I walked back upstairs to Team Death HQ, Vanessa and Alta were talking in the living room, loud enough that I could hear every word from the kitchen. Maybe they hadn't heard me slip back in. Or maybe they didn't mind that I was listening.

"Tell me more about it."

"About being a dominatrix?" Vanessa laughed. "You don't want to know."

"I do," Alta said, eagerly.

I had missed the conversation when Vanessa revealed she wasn't really a consultant. But now I was catching the deeper dive.

"I used to escort." Vanessa paused, moving into uncertain waters with her new, very straight friend. "You know, meet up with men and go to dinner or somewhere with them for money. Or do various things with and to them in hotel rooms that I'd rather not talk about."

"Because?"

"Because those days are over, Alta. Because I do all my work online now. In the tidy trenches of digital desire. Safer that way. No fluids. No fucking. No crazy men in my face."

Vanessa hadn't shared many details about her past except to say that it was too painful to revisit. I took a furtive glance out of the break room and saw Alta and Vanessa standing next to the whiteboard.

"What do you do, now?"

"I discipline submissive men who have a deep need to be controlled, physically, emotionally, and financially. That might mean—"

The marker squeaked on the whiteboard as Vanessa laid out her smorgasbord of domination.

"Oh, you really do that?"

"Yep, all the time."

More squeaking.

"And that? Oh, that sounds painful."

"They love it."

"Is that what you do for Coe?"

I stopped breathing for a moment. Alta still suspected that Vanessa and I shared more than Team Death spirit.

"No. We're just good friends."

"I've heard about *friends with benefits.*"

"That's not a thing anymore, Alta. It was just an excuse for drunk dudes to show up at sorority houses and ask for a contractual blowjob."

"Are you two ... intimate?" Alta's tentative question hung in the air.

"Of course. But do you mean *are we fucking*?

"Yes, in so many words."

"Really just one word, *fucking.*"

"Are you?"

"No."

"Really?" Alta seemed surprised. "I mean, Coe always needed more ... excitement, complexity. Are you two in love?"

Vanessa paused. "Not in the way that you're probably thinking. We're confidantes. We tell each other things. Things that probably shouldn't be heard by other people. We help each other figure them out. That's love, in a way."

"I like that," Alta said.

"Do you?"

"Coe needs a confidante. I keep my thoughts to myself."

"Maybe you should let them out."

"Maybe I should."

Maybe I should have stopped listening, but I couldn't.

"Coe's messy," Alta said. "Loses his phone or his keys all the time. Forgets appointments. That's the easy stuff. He wants to be clever and funny the way other men want to be rich and powerful. He wants to make his dead father proud."

She paused in her searingly accurate X-ray of my personality. "But I can tell he cares about you. You two look so ... so comfortable together. You fit well."

"We do."

An ill-defined ache washed over me as I remembered being alone with Vanessa, watching her work, talking for hours.

"He loves you a whole lot, Alta. The real kind. I know it. Most men give in to temptation when it's right in front of them."

Harup ambled in and opened the fridge to get an iced coffee. I put my finger over my lips and he shrugged, sat down.

"I did," Alta said. "With Zeno. We ... we were *fucking*. It was a big mistake."

Harup put down his coffee and started paying attention.

"I wasn't the only one, of course," Alta said. "He took advantage of lots of other women he worked with. But just once. Then moved on."

"Once men like that get what they want," Vanessa said, "they don't want it anymore."

"Did you come up with that?"

"No, it's a cliché. But how about this. Men are generally miserable. They try to use their power to make us as miserable as they are."

"Why?"

"So they're not alone."

Harup and I looked at each other. *Shit.*

"Coe isn't miserable," Alta said. "He just takes the world's problems personally."

"Hard not to be."

"But he doesn't pass it on," Alta said, an insight I couldn't argue with. I didn't want to make anyone miserable. "I think he'll be a lot happier once he gets the watch cut off."

I winced at the thought of my surgery, just days away.

"I'll need your help keeping an eye on him," Alta said. "I haven't told anyone this yet, but I have a job offer. Genetic research firm in Palo Alto. I'm going to be traveling a lot again. You're welcome to stay here in the apartment after we're done with Team Death. Harup can too, if you want a roommate."

Harup perked up.

"I don't think so, Alta. Seems like my work here is done. Death Watch is winding down."

"If it's about money, we wouldn't charge you."

"No, it's not about money. Never is. Just like it might be the right time to move on."

"Why? You're good for Coe. And you're part of the family."

"You are too, you big freak," I whispered to Harup, who gave me his Hallmark smile. "Now get out of here." I kicked his ankle until he stood up and wandered back to his tech cave.

The living room went silent and when I peeked out I could see that Vanessa was holding her head in her hands, shoulders rising and falling as Alta rubbed her back.

Vanessa rose up and wiped her face with the hem of her blouse. "Got to say, not used to women being nice to me."

I ducked back into the break room, realizing how very lucky I was. Lucky that Alta was back home, after all that we had done and not done. Lucky to have Vanessa as a confidante. I even felt a newfound appreciation of Harup, his annoying quirks transformed into charming eccentricities.

For now.

WHAT'S NEXT?

The city emptied out over the holiday weekend. The only people still working were those Labor Day was intended to celebrate—doormen, drivers, waiters, cooks, cops.

We met in Team Death HQ early, when the day was still cool and fresh—except Wren, who insisted on *having a life*. My date with the D'Issan procedure was just a day away. Alta's new job started in a couple of weeks in California. Vanessa was starting to get her regular clients back.

At about three, we were all slowing down and wondering why we hadn't managed to do anything fun on a three-day weekend. For someone facing surgery, fun was hard to find. But I had an idea.

I walked into the living room and flicked the lights. "Emergency. Emergency. All work must stop. Team Death is needed at Bar Dog. Conclude your work and report immediately."

Alta and Vanessa closed their laptops. Harup took off his headphones.

The four of us took the elevator down to the lobby together for the first time. We looked at each other in the creaking elevator and laughed. What we'd been through, the intertwined connections between us—it was all too unlikely, incredible, and absurd. We passed by Glenn's desk without waking him and stepped out into the thick late-summer air.

"Glad the grandma mimes went home." Vanessa nodded at the crushed signs on the curb, last remnants from Faces of the Faithful.

Alta and Vanessa led the way down 57th, Harup and I just a couple of paces behind them on the empty sidewalk. The street was a wasteland unless you looked more closely. Nothing showed the city's legendary inequity more clearly than the empty boulevard of billionaires on a holiday weekend, its alleys clumped with cardboard hummocks full of unsettled sleepers.

An enormous crane stood silently at the intersection with Broadway, turning another 19th-century building into 21st-century luxury. Alta hadn't mentioned *the plan* lately, since it reeked of Zeno. Instead of a dream penthouse, we had Harup and Vanessa as upstairs neighbors.

From what we could tell, Death Watch was on autopilot, losing altitude and customers. Robert and Surgical Outreach already had a long waiting list for the D'Issan procedure. Watanabe's own watch might go off on some fated day, killing its creator, delivering the ultimate complication—and the world would have heard the last from this *mononoke*. Another demon spirit would step up and fill the void. But I set that thought aside. The future wasn't my problem; it was everyone's.

We turned north on 6th Avenue to get closer to the park. Along Central Park South, parents were walking children to the pond, or over to the zoo. I spent days in that part of the park when I was a kid, considered it my backyard. I could hear the calliope from deeper in the park as we walked closer. Harup cringed at the sight of enough tourists to fill a small town.

"They're just people," I said. "People from places you've never been wearing clothes you don't like."

His fingers twitched.

"Yeah, I know. They're also annoying and they get in the way."

More twitching, and a glance.

"They won't be in Bar Dog. Give it a rest."

We walked on, past rows of hotels, dodging a big group of schoolkids in blue uniforms. I wondered what kind of school had a field trip on Labor Day, when I heard a throttled voice.

"No. *No no no no.*"

I hadn't heard Harup speak in years. I was about to tell him that his voice sounded fine when he stabbed his finger toward my left hand.

A slow trickle of blood seeped from beneath my watch, coursing down to the tips of my fingers and dripping down on the sidewalk.

"Doesn't hurt." My heart pounded as I looked at the watchband, saw only a slowly throbbing red dot instead of today's number.

"Maybe it's done. Just a prototype. Not supposed to work."

The knives pricked my wrist from beneath Death Watch's shining case, with no more pain than an inoculation.

My watch started to vibrate slowly, then faster and louder.

A warm rain sprayed into my face and pain shot up my arm as I looked at Harup and saw his face splotched red, his mouth open wide and screaming. I stared at my glistening arm once then looked away as the watch climbed up my arm like a hungry machine, paralyzing me with pain.

The gray buildings swirled.

Pigeons scattered up into the air.

The blue sky over the park dimmed at its edges.

My hand hung at a terrible angle.

The pain the fucking pain.

I tried to say something but couldn't. Vanessa held me in her arms and Alta tried to grab the watch and pull it away but her hands slipped and then the gnashing stopped but the blood and pain didn't.

Alta shouted over and over for a doctor.

Strangers said it was going to be okay.

More hands touched me.

Arms wrapped around me.

My knees buckled and we all fell to the sidewalk and my face pressed against the warm bricks then darkness pain sirens coming closer. Schoolkids screamed or laughed and I remembered playing here as a boy walking through the park hand-in-hand with my invincible father who sang his favorite jingles to me and I thought the kids were happy because in the end we all hear what we want to hear laughing crying nothing everything.

About the Author

Stona Fitch is a writer, editor, and publisher whose novels include *Senseless, Printer's Devil, Give + Take,* and more. *Senseless* was adapted as a feature film by director Simon Hynd, and produced by Shoreline Entertainment. Many of his other books are currently optioned for film. He also writes a Boston-based crime series under the pen name Rory Flynn.

In 2008, Stona founded the **Concord Free Press**, an all-volunteer press that publishes and distributes original novels for free, asking only that readers make a voluntary donation to a charity they believe in or person in need. Its books have inspired more than $5 million in donations and ongoing generosity around the world.

He lives and works in West Concord, Massachusetts.

Acknowledgments

Special thanks to Ellen Levine, Audrey Crooks, and Trident Media Group for their faith in *Death Watch* right from the start. And to Chris DeFrancesco for sharing his many talents with the Concord Free Press, our ongoing experiment in subversive altruism, for so many years. Thanks to Randall Klein for his expert editorial guidance, Martin Sorger for the fine Arrow Editions logo, and Wyn Cooper for sharp-eyed proofreading. And to Doug Schwalbe, Castle Freeman, Jr., Kevin Ashton, Bill Ciccariello, and Brent Refsland for their much-appreciated early enthusiasm.

Above all, thanks to Ann for sticking with *Death Watch* draft after draft, for decades of encouragement and advice—and for a lifetime of love.

RIP Dr. Murray Goldstone (1934–2022) reader, advisor, and steady hand on the tiller.

ARROW EDITIONS